RESISTANCE
An Apocalyptic Thriller
M.L. Banner

Toes in the Water Publishing, LLC

ISBN (Paperback): 978-1-947510-24-1

ISBN (eBook): 978-1-947510-23-4

ISBN (Audio): 978-1-947510-26-5

V1.1

RESISTANCE: Highway Book #3 is an original work of fiction.

The characters and dialogs are the products of this author's vivid imagination.

Much of the science and the historical incidents described in this novel are based on reality, as are ts warnings.

Acknowledgment

R esistance is for you, Dad. Wish you could have been here to read it.

Author's Notes

T hank you for picking up *RESISTANCE*, the next chapter of the *HIGHWAY Series*.

As the third book in a series, *RESISTANCE* starts right where *HIGHWAY* and *ENDURANCE (Highway Book 2)* left off. I strongly recommend you read the 2nd Edition of these first two books in the series so that you can better appreciate the story and its characters. However, the Prelude of *RESISTANCE* was written with storyline and character reminders for those new to the series and for those who have already read the 1st edition of these stories when they first came out in 2016.

HIGHWAY and *ENDURANCE* have been such a fun ride for me and the tens of thousands of readers who have taken the journey. With *RESISTANCE*, the thrill-ride continues, until its conclusion in *REVOLUTION*.

So, let's lock and load, take a breath and get ready to "Join the Resistance!"

- Michael

Resistance

"A well regulated Militia, being necessary to the security of a free State, the right of the people to keep and bear Arms, shall not be infringed."
- 2nd Amendment, US Constitution

"If Tyranny and Oppression come to this land, it will be in the guise of fighting a foreign enemy."
- James Madison

"When injustice becomes law, resistance becomes duty."
- Thomas Jefferson

July 12th

8 Days After the Fall of America

JOIN THE RESISTANCE

Prelude

"The fall of America started on July 4th, when terrorists attacked with suitcase nukes at multiple locations including DC, Chicago, New York City, Jacksonville, along with two atmospheric blasts by Russian missiles over Kentucky and Uta..."

A staticy background tone briefly replaced the radio broadcast which had faded away. Lexi Broadmoor's left hand shot from her lap to the frequency selector. She had intended to tune in the station better, but then the broadcaster's Texas twang boomed out of the Plymouth's speakers.

"... caught us off guard, bringing down the US power grid, severing the Internet, stopping all commerce, and ceasing emergency and law enforcement services.

"It was not a fluke that the Islamic Caliphate of America or ICA chose July 4th to attack. On that day, a planned celebratory signing of the Freedom for Americans Act was scheduled, bringing together nearly every member of the Senate, Congress, and the Administration. So, by all measures, the US government was destroyed with one bomb on that fateful day.

"Days later, using our own advanced drones from two Air Force bases, they sarin gassed military installations all over the western and southern US. Then their land assault began.

"Still no official response from anyone claiming to be part of the federal government or the US military.

"It shouldn't have come as a surprise that for years, mixed in with the millions of illegal migrants, ICA invaders have been silently entering through our southern borders and southern and eastern coasts. What is surprising is their current march from town to town, dressed as US Army, driving older-model Army trucks, killing citizens with weapons, all to quash any possible resistance by US citizens. And still the attacks continue.

"Therefore, my fellow Americans, just as it was during the American Revolution, the fight rests upon you, through our private militias, to resist these terrorists and their plans to conquer America. Yesterday, we resisted the invaders who attacked us in our own town, and we've been hearing reports of similar stories by citizens in other towns. It is up to each of *you*, American patriots, who are listening... Join the resistance! Your country needs you. Monitor Channel 9 on your CB radio to find information about your local militia. If you have any military training, you are especially needed. Regardless, everyone who is able is asked to become part of the resistance. Together, my fellow patriots, we can wi—"

An ear-piercing, warbling tone, like electronic pulses, blared from the car speakers, cutting out any further broadcast.

Lexi reached over, this time switching off the radio.

"So," Lexi projected her voice out to be heard against the loud whoosh of air coming through the open side windows, "do you think—"

Bang! Bang-clank! erupted from the driver's side.

Frank Cartwright didn't hesitate: he jammed down the accelerator. The Fury's three-hundred-eighteen cubic inch engine pushed them to their seat backs and shot the vehicle up to an unsafe speed. Frank eyeballed Lexi, who had slunk down out of her seat, her knees punched into the floorboards.

At one-hundred miles per hour, Frank laid off the accelerator, heaving them forward. They coasted. The air continued to scream in, drowning out any other possible sounds.

At fifty, Frank turned off their headlights and they cruised silently in the dark. The breeze whirled inside in spits and spurts.

"Are you hit?" Jasper asked. He was perched above Lexi, claws dug into the front bench seat, his head hung forward, eyes focused on her.

She didn't answer, remaining in her position off the seat, head just below the dash, hyperventilating.

When the car had come to crawl, Frank reached over and squeezed her arm hard enough to elicit a grunt. "Are—you—hit?"

She shook her head and then glared at him through the darkness. From just the slightest glimmer of light that leaked out from under the dash, Frank thought he might have caught some tears in her eyes.

"Was... that Uncle... Abdul's group?" she said, nearly breathless.

"More like a couple of yokels with guns, taking potshots at anyone who happens to drive by."

Finally, the car lurched to a slow stop, and Frank turned off the ignition with it still in gear.

"But how could you know?" She pushed herself back

up onto her seat. "Abdul knows everything… He knew where… we lived… He doesn't die…" Every other word came in high-pitched shudders, "and I… couldn't protect… Travis."

Frank wrapped his arms around her and squeezed, even though it hurt. He glared at Jasper, still ominously hovering over them from the backseat, doing nothing. "You could chime in anytime now, buddy."

Jasper cleared his throat, his features unrecognizable in the dark. "Um, yes. I doubt Abdul Farook" —the name rolled off his tongue, like if pronounced by a native— "knows where we are at this moment, much less would he send people out to shoot you. He wants you… Uh, as you already said, he doesn't want to hurt you."

Frank wished he could see Jasper's face, because his words were odd, but he couldn't chance their alerting anyone else to their presence by turning the dome lights on. It was why he refrained from touching his brakes.

He shrugged off the odd feeling about Jasper—he had no time for this—and made a mental note to remove the fuse for the taillights when they were safe.

"But neither of you know it wasn't an ICA unit?" Lexi continued, her voice still quavering. "They're everywhere, so you have to admit it's possible."

Although Frank didn't genuinely think an ICA soldier would be shooting randomly at a lone car driving by at night, he did have to admit he couldn't know for sure. They *seemed* to be everywhere: they had already seen at least four different truck convoys of theirs today.

He stared past Lexi into the darkness, where the crickets were strumming a particularly loud song this evening and considered the implications of this.

Speculating on the number of people Abdul recruited and brought into the US, mixed in with the hordes of illegal aliens that had come across their open borders the past few years, was truly mind-numbing. Then to stealthily train what had to be the equivalent of at least two divisions, all while waiting for this day.

"You're right," Frank said at a whisper. "I don't know. All the more reason to get off the road." He started up the car. "We'll go just a little way longer, till I can find us a place to pull off the road for the night."

The whole time he mentally chewed on Lexi's questions about Abdul and his invaders.

Lexi

Meanwhile, Lexi was attempting to get her mind off of her nightmares about Abdul, by focusing on what led up to this day...

Was it only eight days ago?

She was so different then. Another person really: an obstinate child, filled with anger, all wrongly directed at her father. She thought he abandoned her and Travis after their mother died, when he sent them to live with their aunt and uncle in Tucson.

Disgust filled her when she thought of her former self. Yet with all the secrets, how could she have known? She had only just learned, through the clues her father had left after his death, that he was, in fact, a hero.

The whole time he'd been MIA from his family, he'd actually been deeply embedded in a US terrorist cell, searching for—.

Lexi's mind froze once again on the image from her dreams. The one she saw all the time in her waking consciousness. The image she couldn't avoid, which seemed to manifest itself day and night now... Abdul.

Her stomach hitched, and she involuntarily gagged like some ally cat hacking up a furball.

Abdul Raheem Farook was the leader of the terrorist cell that her father had been investigating. He also turned out to be her father's brother, and therefore, Lexi's uncle. It was Abdul who had stolen everything Lexi had cared about: first murdering Lexi's mother, by poisoning her in public; then slaughtering millions of Americans, and in the process, killing Lexi's father too. Her father had been frantically attempting to bring Lexi and her brother to the safety of a secret bug-out home in Northern Florida, when Abdul's nukes went off and her father died in a car accident, stranding them on the highway.

Travis and she had stumbled across Abdul's place—before she knew his true identity as her uncle and America's mass murderer—just as he had planned.

But their godfather, Frank, ended up saving her and Travis from Abdul's clutches, before her uncle could force her into marrying him. It was Frank who had finally taken them to the Florida house north of Endurance, Florida.

Frank immediately began teaching her how to defend herself and Travis. Most of all, Frank became her strength and helped her to become tough enough to survive in a ruined America.

He too would be the one who helped her through the fear. Her brother on the other hand…

Lexi's gut hitched up again, not just from the last memory of her brother, but what it meant she had to do next.

Why couldn't you have died? she begged Abdul's reoccurring image.

She had stabbed Uncle Abdul and left him for dead, but this evil man struck again, somehow surviving, and then abducting her little-brother, Travis. Worse, Abdul maimed him by… She shuddered at the gruesomeness of the note and her brother's severed finger. It was Abdul's proof not only that he had Travis, but that he was capable of all types of cruelty.

"How could anyone who claimed to have wanted to adopt my little brother, at the same time injure him so horribly?" her brain yelled silently.

Red-hot rage boiled inside of her once again. It felt so much better than the fear.

Abdul had murdered her family and millions of Americans; he was going to force her to marry him, even though he was her uncle; and then he abducted Travis and severed his finger to prove he had him…

"Sick mother f…" she hissed into the wind.

That's why Frank, Lexi and their new protector, Jasper were on the road again. They were going to save her brother and then once and for all, kill Abdul. That was if they didn't encounter any more of Abdul's invaders, like those mentioned on the radio.

They had experienced them just south of their new home in Endurance, Florida. If it hadn't been for Jonah, Emily, and others from the town, they would have perished. And now, they appeared to be everywhere.

Lexi once again wondered how so many troops could have entered the country, without being noticed before. It must have taken many years of planning to get that many men into the US...

Chapter 1

Three Years Before the Attacks

The Mexican's military rifle cracked from an unexpected burst of several quick rounds. The American border patrol agent, who had just told them to halt, crumpled to the ground where he stood.

"*¡Ándale-ándale!*" the Mexican gunman barked at Faisal Shahzad and the others trailing behind him, before stomping forward again. None of them needed any prodding. They marched past the fallen guard, apparently leaving the guard to be found by whatever wildlife lived out here or some other patrol.

As the Mexican strode past the sporadic patches of Buffelgrass and Jumping Cholla, he snapped a cell phone to his ear and rattled off a flurry of words in Spanish. Faisal and his group silently followed on the well-trodden path, fully illuminated by a sun which had long since sprung over the distant mountains on their right.

Faisal wiped his forehead with a soaked handkerchief and glared at the cause of his discomfort. This place was every bit as harsh as his homeland of Iran. He just wasn't used to walking as many miles as he had today, nor in shoes with strips of carpeting strapped to them—to "hide your footsteps"—their Mexican guide had explained. Yet other than the heat, and the odd footwear, this whole journey was easier than he had thought it would be.

They had just crossed the American Mexican border, which was open for as far as the eye could see. Its only protections were steel barricades to keep vehicles from driving through, and a little barbed-wire fence, which had long since been sliced open. It had been this way for years from what Faisal had been told: some sort of break-down in American politics, that allowed tens of millions of undocumented immigrants to pour into their country unhindered. More importantly for Faisal, mixed in with those millions were many thousands of their fellow be-lievers. Like them, Faisal and his men would settle in pre-chosen locations throughout the country. There they would train, live, and patiently wait for when it was their time to act.

Their leader, Abdul Farook, had planned well for their crossing. Still, Faisal couldn't believe how effortless it was. He was told that this was just one of many American weaknesses, all of which would make them so easy to conquer. He could barely wait for that day.

Faisal looked up and jolted to a halt. Their Mexican guide, was looking right at him, waiting. One of the man's eyes twitched before he spoke.

"I get my men to pick up," the Mexican said, probably referring to the dead border guard. "*Este no problemo*," he told Faisal while shaking his head, as if he didn't believe his own words. Both of his eyes were twitching now.

Faisal nodded, completely understanding the man's part English part Spanish sentence, and his nervousness. Although this man was part of a vast and very powerful Mexican cartel that ruled this area, they were still interested in keeping Farook and his people happy—because Farook paid very well. The Mexican knew Faisal, as the leader of this group, needed to be pacified. But Faisal couldn't imagine Farook would be too pleased with an American border policeman being killed years before he had planned to let the world learn about the ICA. Faisal had no doubt that word would eventually get back to Farook, who would tell the Mexican's cartel leaders... Yes, Faisal suspected this man's days were numbered.

However, none of this was Faisal's concern. He was confident Farook would make sure their fighters remained hidden for as long as they needed to be.

The Mexican, after getting the go ahead nod from Faisal, continued them on their march for another kilometer, maybe two.

They came upon a clearing where a faded-red pickup truck, coated in dried mud and dust, was parked under the canopy of a spacious mesquite tree. Emblazoned on the pickup's driver-side door, a worn away insignia with three acorns and below this, the words, Tres Bellotas Ranch.

Two men sprang from the well of the tree, one immediately opening the truck's tailgate and the other yanking a box from the bed and tossing it on the ground, a few inches away.

Their Mexican guide rattled off several more strings of garbled Spanish to the two animated men, who subsequently offered to help Faisil and his men up and into the truck.

From what Faisal understood, this was the end of their long walk. After this, they would be transported directly to their base in Arizona, where they would spend their days training to kill Americans with precision. All under the noses of the Americans.

"Almost at your new home," the Mexican said, grinning at Faisil through a set of brown teeth.

"*Ash-shukru lillah*," Faisal replied loudly for his men's benefit, as he grabbed the sweaty mitt of one of the helpers who pulled him up into the truck bed from the ad hoc step. He knew the Mexicans wouldn't understand his giving *all thanks to Allah*. As long as his men heard him.

Tres Bellotas Ranch

In a flurry of Arabic, a beefy man who introduced himself as Khalid, welcomed their newest recruits, who were carefully piling out of the truck bed.

Before hopping down last, Faisal eyeballed his surroundings. It was greener than the lengthy stretch of desert they had just hiked through. Past the gate Khalid stood in front of, a long stretch of road that terminating at a group of ranch styled homes and vast bunk houses. All around them were lines of mesquites surrounding open fields that were carpeted with hundreds of men training.

It had been a many-year journey for him that started when he first met Farook, who had traveled through Iran recruiting for his cause. When he heard that Farook would usher in the destruction of the United States, he volunteered immediately. When others began to regard Farook as the messianic Mahdi, Faisal vowed that one day he would make sure Farook took notice of him. Yes, he would fight as well or better than all the others, but as a leader he would also be smart so as to survive and shine. Rather than becoming a quick martyr like many of these men joyously would, he would rise up to become important to Farook and perhaps one day, be part of the Mahdi's inner council.

He was now in America at this place, where he would train until that day he would lead a group deep into this country's heart, at which point he and his ICA brothers would stop it for good. His plans were coming together.

"You are Allah's newest fighters in the Jihaad." Khalid's Arabic rolled off his tongue like an Imam at Friday Mosque. "You will be joining many thousands of others from all over the world to train for the day when our Mahdi tells us it is time to fight."

Faisal and his men had already heard this same speech before they started this journey. But it was good to hear it again.

"We had learned from the Taliban and then ISIS that to win against the Americans, we had to fight them in their own country. Just like Mohammad—peace be upon him—who took his fight directly to his enemies, we too will take the fight directly to the infidels, on their own soil. Because they will not expect the fullness of our attack and their many other weaknesses, including their godlessness, we will be victorious."

Several of Faisal's men murmured under their breaths, obviously wanting to say more, but waiting to be told that they could respond.

Faisal held up a hand to quiet their murmurs and addressed them. "Your job is simple, my brothers. Train, pray and wait until we are called upon by Allah and our Mahdi to begin our fight. When we have all completed our training and it is time, we will usher in a new Caliphate here, in the Americas.

"*As-salaam 'alykum*," Khalid hollered.

Faisal and the ten others who had followed him and the Mexican through the desert, and now stood beside Faisal, responded immediately and in one voice, "*Wa 'alaykum as-salaam*."

Chapter 2
Somewhere in South Carolina

Lexi

Present Day

Their car's engine was switched off, its tires grinding on asphalt until they came to a stop. A symphony of cricket chirps flooded through their side windows, drowning out any other sounds their hypersensitive ears might have picked up on. But there was one other note, almost imperceptible among the cricket's din...

"Why did we stop? What did you hea—"

"Shhh!" Frank cut off Lexi and pointed forward, not that any of them could see his hand or to what he was pointing. But there was a sound, which was rising steadily above the rhythmic cadence of the forest's insect concert. A mechanized rumble that grew, along with a momentary flash of lights, in the distance.

The three of them sat silent in the car, eyes now drilled forward toward the amplifying machine-like thunder.

Less than a mile away, the roar of one truck after another burst by, at what looked like a T-intersection. The peripheral sparkle of each truck's headlight beams momentarily illuminated their own path to the T. Each passing truck's light completely exposed them, a silent ghost-like vehicle in the middle of the otherwise empty wooded road. With each flash, the three of them sucked in hitching breaths, but remained otherwise motionless, afraid their movements in the murk would somehow give them away.

When the last truck zoomed by and out of sight, they let out their collective exhale. They remained unmoving even as the convoy's diminishing clamor was once again consumed by the staccato thrumming of the woods' cricket chorus. Frank took in a quick gulp of air, as if he were about to speak, but then the convoy's dull echo was abruptly drowned out by the tortured squealing of old brakes. It told them the trucks were halting not too far away. *But why?*

"Did they see us?" Lexi asked the rhetorical question she suspected they were all thinking.

The crickets' unending song was momentarily cut by the yell of a man in a familiar foreign dialect, followed immediately by the distinctive *ra-te-tat, ra-te-tat* of automatic gunfire.

Frank didn't offer a thought or explanation. He started up the car and moved them forward a few feet, headlights still off. Then he took a hard turn, as if he were going to pull a U-turn, but stopped. The headlights were flashed on and off once to light up a small path Lexi hadn't seen. He took them in that direction, at a snail's pace.

"We're getting off the road and stopping for the night," Frank announced, barely above the crickets' roar and the crunching tire-sounds which seemed much too loud. "We'll find a spot where we're not likely to be heard or seen from the roads. Then we'll leave at first light.

"Was that an ICA convoy?" Lexi whispered.

"Think so."

"And who do you think they shot?"

She didn't really want an answer, but as always, he gave one. "It was probably another idiot with a gun, who tried to jack the lead truck of their convoy and didn't realize they were terrorists with automatic weapons."

None of them said a thing during the mile or so that they proceeded down the dirt path. When they stopped, Frank announced this was it and he deliberately stepped out of the car. He marched away from the car, with a specific mission in mind.

Jasper

Frank barked off a couple of whispered orders to Lexi, who obediently grabbed her pillow from the car, while Frank moved rocks away from a small tree just in front of them.

"You think we're safe here?" she asked for the second time.

"For the night, yes. But let's keep the chatter down to a minimum."

Jasper trained his light around the somewhat open area Frank had chosen for their so-called campsite. "I'm going to do a walk around the perimeter of our site to make sure there are no surprises for us," he gruffed in a low voice.

"Sounds good. Thanks, Jasper," Frank said, while placing his Maglite on the car's hood and focusing its beam onto the small tree from which he'd cleared rocks away from its base. Lexi followed Frank as directed, still holding the pillow she had been told to bring to him.

Making sure neither of them were looking his way, using the car to shield his movements, Jasper abruptly grabbed a couple of items out of his large duffel and put them in a separate canvas satchel that he had slung around his head and shoulder. After zipping this up, he hoisted his heavy Thompson submachine gun over his head and around his other shoulder. Finally, he clicked on his surplus Army flashlight. Like the Thompson, it was pilfered from the resident he'd killed when he took over the house next to the one Lexi, her brother and uncle recently occupied. He cursed Frank for the Thompson's weight when they could have had one of the new AK's offered by Jonah. But Frank had insisted that Jonah and the residents hold onto the AKs to defend their town against any future attacks that might come their way.

He glanced back, this time to figure out what Frank was doing and saw that he had been preparing Lexi for another hand-to-hand combat lesson.

Jasper had sworn to himself and his Mahdi that he wouldn't let Lexi out of his sight, but part of protecting her was to make sure there were no threats around them. It was also the reason why he hadn't killed Frank yet. With all the crazy Americans wandering around these parts with guns, it was easier to have two people looking after Lexi than one ... at least until they finally reached

Mount Weather and his Mahdi. Then he would personally dispose of Frank.

Not much longer, he told himself. Jasper kept his back to them as he marched a hundred meters away, at a diagonal, intending to then walk a circle around them and look for anything and anyone who might pose a threat. But before he did this, he needed to check in and provide a long overdue update.

With his focus trained toward Frank and Lexi, just out of his sight, He pulled the satellite phone out of his satchel and keyed in the number.

As he waited for it to be answered, he also listened to Frank and Lexi, as well as any other sounds. Other than the incessant insect chirps and the sound of the other side of the line ringing, he heard nothing.

When it stopped ringing and no one answered, he said, "It's Imran." He had taken special care not to use his real name all this time so as to not mistakenly blow his cover. But this was how his Mahdi wanted him to answer in case someone else might pick up the phone for him.

The familiar voice of his friend and now leader of their new Caliphate in America answered him warmly. "I only have a minute," Jasper said, "but I wanted to check in."

Before continuing, he paused to receive praises back from his Mahdi, Abdul.

"We're headed your way, and we should be there by late tomorrow or the next day, if we don't get stopped by one of the many groups of Americans with guns or one of your many ICA units in the area."

Jasper listened for his instructions, nodding but not replying verbally to what he was told to do. Finally, he said, "no they do not suspect."

He listened again.

"Yes, I will kill Frank Cartwright the moment I believe he questions my fealty is to anyone but them."

He listened for a longer period and nodded.

"Yes, my Mahdi... Yes, of course, Abdul. I must go before they question my being gone."

No farewells. He turned off the phone and snuck it back into his bag.

When he heard the crack of a branch breaking behind him, he swung his Thompson in the sound's direction.

Lexi

"**I**'m going to teach you how to punch."

Lexi's hands balled up into fists.

"Nope," Frank stated. "Not with your fists like you see in movies. If you miss and hit your enemy's forehead, you'll break your own bones."

"You want me to slap my adversary?" she asked, trying not to sound smug when that's what she felt like saying in response. She had already learned not to heckle her drill instructor.

"No, you're going to strike with the heal of your palm. Come here."

He ushered her over to a small tree, about twice as tall as her, on which he had duct-taped her pillow around its middle.

"Pretend this is your enemy's head." Frank stood on the other side of the pillow-headed-tree, and he struck like lightning, pummeling the faux enemy with a combo of blows from the heel of an open palm from his uninjured side.

He turned his head to her. "Here's how you do it with both hands." He demonstrated snail-like. "You drive forward, with an arm straight, palm first, into the man's nose." He did this with his weak left palm. "Then immediately with a counter hip twist, drive your power punch with the other palm to the side of his head."

He took a step back. "Okay, now you try."

As she approached, he said "keep both hands up for protection."

She did and tried to mimic what he did and said, driving her left palm into the enemy sapling's fake imagined nose.

Frank had come around to her side. "Drive from each side so you can see him plainly."

Lexi did exactly as he had said. With her last punch, she imagined it was Abdul's head and she hit so hard the tree gave a satisfying crack, like she had broken it with the power of her punch.

Then as if picking up and echoing this sound, there was a crack of a not-too-distant gunshot.

M oments later, Jasper reappeared. He told them the sound was nothing to worry about; probably a small animal that surprised him and that the convoy was at least several miles away now.

Frank seemed to accept that and then handed each of them their MRE pouches. Although Chili Mac was Lexi's favorite, she couldn't calm her nerves down and enjoy it. Every sound, other than the constant chirping, made her jump.

Sleeping would evade her most of the night too, even though Frank and Jasper were staying up all night to watch and she was given the front seat to herself.

When she finally nodded off, the reoccurring night-mare, involving her Uncle Abdul, took over.

Chapter 3
Endurance, Florida

Emily

"Jonah Price," Emily Stone hollered, her voice echoing down the clinic's abnormally quiet hallway.

Jonah's footfalls were immediate. Even though he and a few of his men were busily helping to resecure the clinic this evening in preparation of the unlikely event of another attack, he always jumped when she called; especially when she used his full name. At any other time, she would have found this humorous, but not now. Her stunning discovery was the only thing on her mind. She was hoping that Jonah could find a hole in her logic and somehow prove her wrong.

"Em, are you all right?" Jonah huffed from the doorway, his eyes bloodshot but full of their usual empathy and concern when he was in her presence.

Upon taking her in, his expression changed: eyebrows furrowing, mouth pursing, as he paddled over to her. Softly laying a hand on her shoulder, he said, "What is it?" He controlled his breaths to forcibly hide his need to gasp.

"Sorry to worry you, Jonah." She held out a document she had been studying when he came in. "Look at this and tell me if this screams out to you what it does to me?"

He accepted the single piece of paper and hesitated, before pulling out a pair of spectacles from his shirt pocket. He snuck them onto the bridge of his nose. She implored him to stop trying to hide issues like his near-sightedness. She accepted him as he was, with all his faults and frailties. He swore he wouldn't, but old habits die hard.

Using a finger to trace each line, he studied the Endurance Health Clinic admittance form. At the fourth line, the address, he stopped. His eyes suddenly wide, flicked up to meet hers above the tops of his specs and she nodded, telling him he had found it.

"Who the hell is Qwan Lee? This person lists his address as the same as Jasper's. That is Jasper's address, right?"

It was a rhetorical question because he knew the address better than she did. Meanwhile, his finger searched for more insight, tracing down the form to the age question. The answer written was *96.* Way too old for Jasper. "It has to be some sort of clerical error... *right?*"

"That's what I thought too," Emily said. "As you know, I had taken some time to get a handle on our paper records, because all our clinic's computer files were on the cloud, which doesn't seem to exist anymore. Anyway, I ran into this." She picked up another sheet of paper and handed it to him. "It's Mr. Lee's admittance form for a mild stroke three years ago. Seeing that he listed his address as the same as Jasper's and his age, I dug some more, and I found this." She handed him another form. This one for new patients.

"Holy shit, Em! Mr. Lee was a new patient five years before that at the same address..." Jonah yanked his specs off his nose and glared at her. "If I remember right, Jasper told me he'd been living there for five years, which was always weird to me because I had never met him before the attack. Until now, I had reasoned that he was some sort of hermit who kept to himself."

Emily nodded. "Me too."

"You know what this means?" Jonah asked.

"That Jasper lied to all of us?"

"More than that. He just happens to be in *that* specific house in Endurance, conveniently next to our new friends, but for the wrong reasons."

"I'm afraid to ask what you mean." She shot Jonah a glance that reflected his own fear.

"Stanley never mentioned anything about his neighbor; only that he had chatted with him a couple of times. He certainly wasn't close enough to really know the guy. However, Jasper seemed to know a lot about Stanley and his family. And what happened to Mr. Lee?"

Emily hadn't considered any of this. She just wondered what else Jasper—or whatever his name really was—wasn't telling them. But now her greater concern was the potential threat this man might pose to Lexi and Frank. Worse, since they weren't able to communicate with them, she began to worry, and she suspected Jonah was as well, though he didn't say.

Her mind was whirling as she drilled her eyes into his, until Jonah broke it off. He pecked her on the lips and said, "Thanks, Em."

"Where are you going?"

"To get some men and check out Jasper's home firsthand. We need to find out why he's here before our new friends continue much further." He dashed out the door.

Lexi

Lexi attempted to make herself comfortable in the front seat, but it was no good. She couldn't sleep any longer.

She lifted her head and peeked up over the dash, seeing Frank still holding vigil, seated on the hood of the car. His head occasionally swiveled from side to side, searching for any potential threat. Jasper was out in the woods somewhere, looking for any other perils which might stumble across them. They helped her to feel physically safe from Abdul's thugs, at least for now. If only these two men could patrol her dreams and kill the ever-present psychological enemy residing there.

She lowered her head and eyeballed the lights of the display of the HF transmitter Jonah had installed for them. It was on, the volume turned down low. With the windows closed, she would be able to hear it if anything was transmitted. But the damned thing hadn't worked after their first potty stop yesterday. Jasper said he checked it thoroughly, though he admitted not having any skill in this area. None of them did. *If only Travis was here*, she thought and then she felt immediately sad.

Even though it was fruitless, she would check out the radio once more. She didn't know anything about it, but she was smart at figuring things out. Plus, it would at least get her mind off things... *or thing.* She turned up the volume and played with the frequency selector, moving it from one side and then the other. When Jonah had shown them how to use this, there were whistling noises and overall static sounds as he moved the selector. Now the radio only emitted a hiss, like it wasn't receiving anything.

A thought occurred to her: *maybe something was loose on the radio.*

She reached behind the chassis to feel what cords were coming out of it. She felt what she guessed was the power cord, which was permanently attached to the back. The tips of a finger fell upon a circular connector, which was part of a thick round cable. *The antenna!* She thought of the cable that temporarily snaked along the underside of the dash, and then up and out the front passenger window to the magnetically attached antenna on the top of the roof.

Could it be that simple?

She twisted the round metal connector, feeling it tighten itself to the back of the radio. The hiss-sound turned to whistles and static.

She wanted to yell out, but Frank told her to keep quiet. And neither he nor Jasper were visible now. Plus, using the radio was Travis' thing, not hers. And she couldn't remember the damned codes. So, she would monitor and listen to their frequency. She would answer if there were any calls on their preselected frequency.

She laid her head down on her pillow wondering if Jonah or Emily would call for them... Maybe she could somehow talk to Travis... She smiled at this.

Lexi finally nodded off peacefully. But her peace wouldn't last long.

Jonah

It didn't take more than ten minutes before they uncovered more proof of Jasper's fraud.

They found an old chest in a bedroom filled with personal effects, including framed pictures of an oriental family. Front and center of the picture was a 90-something year old man. The background looked familiar, like somewhere around the rear of this property. Jasper was not present in any of the pictures.

Just as the home's worn interior did, its smells also supported the profile of a house being occupied by a single old man, like Mr. Lee.

"So where did you go, Mr. Lee?" he asked the family picture.

Before he and his men arrived, Jonah was working on the hopeful theory that Jasper—who was not as old—and Mr. Lee were roommates at one time. But that hypothesis had little evidence to support it.

The more Jonah and his men looked, the more they found of Mr. Lee's personal effects and nothing of Jasper's. That was until they uncovered the locked case, or rather when Jonah ran into it.

He had thought it was an old coffee table, with a rug thrown over it, in the middle of the living room. They had walked past it several times, giving it no notice, until Jonah banged his foot on the solid side of the chest. Peaking under the rug, Jonah yelled out, "Grab a crowbar out of the truck and pry off the lock."

"Jonah," a voice hollered from outside, through the back door they had left open to air out the place. "Come here, quick."

Jonah trotted outside, into the overgrown backyard which at one time, must have been very beautiful, but had been not kept up for the past year or so. *It was one more of the many clues that something was amiss.*

He found two of his men under a giant willow, standing before a mound in the ground.

"I think it's a grave," Bagley said. "I'm guessing it's maybe a year old. Not much more."

"Dig it up and let's find out if that's our Mr. Lee or if—" Jonah began. But before he could finish his sentence, one of them dashed off, grumbling about getting shovels.

"Alright Jonah," Randell said from inside. "You've got to see this."

Jonah trotted back to the living room, where Randell White was standing over the now open chest "I'm calling this a strike." Randell announced. "Our Jasper is a practicing Muslim," he said, carefully handing him with both hands a well-worn Koran.

"Great work. Would you help them dig up the grave they found in front of the big willow tree? You might need to find more shovels. I got this."

It all clicked in his brain. Jasper was a plant, and he was pretty sure that he killed Mr. Lee and took over this house to be close to Stanley and his family when they arrived. And whoever planted Jasper made sure that he knew as much as he did about them. *But who sent Jasper and why?*

While he waited for confirmation that Mr. Lee was the occupant of that grave, Jonah knelt down to the open chest and proceeded to take out what he suspected were the true belongings of Jasper: besides the weathered Koran, there was a prayer rug, a ceremonial type robe he'd never seen before—"Except like the one worn by the Iman in Crystal Springs when I was forced to shoot my son," Jonah explained to the open chest.

All of it pointed to Jasper being someone important to an Islamic group... *Maybe even Abdul Farook, the terrorist leader,* he pondered.

Jonah must have been lost in his thoughts for a while, because the next announcement from Randall was, "we've uncovered a skeleton."

Jonah dashed outside to see for himself, not really knowing what an oriental skeleton would look like compared to an Anglo one.

The men were carefully uncovering a hand now.

As the skeletal remains of this person were revealed, he could see the size of it was very small. *Like an elderly oriental man*!

Then his men stopped abruptly, Bagley stood up from the hole and murmured, "Jonah, take a look at his head."

"Strike three," Randell stated.

Jonah shuffled around the dirt pile, which looked like sacks of trash, though it was hard to see in the dark. He was handed a flashlight and shown it at the skeleton's head. It was instantly obvious. A perfectly round hole right in the skeleton's forehead.

They now knew Mr. Lee was murdered, and he was sure Jasper did it.

Chapter 4

Lexi

July 13th

Lexi couldn't quite make out Jonah's disquieting words; some sort of warning interrupting her repetitive nightmare.

She glimpses behind her, catching Jonah in the distance, yelling his warning—she still can't hear what he's saying. When she returns her gaze forward... *it's Abdul.* He's standing directly in front of her, like some unmovable force. She dead stops only inches from him. He's caught her, again. He always catches her.

Abdul snickers. The dark whiskers of his beard and mustache framed his mouth like old moss surrounding the opening of a black cave. They flutter with each mocking laugh. He lifts one of his hands to his cheek, where a knife is half sticking out. It's her knife. She had stabbed him there with it.

He smoothly slides the knife out, releasing spurts of his own blood. She panics and tries to run away, but she cannot. She's locked in place, so that he can do what he wants to her. A wave of shock and revulsion possesses her entire body, just as he *would* possess her.

Tremor-filled laughter fills his lungs and then pours out as a howling cackle. "You silly girl, ha-ha-ha." He points the knife at her. Blood is dripping off it and his hand. "Don't you know, Suhaimah, I cannot be killed. Nothing will stop me"—He surprises her with a quick step forward— "until we are reunited as husband and wife." He stabs her in the belly.

The sharp pain was as unexpected as his move, causing shudders throughout every muscle.

Her hands reflexively explored for the knife wound, but there was nothing there. She glared at her gut and saw no evidence of an injury. Her eyes flicked up and rather than seeing Abdul, as she expected, it was Jasper, looking down at her. She felt below her to confirm she was lying on the Fury's front seat.

It was all a dream.

"Oh good, you are awake." Jasper said and pulled a hand away from hers, clasp around her belly. "We are going now. You are driving while Frank and I sleep."

There was no waiting for a response. He backed away, slammed the driver's side door and walked around the front of the car, toward the passenger side.

"Glad to see you slept," Frank said from the back seat, "but it looks like you were having another bad one."

Lexi sat up in her seat, letting her boots fall to the Plymouth's floor mat, and attempted to collect her thoughts. Her brain was a fog, clouded over from sleep and what was obviously now another nightmare about Abdul. But this time it was different somehow. *Wasn't Jonah in this one?*

"Are you good to drive?" Frank asked, seeing she wasn't entirely with it.

"Yeah, just trying to sort out my drea—" Her eyes shot to the radio, which was now off. "Why is the radio off?"

"Jasper found it on before he woke you. He said that it was shorting out and he had to turn it off because he was afraid a fire might have started."

She could smell the faint scent of electrical smoke. "But I got it working again; the antenna was loose."

"Guess there was more wrong with that thing," Frank responded. "Don't worry, if we don't find a radio on the road, we'll notify our friends in Florida and Texas right after we defeat Abdul and get Travis. Come on. We need to get in some mileage today."

Jasper punctuated Frank's statement by dropping onto the bench seat and slamming shut the front passenger door. Jasper stared at her with his unreadable eyes that seemed insistent on something... Probably that she get going. She could never tell what that man was thinking. Whereas Frank was an open book: he was either pissed at her, which was most of the time, or somewhat pleased. But always readable.

"Seems like all I do is worry," she said and then fired up the Fury's engine. "I'll take any suggestions as to our best route." She spun them around and headed down the small path they had come in on. Other than their faint tire tracks, it seemed less road-like and more game trail.

"Just continue northeast along the same route we planned to I95. And watch out for blockades. I'm going to catch an hour or so and then I'll take over. Wake us if you see anything that seems off. And do *not* speed." Frank laid himself down on the back seat, out of view of the rear-view mirror. Jasper turned his head away from her and rested it against the back rest.

She was on her own.

Endurance

Jonah

"Did you try them more than once?" Emily asked, her voice abnormally high-pitched and piercing, as if she were physically hollering right in his ear.

Jonah glared at the radio, frustrated not at her but his inability to reach their friends. "Of course, Em." He took a breath and considered seriously again jumping into his Vette and racing North to catch up with them. He just didn't know if there was something else he could do to get word to Frank and Lexi that Jasper wasn't who he said.

Then, he had an idea, and he pounded the mic button. "Em, I'm going to try Frank's military buddies, in Texas. Maybe they'll have a way to reach them that we haven't thought of. Otherwise, I'm tempted to drive there myself to warn them."

"Please don't do anything rash. I need you here. Go and try Frank's friends and then let me know. Out."

She was gone.

Jonah thumbed through Frank's hand-written notes

about how to reach someone named Grimes… Finding what he was looking for, he turned the dial of the Kenwood to the frequency Frank listed and pushed the microphone button. "Calling Mr. Gri—ah, Mr. G. This is ah, J. I'm calling with important information about F and L. Do you read me."

Barely a couple of seconds passed. "This is G. J, please give me the password and then dial to the second frequency F listed."

Jonah didn't understand what it meant, but Frank's writing was clear enough. "Chicken Foot." He didn't officially sign out or wait for acknowledgment that it was correct. As Frank said, if Grimes accepted it, he would be at the next frequency specified.

Jonah homed in on the frequency, turning the big frequency dial with the attempted agility of a safe cracker, and immediately depressed the mic button, "This is J. Is G there?"

"Thank you, J. F said, you or another friend from town might call on his behalf. We're going crazy for news. You got any?"

Jonah cleared his throat first and then clicked on the mic. "Unfortunately, I don't have any good news. In fact, it's bad. Firstly, I haven't heard anything from them, even though I installed an HF unit in their Plymouth with instructions to check in once per day until they arrived. But nothing since yesterday. And that's not the bad news… The bad news is that Jasper, their neighbor and supposed friend of Stanley—who was a friend of mine by-the-way—is in fact one of Abdul's men. He killed the neighbor and buried the body in the yard and waited for Frank, Lexi, and Travis to get here. And Jasper is with

Frank and Lexi... I'm all out of ideas, short of sending someone up there to catch them by car. Do you know of any way to reach them?"

There was a staticy hiss that undulated up and down, much like Jonah's nerves had been the last few days. He was about to ask if G had received his broadcast when the signal boomed in.

"I have an idea or two..."

It was only then that Jonah recognized the voice was that of Lieutenant Grimes of the American Freedom Network. *THAT Grimes?* he thought.

"... I'll work on finding a way to reach them. But sending someone their way to intercept maybe the only way to be sure they get the message."

Jonah thought of Emily's request to stay with her before answering. "I'll see what I can do on that front. We're preparing in the unlikely event of another assault on our town from the Islamic town just south of us."

"Hear you. Got to protect your town first. Frank and Lexi are pretty smart and can take care of themselves. Let me work on contacting them."

"Thanks G, and I'll keep trying on my end."

Lexi

L exi pulled down her *shemagh* to take a sip of water and yanked it back up again. It was Jasper's idea that they wear them to protect against the dust from the open windows—which were left open so they could hear better what's going on outside. And with the enemy so close, Jasper suggested they look a little like them, if they get stopped. He said it would give them an element of surprise. She thought other than the dust thing it was a bad idea, but Frank went along with it. So that was that.

She glared at both, wishing one of them were awake to talk to her, so as to dispossess her from the nightmare seemingly forever imprinted on her conscious mind. Instead, her only mental diversion was the endless landscape of trees and the highway, clogged with dead cars.

But that damned image of Abdul, with his cheek squirting blood, while he pointed the knife she'd stabbed him with at her, calling her by the name he had given her.

Stop! she admonished herself.

She let her eyes wander to the side of the road, focusing on the blur of the trees as they rolled by.

When she returned her gaze to the road ahead, she had to rough swerve the car, narrowly missing what looked like a person standing in the middle of the access road. But it wasn't just any person.

It was Abdul.

She glared at the rear view, of course seeing no one.

The hyperventilating started again, just like last night.

She gasped for air, even though there was plenty of it pouring in through the side windows. An end of her *shemagh*, was being yanked at by the blowing breezes, while simultaneously whipping against her cheeks.

She quickly eyeballed Jasper, in the passenger seat. He was awake now but appeared unfazed by her erratic driving. He simply scowled—as he always did—out the windshield. Movement again in her rearview mirror revealed Frank, at first frowning at her from the back seat, then hissing his constant warning, "Don't speed." He must have sensed there was no real problem because he turned his head away and closed his eyes. Like Jasper, he too seemed only concerned with sleep right now.

Once again, she was stuck dealing with her nerve-wracking anxiety about Abdul, on her own. All she'd been doing is stressing over Abdul. Every waking moment she's been reminded by her nightmares or by Frank and Jasper that she was going to have to deal directly with the man who had taken everything from her, now including her brother.

Frank and Jasper were doing their best to look after her, but Frank's nonstop training and both their hawk-ish watching of every move she made were a constant reminder of the giant millstone she was forced to carry. She didn't want any of it. As much as she relished the thought of killing Abdul and retrieving her brother. She almost wished she could embrace her old self and run away... to where she didn't know; just away.

She looked up to the sky and thought a little prayer might help, as Frank had suggested... *Allah or God or Whomever you are, could you get me out of this whole thing. I just don't think I can do it. I'm so scared...*

Lexi instantly felt pangs of guilt from this. Did she really want to run away from her brother and not deal with Abdul?

"Yes!" she silently yelled.

From her periphery, she caught the glitter of flashing dots on the road.

"Spikes!" she huffed, while jerking at the wheel in a vain

attempt to swerve around them. *No chance.*

The Fury's tires exploded and now she had to wrestle control of the same vehicle that her father couldn't, in the process losing his life when he had crashed into a highway sign.

She slammed both feet on the brake pedal and held tight to keep the car pointed in one direction, the car's drums locked up and tried to spin them around the other way. But she held on with everything she had.

They came to a screeching halt.

At the same moment, a swarm of masked men came at them from all sides, guns drawn.

Chapter 5

American Eagle Patriots

Their car's tires were blown out and they were surrounded by men with guns. Trapped.

Four men, two in front and two in back had their rifles pointed at Lexi and her group, with one barking orders. *In Arabic!*

The men were brandishing AK-style rifles, and their faces were covered by Middle-Eastern *shemaghs*, which would seem to indicate they were the enemy, and not just some thuggish group intending on stealing their supplies.

Lexi had involuntarily jerked her revolver from her holster and pointed it toward the noisy one. Without looking, she suspected Frank in the back seat and Jasper in the passenger seat, were doing the same with their weapons. But there was no way the three of them could lift their weapons above the car's frame and shoot all four men before at least one of them would return fire.

After the leader's command, the only sounds were the mind-numbing chorus of the summer locusts.

She couldn't see their faces, but the blue eyes of the loud one seemed dead set and determined. The others were different: their eyes flitted around like fireflies trapped in little jars, and their weapons appeared to be twitching. Other than the leader, these men were nervous.

For several long moments, there was not a peep from anyone inside the car or out. When the noisy one yelled again something that sounded like "Identify yourself!"—though her Arabic was already too rusty to be sure—she noticed something both peculiar if they were really Islamic… and familiar.

On each of their forearms, just below their shoulders, were roughly hewn, almost hand-drawn patches of an eagle.

An American Eagle!

"Hey asshole," Lexi belted out in English, while lowering the scarf covering her face with a free hand so that her words were clear. "You may have us out gunned, but I'll get you in your nut-sack first. So, stop pointing your rifles at us, eunuch!"

Frank snickered from the back seat. Jasper let out a loud sigh.

Blue Eyes lowered his weapon and pulled his *shemagh* down, revealing the stubbled mug of a very pleasant-looking man—not much older than her—framed by a wide grin. He chuckled and then in a smooth voice said, "Okay guys, they're not rag heads." He made a twirling motion with his hand above his blond head and gave a whistle. The other men, except one, relaxed and motioned like they were relieved and ready to walk away from their car.

"Jay, you good?" Blue Eyes asked the man on Jasper's side, whose rifle was still pointed in Jasper's direction.

"Tell this one to lower his scarf so we can see he's not one of them," demanded Jay. The man's giant brows furrowed into one V-shaped, weed-ladened hedge to show his seriousness. Yet, his rifle quivered even more than when she'd first noticed.

Jasper slowly raised his Thomson above the dash, ensuring it was visible to Jay. "My machine gun says, 'No!' And you do not want Thompson to say anything more to you."

"Hey Jasper, back off," Frank calmly stated in a measured tone, "These folks are not our enemy."

"Jay," Blue Eyes yelled, "stand down!" He marched around the front of the car, toward Jay.

Jay's rifle barrel fluttered in the air like a leaf, but his finger was no longer on the trigger. *At least Blue Eyes taught good trigger discipline to his militia*, Lexi thought.

With an extended hand, Blue Eyes guided Jay's rifle downward. "Come on, the convoy could be here at any moment. We need to get into our positions."

Jay's shoulders sagged. He nodded and turned his back to them.

The four men quick-shuffled toward the overgrown area they'd just sprung from.

"Hey, wait!" Frank hollered from the back seat. "Haven't you forgotten something?"

Blue Eyes halted, turned, and glared back at him, acting as if he were being delayed from a date. The man's eyes turned into slits, as he waited for Frank to give a retort as to why they were being further inconvenienced.

At first Lexi didn't know what Frank meant either, but then she nodded when she figured out his point. "Yeah, you guys blew out our tires. *You* need to fix them."

Blue Eye's glare went from serious to curious to downright stupefied, as if what Lexi's suggested was the dumbest thing he'd ever heard. Then he started to smile again and his smile turned into a cocky smirk. "Maybe you shouldn't have been driving so fast. You never know what you're going to run into."

"You mean, like the tire deflation spikes you threw under our tires?" Frank stated more than asked.

Blue Eyes shrugged his shoulders in defeat.

A radio chirped and Blue Eyes yanked a walkie from his side and turned up the volume to better hear the barking voice. "Where the hell are you?" a man demanded in a gravely roar. "The convoy will be here in a few minutes. Report!"

"Come on, Slim," insisted Jay to Blue Eyes who seemed hesitant to answer the voice on the other side of the walkie.

Finally, Blue Eyes/Slim barked back at his radio, "We're on our way, Cappy." Slim returned it to his belt and turned back to address Lexi's car. "Alright, if you'll follow me and be quiet, we'll see what we can do about getting you back on the road. But we gotta go now."

"Where are we going?" Lexi asked, already out of the car, holstering her revolver and snagging her pack from the front seat.

Slim paused to eyeball her from head to toe before answering, again with a big overconfident smile. "We're going to kill ourselves some terrorists."

He spun on a boot heel and darted into the overgrowth, following the path his men had already tread before they disappeared moments ago. Frank grunted something from behind her, but Lexi ignored it. She couldn't move fast enough.

Leaving her driver's side door wide open, she darted to Slim, not even looking back, or addressing Frank's and Jasper's voiced demands that she stop. Their noisy footfalls told her they weren't too far behind.

Following strangers, who had moments ago been pointing guns at them was probably a foolish exercise. Her logical side told her this. Yet this also felt right to Lexi: these people were some sort of militia fighting the same bastards they were. More so, with each bounding stride through grass and weeds, she felt... free. She was doing what *she* wanted to do, not something she felt obligated to do.

The foliage was dense, not allowing Lexi to see anything, except for Slim's backside—he wore desert-patterned, military fatigue pants, just like hers—as they raced over a path that was no bigger than that of a small game trail.

For the first time in the 48 hours since Abdul had come back into their lives, she felt both exhilarated and happy. Then a distant gunshot brought her back to reality.

All the anxiety flooded back.

The exhilaration was still there, but she felt at a knife's edge, not knowing where she was going or where these strangers were taking her. There were rustling noises all around.

Finally, after fast-jogging for a couple of long minutes in a straight line, Slim dashed to his right. She followed.

Immediately in front of them, the brush thinned out and the trees opened.

Slim didn't slow at the canopy's edge. He burst through the trees and then darted across the same highway access road they'd been traveling on and started up an overpass road. He hung low as he ran, keeping his head below the roof lines of the dead cars and trucks lining the overpass. At a white van, near the top middle of the bridge, he stopped and disappeared inside its side entrance.

Lexi mimicked Slim's movements as she made her way to the same white van. Before reaching it, she peeked back over her shoulder to check on her protectors. Neither Frank nor Jasper were in sight, having not yet come out from the tree line. For a moment, she considered going back to check on them. But then she decided the delay was because of Frank's bum knee, which had been bothering him even more the last twenty-four hours.

They're fine, she reassured herself and continued back up the rest of the way to the excitement.

She felt exhilaration at what she was expecting to witness. These people were part of a militia, just like Grimes on the radio had reported. They were fighting the terrorists to save her country. They were on the front lines, just like she was now.

When she reached the van, she doubled over sucking in several breaths of humid air. The van's side door was open wide, revealing Slim, who was kneeling beside another man in a wheelchair. He had Slim's shade of hair, only a lot longer. Slim was glued to long lensed binoculars, pointed out a window facing south, down the highway. The long-haired twin, who looked older, had one eye up to the eyepiece of a scope attached to a bolt action rifle also pointed out the window. "I see 'em," Slim mumbled, his voice an octave higher than earlier.

Without moving his head, Slim lifted his radio and stated, "Okay, everyone. Remain in position. We don't want Hajji to see us before they reach our trap." His voice was now as smooth and calm as before, like a seasoned quarterback calling the next play against an inferior team.

Lexi looked past the men, out the van's side window, squinting hard to see what they both easily saw through their telescoping lenses.

At first it was just a small moving reflection, like a mirage, in the middle of the road, a couple of miles or more away. Then she caught several glints of light, from a long line of large truck windshields, moving toward them.

Without thinking, she withdrew her revolver and revealed a smile.

Jasper

Jasper was ready to kill all these militia members himself, just for putting him through this escapade.

He finally caught up enough to see Lexi, but remained hidden so that she wouldn't see him. He had taken care of Frank so that he wouldn't get in his way. Now, Jasper felt it was time to act further. But first he had to get Mahdi Abdul's approval.

There were just too many possible problems before him, which if he didn't step in and intervene, this situation could rapidly spin out of his control: Namely, Lexi could get injured interjecting herself into what was obviously going to be a battle. But he also didn't like what he suspected was one of Mahdi's group of fighters about to be ambushed by this American militia.

Jasper felt sure that the militia members wouldn't survive a full confrontation with the Mahdi's better trained soldiers. They may surprise them, but it was what would happen after the ambush that concerned him. Playing out the scenario further, upon witnessing this imbalance, their young leader Slim, would want to engage, and Lexi would as well. That's when Lexi would be in the greatest potential peril.

It was time to end this thing now. Not the ambush: there were too many pieces already in motion. But he would stop any chances of Lexi getting hurt, by quickly taking out Slim and his wheelchair-bound comrade in the van.

Jasper had set himself up behind one of the vehicles on the bridge and had Slim and the other man in the sights of the M1 Garand he had pulled from their car. Lexi was in between them, but he had two easy shots. So other than being startled, she would be fine.

He pulled out his satellite phone and dialed the Mahdi's

number.

Chapter 6

Faisal

Faisal Shahzad's truck was nearly glued to the taillights of the US Army truck in front of him. After every few seconds, he shot sidelong glances out each of his open windows. His years of training at the ranch taught him to look for anything out of the ordinary which could hurt their mission.

Even though he was only second in command and bringing up the rear of this convoy, he took his role very seriously. He knew that at any moment some opportunity might present itself and change his standing, and maybe even shine the light on him to his Mahdi.

When the brake lights flashed in front of him and then burned bright, Faisal had to resist the urge to jam on his own brakes for fear of rear-ending the truck. Since twenty of the ICA's finest fighters were in his cargo hold, he also didn't want to do anything that would imply that he was weak or nervous. So, he pumped his brakes smoothly, bringing them to a quick but controlled stop, while also jogging the truck slightly to the left so that he could get a better angle on the front of the convoy and why they had stopped.

Ahead of their lead convoy truck was a blockade of cars and trucks, just before an overpass. Their commander was in the lead truck's passenger seat, no doubt considering whether to force their way through the blockade or take the highway exit about one hundred meters away. Like him, the other trucks were lined up in single file, waiting for their commander to make his decision.

To Faisal, neither option felt right. But it wasn't his call.

Finally, there was movement up front.

The commander's lead truck turned away and out of sight. Faisal leaned over, onto the empty passenger seat to see the truck was headed off the highway, onto a parallel road, which he presumed would take them around the blockade.

That was the wrong decision, Faisal's brain screamed. But he did not know why.

Yet, each truck dutifully followed the same path, one after another, until it was Faisal's turn to fall into line.

The sparkle of something caught Faisal's attention and he crooked his eyes upward, at the top of the overpass. There, not unlike so many other overpasses they've driven through, was a line of dead vehicles. But this line looked different.

Most grouped cars had space in between them, because until the cars or trucks died, their drivers would have kept a distance to allow for time for braking. But this line of cars, trucks and vans on top of this overpass appeared to be connected. As if they were pushed together.

Another glint of light.

It was coming from the side window of the van. There was someone inside the van with binoculars.

It's an ambush!

Faisal completely lost track of the fact that he was stationary on the highway, while the rest of the convoy had taken off without him. All he could do was glare at them right when the attack came.

Aalim Mohammad

Aalim Mohammad was overanxious, but he didn't know why.

The second in command of their convoy, bringing up the rear behind him, Faisal warned him about keeping his eyes open out his side windows and being aware of anything out of the ordinary. But Faisal always struck him as being too cautious. Besides, they were far better trained than the Americans they were likely to encounter.

He harkened back to reports they had received earlier from their commander about many of their divisions encountering pockets of American resistance. However, they were told not to worry about this as these so-called militia groups were composed entirely of untrained infidels, who were old and using ancient weapons, because their government had recently made military-style weapons illegal. Even better, they allowed women to join in their militias. Not that this detour in the road had anything to do with a militia.

This is nothing, he reassured himself.

Their own unit had encountered very little resistance as the American infidels had done exactly what they were told they would do: submit to death.

Aalim Mohammad of course wanted more from his enemy. He wanted resistance. He wanted to fight his enemy, even if his enemy was composed of women and the elderly. He licked his chops imagining what it would be like to engage women in battle, as he kept his truck close, but still a safe distance from the truck in front of him.

He was jolted out of his daydream when he heard a low rumbling sound ahead, like a desert thunderstorm that grew stronger in the distance. Several voices called out in the convoy.

He shot a glance at his side mirrors and noticed that Faisal's truck was no longer behind him.

Where did he go?

Something caught his eye, and he refocused his glance upward to an endless expanse of trees and grass. Probably nothing.

Then he saw it.

It was a little thing that looked out of place. A flash of black that didn't belong, beside a brown tree-trunk.

He craned his neck forward and saw it about fifty meters away. It was a man with a gun pointed at—

He crashed into the back of the truck in front of him, sending him forward against the large steering wheel, the only thing that kept him from going through the windshield.

The tumbling sound of men and equipment, rattled in the back of his truck, followed by angry yelling in multiple languages. All were somewhat blotted out by crashing sounds and more hollering in front of him.

"Logs!" wailed one of the voices, as Aalim Mohammad attempted to back his vehicle away from the truck he was now connected to. He couldn't find the gear, causing grinding noises. Then he caught a flash of several figures running toward them on his right side.

He ground his truck into reverse and put some distance between him and the truck in front of him. But he hit something hard from behind, bringing him to a stop.

At the same time, the truck in front of him had moved to his left, revealing a sight he could not explain, nor believe.

All the other trucks of the convoy were knocked off the road, either turned over, partially crushed, or rolling down the embankment. Headed toward him were many giant log polls, rolling down the road.

We drove into a trap, he thought and yanked at the steering wheel and stomped on the gas pedal, lurching his truck to his right, toward the figures with rifles closing in on him rapidly.

Aalim Mohammad looked up just as one of the log polls rolled past him, barely missing him. Another immediately followed, but bounced up and over his truck, just grazing his roof. Then another hit him dead on, stopping him like a stone wall. Once again, he was sent forward into the steering wheel, this time breaking something inside of him.

He gasped for air and then coughed, sending nail-point pain through his lungs. He reached for his weapon, ignoring the hurt.

Shots rang out everywhere, several of them finding his windshield. And now he could see the figures were coming at him not just from one side, but everywhere. They weren't old people; they ran like the young. Their weapons weren't old either; they looked new enough and plenty lethal.

Aalim Mohammad jumped out of the cab, bracing himself on pavement that seemed to move, while attempting to bring his rifle up, but he was punched in his belly. It seared with pain. Then something like a brick hit him in the square of his back, knocking him down to the ground, where his weapon popped out of his hands.

It all happened so fast he couldn't do anything but watch: the figures raced up to each of the damaged or destroyed trucks and fired their weapons into the cabs and into the backs of each truck. Their beloved fighters, who had been trapped in the trucks, had little chance of escape. One or two attempted to hobble away but were cut down like dogs. The black and gray figures swarmed all the trucks, including his, while firing hundreds of rounds at them.

One of the figures stood above him. This one was a small form, almost feminine looking. The shadow pulled down its scarf to reveal the smiling face of an impudent old woman, her long gray hair billowed out all around her like a proud harlot.

Aalim Mohammad couldn't believe this. It was impossible. It was *their* time to establish their caliphate. That's what their Mahdi told them. The Islamic Caliphate in America would crush the American infidels, who were so weakened by their corrupt culture, who were like children who desired to submit to anyone who volunteered to take care of them. Aalim was destined to be a hero in their victory, or he would have happily died as a martyr, taking many infidels with him on his way to paradise. But that wasn't going to happen.

The ultimate insult was that he would die in a battle where he didn't even fire his weapon, and at the hand of an old woman. It was too much for a proud warrior to take.

He spat a mouth full of blood and saliva in the woman's direction, not even getting close to her.

The old woman's shameless grin enveloped her whole face, as she smiled even bigger and steadied her rifle toward his head. She pulled back the charging handle, just to add to his misery and rub in the fact that she was the one who would take his life.

He glared at her barrel, waiting for his miserable death.

Chapter 7
Somewhere in North Carolina

Cappy

"Don't shoot, Gladys!" Cappy commanded. "We need one alive for interrogation." Simultaneously, Cappy blew an air-horn for a full second as the signal to his Patriots to halt their shooting. They had won.

Gladys lifted her head to acknowledge Cappy's command and gave a nod. She moved her Stag Arms pistol—a gift he'd given her only a few days ago—to her side, while she glanced back at the fallen terrorist. "Your life was just saved by a seventy-year-old grandma... Let that sink in, buddy." She spat back at him and turned to two of their Patriots who were inspecting the closest truck for survivors, "Hey, I need help securing this live one. And Ferg, call Doc and tell him we need to patch up Hajji ASAP and keep him alive so that he's ready for interrogation."

Cappy couldn't help but smile as he watched his men jump to it and do exactly as Gladys had requested. Within seconds, they had triaged the terrorist's wounds, loaded him onto an ATV and drove him back to base.

Gladys may have been seventy years old, but she was really no different than most of his militia members: red-blooded Americans, who lost so much to this enemy.

Gladys' home and family were nuked, along with the rest of DC. Cappy found her when she had broken down on her way home in North Carolina.

At that time, she had never fired a gun. But she took to shooting like an alcoholic takes to their first drink of the day. She was a natural. Even more valuable to him was her management experience and natural leadership skills. When his Patriots started to defend their country, he made her one of his team leaders and gifted her one of his favorite Stag pistols. More than a want for her, because of her personal losses, she *needed* revenge against these foreign invaders, and to win back her country. Like most of them, winning was everything to her. Even if it led to her own death.

Just like the rest of his unit, she performed to perfection during this exercise. As far as he could tell, there were only two injuries, all the while they exacted one hundred percent casualties to the enemy. He couldn't wait to join his men and women in celebrating their well-earned victory.

Interrogate the prisoner first, then celebrate, he told himself.

Cappy jumped in his Willys and sped to his tent.

Lexi

It all happened too fast; Lexi couldn't even comment on what she had seen.

She held her breath as the convoy stopped and Slim said, "Let's see if they take the bait." They did.

The whole group took the detour. She was going to ask if Slim had seen one of the trucks pull off, but then their ambush came so fast and furious that she lost herself in it.

She couldn't hold back her excitement. Not only was she witnessing the destruction of many of Abdul's troops, but it felt like she was a part—even though it was so small—of a much larger movement; that she was doing something that was bigger than herself.

Now, instead of driving slowly to a gloomy destiny that was predetermined by others, she was here. All she could do was stand in her place and watch it all unfold before her in awe.

Every one of the terrorists were ambushed and killed so fast, most didn't even have a chance to exit their trucks and put up a fight.

This is fricking awesome, she thought. Not because of the death, but the precision displayed by so many to take down nine trucks filled with several hundred well-armed fighters. And the whole rolling-tele-phone-poles-down-the-hill thing was brilliant too. But what struck her was that a non-military group of citizens were taking it to Abdul's great warriors. And rather than being overwhelmed with fear as she had been every mo-ment since Travis had been taken, she was exhilarated.

With each step of the exercise, Lexi couldn't help but glance over at the good-looking guy, known to her only as Slim, and wonder if he orchestrated the whole operational plan or if that honor belonged to the rough voice on the radio, who was called Cappy. Regardless of who came up with this surgical strike against the enemy, the whole thing was carried out to perfection.

Yet, as much as she thoroughly enjoyed watching this operation executed so flawlessly, Lexi had difficulty quelling a kind of apprehension she wasn't used to.

Rather than being on the front line, with the other American fighters, she was stuck here, watching all the action take place from a safe distance. She wanted to be down there with the fighters, taking the fight directly to the enemy instead of watching from a bridge, out of harm's way. She understood that Slim was a leader, and he was overseeing the operation from this station. She just couldn't stand to wait until, as Slim had said, "The horn was sounded."

So, Lexi waited.

When she heard the trumpet-like blast, which she now realized meant the whole thing was over, Slim finally sprang into action. He hopped to a stance and tapped the shoulder of the long-haired man seated beside him, "How many you get Mike?"

Mike pulled his head from the eyepiece of his long scope, attached to a beat-up looking rifle that was wrapped in camo tape. "Enough," he said. "But you stay frosty. I've got your six, brother."

"Check," Slim said, and he swiftly snatched a can of white spray paint from the floor and dashed out of the van, shouting back to her, "Come on. Follow me."

With gazelle-like movements, Slim darted across the bridge, and then down the off ramp littered with de-stroyed trucks, many of which were overturned, but all were battered. He slowed at the last one still standing up right. He turned toward the embankment, jogged around to the highway side, and stopped. There, he began spray-painting over what remained of the truck's olive-green canvas. It took shape almost instantly: that symbol she'd now seen many times: the American Eagle. It must be their adopted symbol. Ironically, it was also the symbol her father used. Slim's actions reminded her of something she'd seen in a movie. Then she remembered.

It was, *Red Dawn*, where the American insurgents painted a Wolverines caricature rather than an Eagle on the abandoned vehicles at each triumph. Strange how their situation was so eerily familiar to this, where they were now the insurgents, resisting their captors, who had successfully taking over. Until now.

She watched him scoop up a rifle and a couple of magazines discarded on the asphalt beside the truck he had just tagged. Then he sauntered up to Lexi. With a smile spread ear to ear, he held out the rifle and magazines. "Here, my present to you. You'll find this AK a lot more useful than your revolver."

She reached out to accept them, but he held on for a long moment, shining his white teeth, "And with full auto, a lot more fun too."

She mumbled her thanks and slung the AK over her shoulder. **The** magazines were hurriedly shoved into her pack. When she cinched it closed, he snatched her free hand and his eyes held hers. "Come on, Lexi. Now you'll have to join us in our celebration."

They shimmied across the highway and presumably back to their camp, both feeling euphoric but for different reasons.

She glanced back down the highway's blacktop.

It was a small tingle she couldn't shake, not unlike when she'd be alone in the dark and she'd imagine someone was watching her. She felt that now.

Then Slim tugged at her, and the feeling was gone.

Faisal

"Why are we not engaging the enemy?" huffed one of Faisal's young warriors. The man's breaths were uneven and heavy. He shared the man's anger.

Their eyes were glued on the two young people holding hands and walking back across the highway. "Patience. Mohammad—peace be upon him—saved us from the same peril as our brothers to allow us to get retribution, and retribution we will get. I assure you. But now is not the time."

The warrior started to rise, and Faisal grabbed his arm. He glared fire at Faisal and huffed, "We need to kill these infidels right now. And if we die; we die as martyrs as we are commanded to do."

Faisal kept hold. "Remember, what we are taught in Surah chapter 3; verse 125. 'Most certainly, if you believers are careful and patient and the enemy launches a sudden attack on you, Allah will reinforce you with five thousand angels designated for battle.'

"We are dealing with a greater force than we were told.

And because we misjudged our enemy and they attacked suddenly, we lost this battle. But they do not know about us yet, only because we have been careful and patient."

Faisal turned to face the rest of his men, each of whom was also desiring to run from the shadows of the tree they were hiding under to kill their enemy. "So, we will continue to be careful, and we will wait to see where their camp is located. Then tonight we will take 250 bullets each or a total of 5000 and surround this enemy and kill every single one of them."

Chapter 8
American Eagle Base Camp

Frank

Frank sat stewing alone in one of two director's chairs, under the camp's most expansive canopy, waiting.

He sucked at this. Waiting was a far worse exercise than participating in any battle. This made him anxious. Waiting meant depending on others. That was hard for an old warrior like Frank because others were often not dependable. He hoped this wasn't one of those times.

With nothing better to occupy his mind, he glared again at his surroundings, which were the open confines of a huge but empty tent-structure. Beside his seat was a small collapsible table and on the other side, the other director's chair. On top of the table sat something most unexpected, and it continued to draw his attention.

It was the last thing he thought he'd see in any militia's tent, even one that appeared to be as well organized. When he first recognized it, he did a double take.

It was a SINCGARS. A hardened portable transceiver used only by branches of the US military. Unlike the older amateur radios, which have large frequency dials and were intuitive to use, this one had a keypad that only a trained radio operator would find understandable. More importantly, amateur radios are available to anyone to buy and then operate, if they hold an FCC license. This unit was strictly military hardware and not available for civilian purchase because of its encryption capabilities. That's why seeing this radio in this non-military tent was so unexpected.

It could only mean that someone in this militia illegally procured this radio from the US military.

But that wasn't the source of his anxiety.

Since being deposited on his chair by Jasper and one of the group's militiamen, he'd been restlessly waiting for some word as to what had happened, and most important, if Lexi was safe.

Jasper assured him that he would make sure he kept her out of harm's way. But Jasper couldn't be everywhere at once, nor could he protect her from a stray bullet. Jasper had proven himself capable, but he was far from perfect: he was the one who had accidentally knocked him to the ground.

Not like I could have kept up, he lamented and then once more rubbed his constantly aching leg.

As much as he hated it, he would have to depend on Jasper as they made their way north to their face off with Abdul.

Frank's anxiety plateaued when the rumbling began outside and under his feet. It peaked further, if that were possible, when the gunfire started. Lots of gunfire. Then just as sudden, there was a distant blast of a horn, and it was quiet again. The quiet was equally disconcerting.

An excruciatingly long number of minutes passed before a cheering roared in the distance and then grew. Almost like the home crowd pouring out of a stadium after a winning game. The revelry swelled until it was just outside the tent. Jasper was the first one who bounded in. He flashed Frank a glance and mumbled, "She's fine," continuing to the other side of the tent. Before Frank could ask him where Lexi was and what the hell had just happened, a cacophony of voices entered the canopy from all directions, followed by the members of the American Eagle Patriots, all seeming to flow into the canopy at once.

He knew well the sounds of a military victory. He'd experienced many victorious battles and witnessed the same beaming faces, congratulatory slaps on the back, and congenial ribbings between brothers and sisters who had just returned from combat.

This group though was very different than the units he'd led in the Army There were certainly a few young faces, but most were older; many were men, but also a surprisingly larger number of women; and there were certainly a few athletically fit, but an over representation of the mildly to the very overweight. In some ways, it felt like a group of mostly misfit toys. But that wasn't a fair assessment as this group not only had a bond; they seemed to have enjoyed success, as a team.

An older woman with long gray hair entered the tent pumping an AR pistol into the air hollering, "Whoot-whoot! Damned good job, troops!"

The tent—now packed—erupted in cheers.

"That's Grandma," crackled a pubescent voice from beside Frank. The lanky kid, standing beside him couldn't have been much older than fourteen. "She's as kick-ass as some of the younger and more experienced Patriots." The kid gleamed a mouth full of wire braces.

Movement on his other side caught Frank's attention, and he saw a diminutive man with metal-rimmed glasses had taken up residence beside the SINCGARS transceiver, put on headphones and started playing with its keypad. Frank looked down, wondering what powered it and remembered catching a glance of a couple of solar panels nearby.

To his right, the crackling voice continued, "I taught her how to shoot," beamed the young guy with braces. He was no longer looking at Frank, his attention drilled into the familiar blond head that rose above all the others crowded in the tent. The group quieted as the young man, who went by the name of Slim, strode to where Jasper had been standing, but no longer was.

Jasper had told him that he didn't care for crowds, so it made sense that he didn't hang around. Knowing him, he was hanging in the dark shadows of a tree, just outside of the tent. Listening and watching.

Slim stood up on a stool to gain elevation. When he had their attention, he raised his hands in the air to quiet everyone further.

Slim was a natural leader.

The charged-up men and women who packed the tent, simmered to a quiet buzz.

At the same time, Lexi pulled up to Frank and put an arm around him. In his ear she whispered, "You good?"

Frank smiled, nodded, and mouthed, "You?"

She nodded back, flashing a grin, and then turned her attention to Slim. Her grin took over all her features. He may have been naive about women, but he wasn't too obtuse to see that she really liked the young man.

Slim flashed a colossal smile in their direction. Then

he worked the room. "Friends, you did it!" he bellowed. Cheers erupted again.

Slim smiled at this and waited patiently for it to subside.

"And with Grandma's idea of using telephone poles..." More cheers, drowning out his words. In the back, where the gray-haired woman they called Grandma was listening, several hands patted her shoulders and back. She nodded acceptance but looked ever more embarrassed by their attention. She seemed completely different than the woman who first strode into the tent. He'd seen this in his soldiers too.

The adrenaline of the battle was wearing off, and that's when the emotions of what happened often caught up and so did the fatigue. And as attention returned to Slim, Frank noticed Grandma look older than she did mere moments ago.

"We have suffered only two injured Patriots, and only minor injuries at that. But we killed one hundred percent of the terrorists and secured more weapons and supplies..."

Slim stopped speaking and did a quick scan of the tent. He leaned down to someone nearby and Frank heard him ask, "Where is Cappy?"

Cappy

"**W**ho gave you your orders? I want details," Cappy hollered, his face nearly pressed up against his subject's.

As expected, Aalim Muhammad didn't answer. Since first telling him his name, Aalim responded the same way to every question, he just quietly smiled.

This time, blood coated Aalim's teeth as heavily as it did most of the surface of his face. But he held his smile, appearing to have no intention of answering the infidel's question.

Purely for his own pleasure and nothing else, Cappy made a fist with his motorcycle glove and drove it with extreme force—the glove's steel alloy nubs connecting first—into the man's cheek, tearing more flesh and breaking at least one bone.

Aalim's head snapped violently to one side and his body lolled forward, held back by his restraints and nothing more.

For a moment, Cappy thought he might have knocked the terrorist out, but then Aalim shuddered. He lifted his head up and glared his destroyed face back at Cappy.

The punch may have been a wasted effort, though it filled Cappy with a modicum of satisfaction. These bastards were going to pay in their own blood and misery for what they had done to America, he would make sure of it if he had to torture each and every one of the terrorists himself. But he wasn't just after revenge. He desperately needed more intel. His little bird in the Army warned him that he wouldn't be able to feed them intel much longer. When his source told him about the convoy, he also said this was all he could give: his superiors were told no more helping militias like Cappy's.

So, Cappy's Patriots would have to collect their own intelligence, and this was the only live semi-senior terrorist he was likely to see. He assumed this man was first or second in command because he was at the back of the convoy, and he understood English. He would have to get serious with this one.

"Okay tough guy. Let's see how tough you really are." Cappy pulled the bloody glove off his hand and dropped it with a loud *thunk* on the table in front of Aalim, causing Aalim to jump in his seat. The terrorist's head lolled to one side before he snapped it back to glare again at his captor.

Knowing he still held Aalim's attention, Cappy stepped around to the other side of the table and reached down to get what he needed next. What would follow was a lot slower but was necessary when the subject was strong like this one. He relished what was coming next, preferring those subjects who thought they could hold out, like Aalim. They never kept silent during this next phase of the interrogation. This was the fun part.

Cappy *thumped* down hard onto the table his roll of tools, relishing Aalim's startled reaction. The thunderous applause from the next tent drowned out Aalim's weak groan.

With care, he untied the red-brown-stained twine that held the leather roll of tools together. After unfurling it he said, "You see Aalim Muhammad, I learned a useful trade during my time in Iraq."

He folded down a flap of leather which covered the handles, followed by the top flap, revealing the business side of each instrument: ice picks, saws, retractors, and scalpels. He let his fingertips methodically run across the tops of each, relishing the tactile feel, while picturing their use. But it wasn't just for his pleasure: this was theater. He knew Aalim was following his movements with great attention. He wasn't likely to pass out at this stage.

More cheering from the other tent and Cappy glowered in that direction as if to will his militia to be quiet now. This would ruin the psychological aspects of what he was doing. When the revelry subsided, Chappy returned his attention back to his subject. "You see, Aalim, one thing I learned is that no one, and I mean not one person, could withstand what I have planned for you next. I know this, and I think you do too."

He withdrew a scalpel and turned to face the subject directly.

"Aalim, have you ever witnessed someone being skinned alive?" He slapped the scalpel's blade against one of Aalim's bloodied cheeks to drive the point home.

Aalim to his credit not only didn't say a word, but his eyes belied the terror he was sure to have been feeling. Unfortunately, to continue Cappy needed to make sure he wasn't going to be interrupted by any further revelry from the celebration nearby.

"As much as I'd like to continue, I must pause to join my fellow comrades for a few minutes, as we celebrate the slaughter of the dogs you call soldiers. While I'm gone, consider how painful it will be for me to remove your skin slowly. Or... you can tell me what I want and I'll give you a good death so you can join your virgins." He dropped the scalpel, now bloodied from tapping Aalim's face, on top of table so that Aalim could stare at it while he was gone.

Cappy repositioned the gag back on Aalim. No sense in having him scream and alert his Patriots at what he was doing. Although these civilians were just learning about the brutality of war, they were still too soft for what he had to do as their leader. And that included his youngest boy, Slim. Mike understood a little of this, but without his legs, he couldn't take over.

"I'll see you real soon, Aalim."

Cappy pulled off his bloodied knit cap and soiled rain slicker, leaving them on a chair as he rushed through the front flap of his tent. It was a good time to leave and let his subject consider what lay ahead. But he also knew he had to make a showing, or someone might enter his tent and interrupt him before he got the Intel he needed.

Aalim Muhammad

A alim scowled at the scalpel, not at all concerned about what the infidel had said. If he could get to it, he just might be able to use it to free himself before this infidel returned and made him say something he would regret for eternity.

Using the weight of his body, he lunged forward, sending the chair legs closer to the table by a centimeter or two, before the carpeted surface grabbed on and threatened to send him over and onto his already damaged face. It took all his might to keep himself upright.

He mumbled a weak curse into his gag and started to lose hope. He felt sure he wasn't going to escape this and was destined for a painful death. What was worse was what he might say. Unfortunately, he knew too much: He knew who was in command and where their orders were coming from. He also knew where they were going before they were ambushed. *If only Allah would take me now*, he thought.

A slight breeze blew through the tent, along with a shadow which passed in front of him. Aalim's eyes searched the infidel's tools.

The scalpel is gone.

Aalim blinked back the blood, which had seeped into his eyes and blurred everything, sure now that he wasn't seeing things properly. Perhaps he had lost too much blood.

He felt the hot breath of someone on the back of his neck. *"Assalamualaikum,"* whispered a voice.

He tried to reply, *Assalamu Alaikum*, but it came out as a murmur.

"Don't speak, friend. You have fought well, and I am sending you to paradise because of your loyalty to Mahdi Abdul, who greatly appreciates you."

Aalim ate up every syllable from this stranger, waiting for his next words, now sure that Allah sent this man in answer to his prayer. A sharp pain began in his back, right around where he'd been shot, and then slid deep inside his body. He suppressed his desire to scream from the pain and the shock.

Almost as quickly, the pain was replaced by a warm radiance that washed over him.

The shadow passed back before him and the scalpel that had disappeared, now reappeared with a *clang*. It was bloodier than when the infidel had held it. He understood why.

He smiled at this and watched the stranger who had given him his release pass through the same flap as the infidel did earlier. He would no longer have to look at that man or worry about giving up his secrets.

Aalim closed his eyes and recalled the picture of what he was sure he would see next; what he had been told he would see by all the leaders of his faith when it was time.

Less than a minute later, Aalim left this world. But what he saw next was nothing like what he was told.

Chapter 9

Frank

The young man everyone called Slim, accepted the adulation of his militia members all the while making his way toward Frank and Lexi. He was holding two cups in his hands.

"Here," he said to Frank, "please enjoy a beer and join in our celebration."

"I'll pass, thanks," Frank said, not accepting the red plastic cup of suds. He would have loved nothing more than to drink a beer and toast what sounded like a decisive win against the enemy, but they had some more pressing matters to discuss, and he wanted to remain clear headed.

"Then you won't mind if your daughter has one in your place, would you?" Slim thrust the cup toward Lexi, who seemed more than willing to accept it.

"She's not—"

Jasper came out of nowhere, pushing others aside, and snatched the cup from Lexi before her fingers could grasp it. He took a quick sip of the drink, holding it away from her as if it were toxic and might spill on her. He appeared to scrutinize the mouthful, not unlike a wine taster might test an old Cabernet out of fear his patron might be about to drink vinegar. Jasper turned his body toward the cup and made a motion like he was going to pour it out, but then returned the cup, along with his normal scowl at Lexi, announcing, "It is not poison." Lexi took a firm grasp of the cup and just scowled back at Jasper. Before she or anyone else could question this odd display, Jasper exited the tent.

"And he must be your bodyguard," exclaimed Slim with a grin.

Frank's mouth hung open for a moment and then closed. Then he looked at Lexi who gave a fleeting look back at Frank. Finally, Frank answered Slim, "Lexi is my goddaughter, not my daughter. And she's a grown woman. If she wants a beer or two at the most, I have no qualms. However, I do have a problem with what you and—"

"Major Franklin Cartwright!" A voice boomed from across the tent, silencing much of the revelry. Heads turned in that direction to find an older man, sporting a regulation haircut, saluting in their direction.

Frank of course knew the man all too well. He stood, using his director's chair frame as his cane, and saluted back with his right hand. "Captain Bedford Horton!"

The two men dropped their salutes and Captain "Cappy" Horton marched over to them, this time with his right hand extended. "Welcome to the American Eagle Patriots."

"You two know each other?" Slim asked.

They shook each other's hands in rapid motion.

"Better question is how they know each other?" Lexi asked.

"The major and I served in Iraq." Cappy turned his attention to Lexi. "And who is this fine-looking warrior?"

Frank just noticed that Lexi had an AK rifle slung around her shoulder, in addition to her pack. "Ah, this is my god—"

"—Lexi Broadmoor, Captain," Lexi stated with a smile and threw a salute at him.

"You're not Stanley Broadmoor's child, are you?"

"You knew my father?" she asked, now letting her own mouth fall open.

Frank knew of Stanley's time under Captain Horton; it was during that time that Stanley received his purple heart.

"Yes, of course I do. In fact, it was your father who saved my life and the lives of several of my men. Plus, he was the co-founder of this militia."

Slim stepped between the Captain and Lexi, shoulder first. "This patch was designed by your father. Rather the eagle was his design."

"You going to introduce me to your new friends," demanded a voice from nearby.

Slim sidestepped away to reveal a man with long blond hair, that almost looked white, rolling in on a wheelchair with big thick tires. It was immediately obvious that he was a jarhead with two steel artificial legs.

"Major," Slim said, "this is my brother, Marine sniper, Corporal Michael Horton. But we call him 'Hotshot Mike'."

"Corporal," Frank said offering a salute, even though it wasn't necessary.

"Major," Mike said offering his hand for a handshake. "It's just Mike now."

Mike looked like an older version of Slim, other than

the legs, a long scar on his forehead and the longer locks. He even had the same blue eyes, albeit more bloodshot. "Okay, Mike. Where did you serve?"

"Marine Sniper in Iraq. Two tours until an IED made me go home."

"He's still the best shot in this militia," Slim said, drinking down the rest of his beer. Lexi seemed to follow, drinking hers down as well and then offering a big yawn.

"And Mike, this is the Major's goddaughter, Lexi, who saw with me earlier."

"Enchanted, my dear Lexi," Mike said, carefully shaking Lexi's hand as if it were a delicate flower.

"By the way, Captain, congratulations on your victory today. I wish I could have seen it. Lexi tells me it was well executed."

"Just Cappy, Major and thank you. As you know, Major, it all comes down to the intel. We had some excellent Intel from an inside source about this convoy." He involuntarily glanced at the radio when he said this.

Frank was glad his host opened the door. He'd just have to be careful how he asked his question. "Speaking of that source, I noticed your borrowed a SINCGARS." At the mention of this, Cappy smirked slightly in acknowledgment of their secret. "Is your Intel source Army or Marine?"

Cappy's smile held, but then his face turned sardonic. "Silly me, I thought you were here to join up. What do I owe this honor of yours and your goddaughter's company, Major?"

Lexi attempted to answer. "We're here bec—"

"—*We* were headed North,"—Frank cut Lexi off, afraid she would give up too much information about where they were headed— "to Virginia to retrieve Lexi's brother. But your son and his men blew out our car's tires. So, unless you have four Firestone Redline tires for a 69 Fury, you owe us a vehicle."

Cappy shot Slim a scowl.

Slim squared his shoulders to his father and then let them drop. "We thought they were a scout vehicle," Slim's voice sounded smaller than his six-foot-three-inch frame. "Maybe it was driving ahead of the convoy. Besides, I was worried they would interfere with our operation. So, I made the call." Slim took a half-step back as if he expected to get struck by his father.

Cappy's face burned with anger for a millisecond and then he regained his composure. Captain Horton's anger was widely known during their service in Iraq, although Frank had not experienced it first-hand. It looked like he went to great lengths now to be more self-composed.

"Major," Cappy said, "You and your goddaughter have my sincerest apologies..." He looked upward, like he was considering how to ask something. Then his face changed, and he flashed an almost imperceptible smirk.

There was some excitement to their left, from the radio operator, which was unnoticed by most in the tent.

"Okay, Major. I will make sure you have a workable vehicle in the morning, if you would transport a friend of the cause up North, to the Virginia border."

Frank was ready to demand the vehicle without any strings attached, but he thought better of it because Cappy could have just as easily told them he was S.O.L. He was about to answer in the affirmative, but the radio operator's excitement boiled over.

The operator pulled his headphone cord out of the

radio and pushed in another cord, causing a feedback squeal from a giant speaker below the table.

He stood up from his chair with a Bible in one hand. Frank almost expected a sermon or some quick proclamation about sin. Instead, the radio operator shouted, "Quite everybody!" He then cranked up the volume to the speaker.

A familiar and reassuring voice boomed from the speaker, blotting out everyone's chatter, "Good morning, America. This is the American Freedom Network. We're broadcasting on this channel to give you the news and report on World War III in America…"

Chapter 10

American Freedom Network

Grimes

R obert Grimes, rose from his chair, even though it was far easier to sit with his splinted leg. He wanted to project his voice and standing was better for this. Drawing the microphone to his mouth, he continued, imagining himself at a podium, before a crowd of thousands. If he were lucky, many more times that number were actually listening to him now. Simultaneously, his mental clock was counting down the estimated number of seconds he had left before he would get kicked off this radio stage. *Better be quick about it.*

"Our nation is fighting a war for its life against Islamists who are focused on taking us over and then subjecting us to their Caliphate. But we are fighting back.

"I know not all of you are Christians. But even if you don't believe, my friends, these words have important meaning for everyone listening. Because there is much meaning within. Do you hear me, *much meaning within.*

"Today's readings come from Second Chronicles, fourteen. Then, we'll go immediately to Second Chronicles, thirty-seven."

Grimes smiled at the thought of the Islamists opening up their Bibles and realizing that there were only 36 chapters in 2nd Chronicles. He hoped they'd think it was a mistake and wouldn't be able to figure out his code. Mostly he hoped and prayed—a lot more lately—that everyone who needed to understand him, would.

"Tomorrow's lesson will start again with Ecclesiastes, chapter 82."

American Eagle Patriots Basecamp

Frank

"**Y**ou got 'em?" Cappy hollered at the radio operator who was busily scribbling down notes on a note pad.

"They're frequencies!" Lexi said at the top of her voice.

"How did *you* know?" Slim shot back. He appeared to be as perplexed as Frank was that Lexi figured it out that easily.

"Simple..." A glimmer of bewilderment splashed across her face, before she shook her head, sighed, and continued, "Simple. There are only thirty..." She flashed a look up at the canopy ceiling for some help. "...six chapters in 2nd Chronicles." She shot a half-glare at both. "I may not be a Bible reader, but I *do* remember stuff like that..." She closed her eyes, and her body swayed a little, like a tissue in a breeze. It was like she was drunk, which was something he had never seen of his goddaughter.

"And..." Slim began speaking, as if he were trying to help her, at the same time gingerly grasping her closest elbow to steady her. "Because the American Freedom Network had to have some way of telling us where to tune in after their signal was jammed. Because the jamming is happening more often now. Our radio operator should now be tuning to fourteen-point-one-four."

"Yes!" Lexi exclaimed with more certainty, releasing herself from Slim. She shook her head again and focused her gaze on Frank "That's what the code meant by the fourteenth book in the Bible, also known as 2nd Chronicles, plus the fourteenth chapter. In other words, 14.14... I guess kilohertz."

"She's absolutely right," Slim added. "That's on the 20-meter band."

"And when that frequency gets jammed," Lexi continued, her voice still loud and demanding attention. "The broadcast will continue on fourteen point three... seven."

"*Shhh*," hissed a long-bearded man standing next to Cappy. His eyes were like daggers stabbing at Lexi, who closed her eyes to either ignore him or something else.

There was a crackle and then the broadcast continued, presumably at 14.14 kilohertz.

"Patriots... We are seeing a change in tides, with private militias across the country taking it to the enemy and winning. We just received a report of a successful ambush of a convoy of terrorist trucks on the East Coast, where over one hundred ICA warriors were killed and none of our militia men and women were severely injured. Congratulations American Eagle Patriots!"

Frank eyeballed the radio operator, knowing now that he must have used the SINCGARS to radio this information to Grimes. It also meant they were in direct contact with Grimes.

Frank nodded at this, glad to have figured it out before he had answered Cappy's request.

"Militias across the country are forming and they need *you*, my fellow patriots. If you can fight, it's time for you to join the resistance. Find a CB radio and tune into Channel 9 to hear where your local militia is gathering recruits to help America fight back. Join the resistance now, Americans."

Frank's arm was bumped, and he looked up just as Slim was thrusting a flyer into his lap. Written all in block letters, it read, "JOIN THE RESISTANCE!" With a larger version of hand-drawn eagle icon in the middle. His mind immediately pictured Stanley who evidently was the originator of this icon. Then at the bottom it emphatically stated, "YOUR COUNTRY NEEDS YOU" and to "GO TO CHANNEL 9 ON YOUR CB RADIO".

He glanced up and saw Lexi had one of the flyers too and she was touching the eagle figure. Her eyes were storm clouds threatening to burst—she must have been picturing Stanley.

"But don't count out our US military. They may have been silent as of late, but I have it from good sources that they are planning a massive counterattack. In fact, any ti—"

The loud tone they had all become familiar with as a jamming signal, blared from the amplified speaker. Everyone pressed their hands or fingers to their ears, until the radio operator turned down the volume. Just as suddenly the tone was gone.

He suspected the operator was already tuning to the next frequency. As they all waited for the broadcast to resume, a thought lingered with Frank: he couldn't help but wonder about the military action Grimes mentioned.

An Undisclosed Location in Alabama

Porter Grimes

The air was hotter than the summer asphalt in Texas, and twice as humid. But no one seemed to mind.

They were all seated inside a small high school basketball court, requisitioned by the US Army. Every space was packed with personnel from different units of the Army, Air Force, Marines and even one unit of the National Guard. All were waiting to hear the OPLAN or Operation Plan for an upcoming joint combat operation conducted by the US military to finally strike back against this enemy.

All the gym's doors were locked shut and manned on the outside by MPs.

Like many of his fellow service men and women, Porter Grimes felt a healthy combination of nervousness and jubilation at that moment. He, too, was privileged just to be sitting here. He glanced at Wallace in the seat next to him. She noticed his beam, she returned his smile, but then her expression changed. She snatched his hand and squeezed it hard—*too hard*. Leaning closer, she whispered, "Grimes, don't go all squishy on me right now. You got us here and now we're finally going to get a chance to get some retribution against these bastards."

"Squishy?" Porter asked. "Me?" He displayed his goofy smile. "Seriously, I'm as glad as you that we're here... Hey, looks like it's about to start."

She released the pressure in her squeeze but didn't let go.

They both pivoted in their seats to face back toward the raised dais. On this, a telescoping microphone was located just below a basketball hoop, which had been elevated up to nearly ceiling height. A four-star general stepped onto the temporary platform and marched toward the microphone.

Porter couldn't wait to hear the details of the operation. So far, all he knew was what led him and Wallace here: some encrypted chatter his dad had picked up about two planned ops. Wallace and he were requested to report to this place to assist in the plan's execution. They raced here, arriving an hour ago. He suspected it was going to be a planned assault on Fort Rucker, just a few miles away.

It was his turn to squeeze, but he didn't look at her. He remained focused on the general, who stood at attention. The man's chest full of medals rose, just before he began speaking.

"My name is General Bennett C. Brown, Commander of the US Southern Command. I want to thank you all for being here. In a moment, I'm going to hand over the microphone to the combat commander leading this operation, which will be the US's first official strike force against the ICA bastards who invaded our country—"

"Let's kick Hajjis' ass, sir!" hollered a deep voice from behind them. "Hooah!" yelled a chorus of Army from the left side of the room, along with scattered laughter. "Oorah!" cheered several Marines.

Porter expected a stern reaction from the general.

Instead, General Brown smiled broadly and held his hands up to quiet the room. "Yes, soldiers, I say, Hooah, Oorah and HUA! You're damned right we're not only going to kick Hajjis' ass, we'll send 'em all to hell."

The whole room erupted. Not a single man or woman remained in their seats.

Frank

The radio speaker was library quiet for an excruciatingly long moment. Then Grimes' voice boomed once more.

"Two more points of warning...

"Watch out for our enemy. Remember he is often hiding in plain sight. Besides wearing Army fatigues, we're receiving reports from multiple sources, including from our own townspeople first-hand, that the enemy are driving in convoys, often comprised of deuce-and-a-halves and other older military vehicles. Most are still painted in Army regulation olive. But they're not Army.

"Assume all to be your enemy and demand to see a copy of written orders.

"Finally, Ma—"—a staticy pulse came and went—"—atch out for a wolf in your midst; he's not who he said he is.

"And to all Americans, stay vigilant and safe out there. This is—"

The loud pulsating jamming signal blared again, until the radio operator yanked the plug.

The tent erupted in chaotic conversations, some discussing what might be the pending military operations, or about the enemy driving around in old US Army trucks, but the majority discussed how quickly Grime's American Freedom Network was getting jammed.

Although all of these were concerns, Frank wondered what Grimes meant with his warning of a "wolf in your midst; he's not who he says he is." It was cut off so he couldn't figure if it was directed to the general audience or someone specific... like Frank.

Stowell, Texas

Grimes

G rimes closed his Bible and fell into his chair. He wanted to say a quick prayer, but Aimes was yapping behind him in a spirited voice. He, too, shared Aimes' anger about their broadcast being so quickly jammed, but he was more worried about his friend.

"Do you suppose he got it?" Grimes interrupted Aimes' fusillade of swearing.

Aimes stopped his tirade and switched off the volume control and therefore the blaring jamming signal that was the spark that ignited Aimes' firestorm of obscenities.

"What did you say, Lieutenant?"

"I said, do you think the Major got our message?"

Aimes trudged around to face his friend. He rested his back against the windowsill, blocking Grimes' view of the framed antenna tower outside. Aimes put his foot up on top of the fifteen-hundred-watt amplifier they had just installed today to make their signal stronger, so it would reach more homes across the US.

Aimes gave his friend a stern glare and let out a long sigh. "Look, Lieutenant. I'm just as worried about our friends. But there is nothing more we can do. We must pray they either heard your message or they become otherwise alerted to Jasper's intentions before it's too late. Our focus now... Really the only thing we can do is find a way to continue our broadcasts and maintain our communications with the military and militias around the country. Everyone is depending on us."

Grimes stared off for another few seconds before he nodded and said, "Of course you're right. Okay, before we address the elephant in the room, have we heard anything more from our Army friends about the pending joint operations?"

Aimes had been working their Vietnam-era PRC-77, which Grimes had put back into service and amplified, along with their 2-meter and CB units. Grimes had concentrated on the longer distance communications through their SSB transmitters. It was Aimes who first got wind of the upcoming joint military operations, when he received the encrypted message for Porter and Wallace. Porter specify any detail, they just left town.

"No, they're keeping everything hush-hush. For good reason. And before you ask again, I've heard nothing from Porter or Wallace since they left."

Grimes banged the heavy bible onto his desk. "I hate

not knowing more."

"Copy that. Now let's address the fat sweaty elephant: what the hell is going on with our signal? You've taken literally every precaution. Do you think Hajji has figured out your code system with the Bible verses?"

"Possible. More likely they've developed some sort of automatic system to target our signal every time we broadcast."

"How are they doing that?" Aimes clenched a fist, trying his best to tamper down his frustration.

"My guess is they've figured out how to use the systems they already had at their disposal at Mount Weather."

Chapter 11
Mt. Weather, Virginia

Mahdi Abdul

The leader of the Islamic Caliphate in America and self-proclaimed spiritual Mahdi to millions of Muslims, marched down one of the complex's primary football-field-long hallways (there were three others above him and an undetermined number below him). His pace was brisk as he couldn't wait to speak to Sal. It was time for the next phase. Though, as before, he would reveal few details, until the plan was already acted upon. Keeping the details secret, even from his most trusted follower, was what kept him safe. It certainly wasn't his Security Detail.

He mused about the sounds other than from the staccato clicking of his custom leather boot heels on concrete. It was the droning clatter of softer footsteps following just behind him. He peeked to see if all his Little Mice were there.

They had even changed their thobes to make sure theirs were simpler than his. His grin threatened to turn into a smile, but this yanked at the stitches in his face, so he ceased this trivial exercise.

As if needing the mental redirect, when he turned into

another familiar look-alike-passageway, there were muffled pops of gunshots.

"Stay here," he ordered. He cracked open the door labeled Accounting. Its use had been changed to what Sal called "other purposes" since they had taken over the vast multi-storied complex. His nose instantly stung from the thick stench of cordite and piss.

Before he could enter, Sal rushed over and made his way through the door opening, slowing only to acknowledge his Mahdi.

"Mahdi Abdul." He gave a bow, appearing surprised at Abdul's presence.

"I came for an update on communications." He could see his Chief Deputy was preoccupied. "Is this a favorable time?"

"Yes, of course. Would you walk with me as I'm already late for a meeting with your military leaders."

"Lead the way, Sal." Abdul said, only too happy to get away from the acrid death smells coming from that room.

They marched in unison, back down the same hallway Abdul had come from, his Little Mice staying far enough away to not appear as if they were eavesdropping on their two leaders. His Little Mice—because they scurried around him like mice, even though most of them were physically much larger than him—always kept him in sight for his protection. They had purpose above ground, but in this place, a security detail was superfluous. They were more his shadows than serving any constructive purpose.

Sal had been silent the entire time and Abdul realized he must have been waiting to be invited to start the conversation. There wasn't much written protocol when it came to the apocalyptic leader of the caliphate on earth.

But it was a common sign of respect and reverence to wait for an Imam to start a conversation.

This rule was insisted upon by Sal. Abdul went along with it to support his Chief Deputy. Like many others, it was hard enough for Sal to accept referring to him by his first name. But Abdul wanted to be approachable to all his people as their Mahdi.

"Were you executing another batch of prisoners?" Abdul asked.

"Yes, my Mahdi. They no longer served any usefulness. After torturing them for days, I believe we obtained all that we needed from the radio servicemen and women who were stationed here. We now have full use of their computer and communications systems." Sal, whose face was a tested network of scars, beamed at this. Abdul knew he was excited to tell him the next part too, so he'd invited it.

"You have solved the codes these infidels are transmitting to American militias?"

"No, my Mahdi. Better than this, we are now targeting the so-called American Freedom Network broadcast directly. Using the American's systems here at Mount Weather and knowing their location, we automatically scan the A-F-N broadcast on all shortwave frequencies and almost instantly send our jamming signal there. They can no longer broadcast more than a few seconds of their messages, which isn't enough time. So, their codes are useless to them. Unless they move, we have effectively shut them down for good."

"That is miraculous news, my most trusted servant."

"However, my Mahdi, the best news yet is that we can do the same to any military installation. And the timing is perfect, because as you know the US military has begun broadcasting."

"That truly is great news. You and your men are to be commended... However, you do not need to worry about the US military. They will not be a problem after today."

"Sir..." Sal's voice changed, becoming deeper. "...as you know, the Americans are planning at least two big military operations soon and probably many more after this. Not only must we disrupt their communications before they strike back against our armies... I would strongly recommend that our armies attack theirs immediately, so that we can achieve a victory for you, even more quick than at the pace we're presently operating."

Abdul halted abruptly, while also grabbing Sal's shoulder, forcing him to stop as well. Abdul drilled his eyes into the dark orbs of his most trusted assistant. "Sal, pay attention. Do *not* stop the American military's communications. Do you understand? I will take care of them in the next phase of our plans, which starts tomorrow. Your orders continue to be focusing on disrupting the US militias' communications next. They are the *only* people I am worried about right now."

"Mahdi Abdul," Sal pleaded. His face, already disfigured, was now twisted in such a way that it appeared as if he were in pain. "Please share with me exactly what this next phase is so I can better understand what you have planned and not do anything to displease you."

Abdul released and then double-tapped Sal's shoulder with his open hand. "Soon, my most trusted servant. I promise you. Soon."

Sal looked like he wanted to say something more, but then his shoulders sagged. "Mahdi, as you wish."

"Thank you, Sal. Now tell me have you set me up for a phone meeting with the new American President?"

"Yes, for later this evening, but I don't understand this either. Are you going to ask her to surrender?"

Once more, he tapped Sal on the shoulder. "Not to worry, Sal. It is all part of my greater plan and again the start of the final phase. Sal, I assure you that not only will you come to understand everything soon, but you will play a critical role in this next phase. I promise to tell you in the fullness of time. And after this next phase begins, the Americans will concede to all of our wishes. Shall we continue our walk?"

Abdul turned to continue his march, but Sal remained in place, eyeing a short hallway that fed into several offices.

"Again Mahdi, as you wish. However, I must go this way to my meeting."

"Do you want me to sit in with you, Sal?"

"No, my Mahdi, that's not necessary. Besides you might want to go speak to your son, Abdul-Aziz right now. He's been very stubborn and continues to resist those you've assigned to look in on him. I'm told, he now says he won't talk to anyone, unless he sees his sister."

"Suhaimah will be here in the next day or two. Imran is protecting her and will make sure she's here as soon as it's safe to do so."

Abdul tossed a glance down the long hallway, which passed by Travis' room. "Yes, I will pay Abdul-Aziz a visit now. He will no longer be a problem. I will make sure of it."

"I know you will. Thank you, Mahdi."

"You can go now, Sal. Thank you for your devoted work."

His most trusted nodded at his dismissal and marched down the small hallway, barely illuminated by only a single light above. Inferior hallways, like this one, were set at a minimum level to conserve energy.

Before going to talk to his son, Abdul remained in place to watch Sal. This would be an important moment when historians examined the ICA. Because after this, everything was about to change.

Sal looked up once before opening the door to a darkened room and disappeared inside.

Sal

The room was purposefully devoid of any light so that no one could see who was conspiring against Abdul. Only the faint glow cast from an exit sign on the other opposite end made it possible to tell that fourteen of the seats were currently occupied. He couldn't see their faces, but he knew who they were as he had chosen each one. All had entered this room quietly, through the back entrance under the lighted sign.

There would be no formal presentation to these men. That had already been done on a one-to-one basis. They all knew of Abdul's failures: his losing his base in Florida, forcing him to prematurely relocate to Mount Weather before they were ready; his nearly getting killed by his niece; his failure to plan on the US Army convoy ruse not working; and especially his not considering that American militias would be successfully coming together to stand up as the lone resistance against their ICA troops.

He didn't need to recite any of these failures. He only needed to give them a few quick words to prepare them for tomorrow. Because Sal felt tomorrow, they would take over. But he was also aware of the dangerous ground they were on, so he'd be quick not to arouse any suspicions of others by keeping these men absent from their posts longer than necessary.

In a soft voice, Sal started. "Gentlemen. We are at a very important stage" —he was careful not to use Abdul's word, "phase"— "but one in which, I fear Imam Farook is about to make several serious errors which may otherwise doom our caliphate."

The room remained silent as it was when he entered.

"Farook appears to want the US military to attack our armies as he is unwilling to disrupt their communications, even though we now have that power.

"Further, he seems more concerned with discussing our plans with the new American President than finishing what he has started.

"I fear Farook may now be following his ego, like Mohammad, peace be upon him, did later in his own life."

"I hope that I am wrong about this. But if I am not, you must be ready to move as early as tomorrow to forcibly take control of this complex and if he isn't compliant, kill Abdul Farook."

"We are ready, Sal," said one voice at the very back. Several other murmurs confirmed their support.

One spoke up. "Ah, sir? What will happen to Abdul Farook's wives?"

Sal responded swiftly. "They will be given to those who want them, in the order of your seniority. But Suhaimah will be mine. Any other questions?"

There were none.

"Very well. Watch your phones for my message. Thank you, my brothers. Together, we will do what Abdul Farook has started: institute this caliphate in America."

"*Assalam Alikum*" they said, sounding very unified.

"*Assalikum Asssalam*," Sal replied and then left the room.

He knew they would continue to talk in hushed tones for a few minutes after he left, of this he was certain. But none would remain for long for fear of being caught. Still he felt all of them would remain strong and resolute when the time was right. Of that too, he was certain.

What he didn't know, until later, was that every one of his men were about to be arrested.

Travis

He reduced the pressure on the point of his shiv, to ensure it had a deadly sharpness to it. Satisfied, he used a smoother portion of his cell's concrete floor to yield the desired result. He pressed its tip to his forefinger at the same time he heard a noise just outside the door. Panic muted the pain of its prick.

Making his movements quick, he slid his new

knife—converted from a spoon—into one of his used socks on the floor and softly kicked it deep under his cot. With his damaged hand, he painfully snatched the open Koran from the old metal desk and placed it onto his lap just as the door to his unit was loudly unlocked and pushed open.

"Assalamu Alaikum, Abdul-Aziz," said Uncle Abdul upon entry. The man immediately headed right for Travis in another disgusting attempt to kiss his cheek, which his uncle did during each greeting .

Travis bit his tongue and closed his eyes, rigidly displaying his cheek.

When the deed was done, Travis opened his eyes and was further assaulted with Abdul's face, barely an inch in front of his own. His breath was a foul mix of jasmine tea—he will never drink that again—and haggis. He vomited last night when Abdul told him what haggis was made from and at this moment, he felt an involuntary urge to hurl once more.

"What do you say"—Abdul spoke slow and succinctly, like a teacher giving a lesson to a slow-learning child—"when your father greets you this way."

You're not my father! You murdered my father, his brain yelled. Travis gave a vacant stare and regurgitated the words he was taught, *"Wa alaykum as-salam aby."* (And peace be upon you, my father).

The urge to upchuck became nearly overwhelming.

"That's much better—Is that your blood?"

The panic was back. Travis just noticed the drops of blood on the floor. Only then did he realize his forefinger was throbbing where he had abruptly poked it with his homemade knife. His intent was to stab Abdul to death with it when the time was right. That wasn't now. Travis thrust his bleeding forefinger into his mouth. The bandaged stub of his missing pinkie stuck out from his fist.

He eyeballed this while making a sucking sound, wanting the murderer to realize this was a subliminal message directed at him for cutting it off. He opened his mouth with his bleeding finger still inside and tried to answer, "I thabbed it on my coth—"

"Take your finger out of your mouth when you're addressing me—and what is that smell?" Abdul crinkled his nose, while his eyes scoured the five by eight room for an answer to his otherwise rhetorical question.

Travis pulled his finger out with a pop-sound and kicked the other offending sock under his bed. "Sorry, I stabbed my finger on my cot."

Abdul frowned, studying the boy's entire display and his disheveled room. Likely he knew—like he seemed to know most things—that Travis was hiding something. Finally, he asked, "How are you coming along with your studies?"

Travis did his best not to groan at this question. He was supposed to study ten hours per day. Luckily for him, it was all familiar stuff as he had read much of it before. He knew he could easily commit enough of it to memory to pacify him. It certainly wouldn't take anywhere near ten hours. Besides, it was all so boring.

"Fine," he answered.

"I expect so. Tonight, as a treat, you will accompany me to dinner with Sarti and Samantha and I will test you on what you have studied today. So be ready."

Travis nodded, doing his best to not show any excitement at this new development. It really was too good to be true. He didn't think he would get his chance this soon. It was perfect.

"I will prepare for you tonight," he said with a sly smile.

Abdul glowered at him, seemingly knowing he was keeping a secret.

"And if you expect to ever see your sister again after she arrives here today or tomorrow…" He stopped and bore his dark eyes right at him. Into him. He did this not just to unsettle Travis. It meant that Travis needed to listen and to heed every word said to him.

"If you cause any of my men any more trouble"—he said again in his you're-a-stupid-child voice—"you won't live to see another day. Do you understand me, son?"

Travis' head nodded and he mouthed the word, "yes." But this was a facade. The rest of him were already doing jubilant cartwheels at the news that his sister was coming for him.

This cinched it. He would get his knife finished quickly and then at dinner, when Abdul lets his guard down and was not expecting it, he would rush over to his fake-father and stab him many times. And unlike his sister, this time he wouldn't miss. He would kill this man who murdered his family once and for all.

Chapter 12
American Eagle Base Camp

Lexi

The conversations converged all around her. A rapid fire of words from seemingly everyone. She could barely keep up with any one of them. Her mind was a lead weight sinking fast. Her arms were too heavy to lift. *Maybe it was all the excitement ...* Fatigue, or something like it, hit her like a car crash.

She turned toward Frank and for a moment it felt as if her head might continue rolling until it popped off the top of her shoulders. *I couldn't possibly be drunk on two beers, could I?*

Frank's face was taut by its usual worry-about-everyone-else anxiety. Most likely the broadcast was his own sink weight. It seemed to be what everyone was talking about.

Frank appeared to be examining the faces of each person speaking. But she could tell that his thoughts were elsewhere. He wasn't listening. Perhaps it was Grimes' warning.

That's it.

A jumble of words tumbled out of her mouth, "What mean 'watch out wolf in yo' midst?'" It all came out louder and more confusing than she intended.

Frank pivoted in his chair, appearing to want to answer Lexi. He stopped when he caught a glimpse of her eyes.

Gladys, the gray-haired warrior-women, now standing behind Lexi, answered before he could say anything. "He's warning all of us to watch out for traitors, especially those pretending to be our friends."

It was as if her words were a slap to his face because Frank looked shocked. Or sick.

His head spun like... he called it *on a swivel.* He turned in one direction and then the next, searching for something or someone around the tent.

"It's because they're fricking Muslims," exclaimed Slim.

Lexi snapped her head right at Slim. More words fell out of her mouth, this time more cohesively organized. "What's because they're Muslims?"

Slim gave another dumbfounded look, as if she asked if it ever rained in North Carolina. "They're all traitors... Muslims. It's part of their religion."

"You know I'm Muslim. So, I must be a traitor den," Lexi's lips spat out another tumble of words, without any thought.

When every conversation abruptly halted, a thought hit her: she would have fared better if she had worn a MAGA hat to a BLM riot.

"What?" was all Slim could muster.

All faces turned to her, demanding an answer, especially ly Dagger Eyes, who now focused every bit of his ire at Lexi.

Frank

He had to stop this before it turned ugly. Before getting here, they'd discussed her not sharing her background with anyone. Most would not understand her origins, much less her connection to Abdul. Even bringing up her Muslim roots might cast suspicion on them in this prickly environment. Their primary goal was to fly under the radar until their mission was accomplished. But Lexi seemed inebriated and unable to control what was coming out of her mouth.

The moment after Lexi's comment stopped all conversations, Cappy returned to the tent and appeared before them. He, too, was giving Lexi a scowl.

Time to deflect.

"Hey, Cappy," Frank announced very loud but friendly, "We'll take the deal…" He wanted to make sure Cappy's and everyone else's attention was on him. "We'll transport your friend to Virginia, in exchange for one of your vehicles. But I'd like to ask for one more thing before we leave."

Cappy reluctantly turned his attention to Frank. "Okay, what do you want?"

"Just a few minutes on your radio. I need to tell some friends that we're okay as our radio isn't working." Frank said this while giving Lexi another glance.

"You got it. Right before you leave, my guy will give you *one-minute* radio time. But no more, because the enemy is listening, and I don't want to compromise our location."

"Copy that. Thanks," Frank said, and motioned to get up. "Now, if it's alright with you, I'm going to unpack our tent and set up so Lexi can lie down. It seems she's enjoyed the celebration but needs to get some rest now.

Lexi moved as if to lodge a protest, but she only wobbled, and Slim grabbed both her forearms to steady her.

"Nonsense," Cappy stated and turned to his son. "Samuel, help Ms. Broadmoor to our guest tent, so she can sleep—If that's okay with you, Major?"

"Yeah, even better. Thank you once again."

"And Samuel," his eyes still drilled on the young man everyone called Slim. "When you return, come back with Chase, so the Major can meet his passenger."

Samuel/Slim nodded and put a tender arm around Lexi for support and she put one of hers around him. She appeared ready to pass out.

"Before you go..." Frank said to Samuel, already a couple of steps away. "What kind of beer was that?" He assumed it must have been something imported with a higher alcohol content and that Lexi was not used to drinking. The one beer he'd shared with her several nights ago, went right to her head then.

"Bud Light," Samuel hollered, his back still to Frank. "It was the only unused keg that they had left at the Legion."

As Samuel ushered Lexi out of the tent, Frank was left to contend with that familiar tingle that had started in his gut which always arose just before the proverbial shit hit the fan. He knew he needed to figure out what it was before it did.

He looked around the tent once more for Jasper.

Jasper

Jasper was watching them all from the growing shadows of a Pin Oak tree, just an acorn's throw from the militia camp's main canopy. The drug he'd put in Lexi's beer would have taken hold by now and soon she would lose consciousness.

Abdul had warned him to take control: gather the girl, kill if he had to and bring her to him right away.

He considered all possibilities and decided the least risky option was to drug Lexi, steal one of their vehicles and drive her north to Mt Weather. He was counting on them finding her a tent when she looked sleepy. He also counted on Frank insisting that she be alone. Then, while everyone was asleep, he would take her and leave before first light. Less risk of someone shooting. He promised Mahdi Abdul he would no longer allow her to get into risky situations.

He didn't have to wait too long. The young leader helped Lexi out of the canopy. She was still conscious, but she could barely hold her own head up. The young man's arm was wrapped around her, his hand below her... his blood started to boil. Jasper wanted to snap this man's neck—perhaps he would do this before he left in the early morning—but he pushed back his emotions and focused his mind on his mission.

He took a step out of the well of the tree, intending to follow them, when he heard something from the next stand of trees, just south of the camp, about 20 meters away. He backed under the tree's cover again, making himself unseen, while watching Lexi being ushered into a tent not too far away. He made a note of its location and drilled into the sound he'd just heard in the darkness.

Another crack of a branch and more movement. But he could tell the noisemakers were attempting to keep their sounds hidden. This was not from one or more of the militia members, none of whom worried about any of the clumsy sounds they made. This was something different. He felt it.

His senses were developed over many years of battle and covert operations in the army. He trusted his senses.

Multiple people, not from this camp, were watching them.

Frank

"Don't worry, Major," Cappy insisted. "She will have a tent all her own, and barely twenty feet from here. My son will make sure she's safe. And I'll bet my right nut, he'll post a guard to watch her tent."

Frank was appreciative of the Captain's words. In truth he really wasn't that worried about Lexi. She was now more than capable of taking care of herself, even in her inebriated state. Plus, he had seen enough to know these were good folks; that they would protect her, despite their obvious prejudices.

But gnawing at him was that feeling that had taken root in his gut. He kept looking for Jasper, perhaps for reassurance that everything was alright.

He may have not known much about Jasper, but the man did have military training, he'd obviously seen some battles firsthand and therefore, he'd probably had similar senses as Frank did. Most important, the man remained in a state of hyper awareness. If something was going on, Jasper would have sensed it too. He was hoping to find him and confirm this.

"Seriously, Major. She's fine."

"No, it's not that. I know she'll be fine. I trust you and your people..." Frank meant that. Cappy may have gotten into trouble with the top brass for being a little too aggressive in his torturing methods, all to give the Army and his unit the upper hand. But Cappy was a patriot through and through. Plus, Frank could see this militia was well run, either directly or indirectly through his son.

"... It's just that I have a sense that things are about to go sideways." Frank was already standing, albeit very uncomfortably, his bum leg offering little support and lots of angry pain. He continued his search around the tent, not so much inside, but just outside. For what he had no idea, and that's what was getting to him. "It's a sense I have in my gut. Every time I've had this sense, the proverbial shit has hit the fan. I've learned to always trust my gut."

Frank had started to take a step forward, intending to

do a perimeter check outside the tent, when someone stepped in front of him. Samuel was trailing, almost invisible behind the looming figure standing before him.

The man looked pretty banged up: a bandage wrapped around his head, a red tint colored two sides of it; several dressings covered parts of his arms and hands; and then there was a parade of bandages covering various lacerations. Purple bruising, especially on his face and arms, were indicative of a blast... or maybe a car accident. Also, there was something familiar about this man's banged up face. But he couldn't place where he'd seen him before... *TV?*

"Major," Cappy interrupted his quiet assessment. "This is your passenger tomorrow, Senator Thomas Chase, the pro tempore of the Senate, and therefore the next in line for the President of the United States."

Frank sat back down.

Chapter 13

POTUS

Eight Days Earlier

An entourage of serious-looking men and woman burst into the bunker's primary conference room, through the heavy door. Abigail O'Neal only recognized two of the faces.

"Evie?" Abbie screeched, while hopping in place in anticipation of her friend getting close enough to wrap arms around her. She needed a hug and evidently, so did her friend.

When they embraced, Evie cried out, "Abbie, they're all dead," Her voice and body quivered violently.

They remained glued as one shuddering mass until they were roughly bumped into by one of the many serious people. Abbie released Evie, who pulled away revealing two painfully puffy eyes and tear tracks of black makeup running down each cheek.

"What do you mean?" Abbie asked, not really wanting to know. She assumed one of the pasty-faced people in this group was about to tell her anyway. But it was far better to get bad news from someone she knew rather than strangers.

When she first arrived at the bunker yesterday, Anton Meer, who had introduced himself to her as the National Security Advisor—but demanded she refer to him as Colonel Meer, even though he'd been out of military service for years—had barely let her out his sight until a few minutes ago. Now, he put himself in between Abbie and her friend, before Evie could gain enough composure to answer the question.

The entire time Abbie had been in this bunker, she was desperate for information of any kind. But neither the Colonel nor the other officials, who all answered to him, had been willing to give her anything. The only news she'd gathered since arriving at this bunker was the one line from a single news alert that hit her phone: "America devastated in multiple terrorist attacks." That was it. The link from this alert went to nothing: apparently there was no Internet or phone service in the bunker. No one had been willing to even explain to her why this was, including

Colonel Meer.

"I'm sorry to interrupt, ma'am," The Colonel said in his now familiar, James-Earl-Jones-voice, "but , at this time, I am authorized to debrief you and to swear you in." He glanced down at a tablet he'd been holding and swiped at its screen to bring it to life.

Swear me in? Abbie wondered. That made no sense. *What could I possibly be sworn into, as I was nothing more than the lowest member of the President's Cabinet, stuck on Designated Survivor duty, while all the others were in DC for the signing...*

Abbie was dumbstruck, her eyes immediately becoming saucer sized.

No, it couldn't be. It was not possible.

"Ma'am, I'm authorized to tell you," the Colonel read deadpanned, "The President and the remainder of his cabinet were killed in the DC terrorist attack; leaders of both houses were also killed in the DC attack; and the planes of both the Vice President and the President Pro Tempore have been confirmed to have crashed, with both now presumed to be dead. Under the Presidential Succession Act of 1792, you are the next in line to the Presidency. So, I'm going to swear you in right now."

Abbie's head swam, as if she were drowning in a cloud of muddled thoughts, none of them her own: *President and cabinet dead; everyone dead; DC attack; I'm next in line... The presidency?*

She needed something or someone tangible to grab onto, but she was alone: her friend Evie had disappeared, and Abbie was now swarmed by the other strangers. One of them was holding up a familiar looking, leather-bound book.

"Please put your hand on the book and repeat after me," the Colonel stated. Then without taking a breath, he continued, "I, Abigail O'Neal…"

Her hand felt impossibly heavy as she laid it on top of the worn cover of the book, she knew instantly was hers, inherited from her dead father. *But how could they possibly have known to bring this here?*

"I Abigail O'Neal…" the words poured from her lips, without any thoughtful assistance.

Like marriage vows, she mused. *I'm about to get married to the most powerful job in the world.*

"… do solemnly swear…"

"… do solemnly swear…"

"… that I will faithfully execute the Office of President of the United States…"

Her legs initially felt wobbly, but now they held firm. Unyielding.

"… that I will faithfully execute the Office of President of the United States…" She knew the rest, gaining even more strength from this. But she waited until she heard it, so she could immediately repeat it back flawlessly.

"… and I will, to the best of my ability, preserve, protect, and defend the Constitution of the United States…" She couldn't remember if the Colonel had ended with the familiar, "So help me God." So she said nothing more and found Colonel Meer staring at her.

"Thank you, Madam President," The Colonel said and offered a hand to shake hers.

And that was it. She was now President. Like in a dream… *Or was it a nightmare?*

"Way to go, Abbie," hollered Evie, somewhere from the other side of the giant conference table, which took up most of the room they were in. She saw her friend's dour face had now been replaced with a smile. "You realize that you're the first woman President?"

Abbie only half acknowledged her friend. Instead, all her thoughts returned to the one day that made all of this possible, when her political fortunes had changed so dramatically.

She had just lost her election for the Texas State Senate, by almost two-dozen points, all because she had been truthful to a newscaster's question in an interview the day before. Her answer was taken out of context. Not that it mattered.

All it took to undo her political aspirations in a small district of Texas was one truthful answer in one interview.

Abbie had wanted nothing more than to hide from the ignominy she knew would follow. But from her campaign members' insistence, she attended what she called the 'Loser's Party' on election night. There, Abbie was visited by a well-dressed, good-looking man who told her that he could give her what she wanted; he could give her back her political career. Abbie had already figured she'd have to go back to bartending. She almost walked away from this stranger who had tossed her a lifeline.

She remembered telling the man, as if it were yesterday, "That's impossible. I've ruined my political career because I was honest in one interview." Abbie knew political realities: Interviews such as hers would live on forever on social media and YouTube, destined to be part of the other party's soundbites for all eternity... Yet, this man didn't bat an eye. He assured her that he could make the interview disappear, as if it never happened. Further, he would get her into a position of political power, so that one day, she would have the chance to go all the way to the top and maybe even become President...

It was just like he said.

The truth was that Abbie had always wanted the Presidency. She craved it, and this stranger was offering her the chance to magically change her past, like burning your old, soiled clothes and replacing them with a new ball gown. She didn't believe it and asked him how he could remove the interview from the Internet and people's memories? He told her that all of that was for him to worry about, but yes, it would truly be gone. Forever.

"What was the catch?" she asked the stranger. In politics, there was always a catch.

He told her not to worry. He was just happy to support up and coming stars of the party. At least that's what he said at the time.

It didn't matter what he wanted her to do. She would have agreed to anything, just so long as she didn't have to go back to bartending.

Without knowing anything about the man or what he would ask her to do in the future, she agreed to his terms.

He assigned her a political adviser, who helped her to polish her image and ultimately became her best friend. Evie was tough at first, demanding that she never again publicly state what her thoughts were, nor share any opinion on anything. She was trained what to say, or as Evie explained, "what the people wanted her to say." She was given all the answers she needed to succeed. For this to work, she had to follow her adviser completely and absolutely. She would, and had of course, because she wanted exactly what her adviser, and who was paying her, was offering. Power.

She had done everything she was asked to do, as well as being surrounded by other advisers tasked to help her.

Every once in a while, the mystery man—who simply wanted to be called "X"—would follow up with her, asking her to complete various simple tasks for him. After he had called her and suggested she take an unenviable cabinet position, in an unpopular administration, she hadn't heard from him again. That was over a year ago.

Abbie shook the memories away to face a reality she could not avoid.

She looked up, seeing Colonel Meer was still speaking, utterly dumbfounded by what had just happened. It was when she heard that her Presidency would last until the now dead President's term concluded in two more years, that it all hit home—*the former President is dead now and so is every other important government official. It's all on you now, Abbie.*

She examined the room, scanning all the strange faces staring back at her, as if they were expecting her to do something immediately. Something presidential.

"Madam President, please take a seat," someone said.

Evie appeared several people away and spoke loudly in an obvious attempt to be heard by everyone. "The Colonel said I could be your Chief of Staff, if you want me... Madam President?" She enunciated every letter of this, like a performance.

Evie being her Chief of Staff, among the millions of other thoughts, had crossed Abbie's mind. Evie was with her almost from the beginning. She helped her to get where she was today. She was perfect. "Yes, of course. You're the one person I trust. Please sit down beside me."

Evie pushed her way past the clog of people who were

crowding around the table to find a seat, all the while she attempted to clean the streaks of her runny makeup with a Kleenex she had pulled from a pocket. Her whole demeanor changed from sadness to seriousness. Then she took a seat and whispered in her friend's ear. "But don't expect me to fill in any details: I've been blind folded the whole way here and before that I was locked up. I heard DC was nuked, and that almost everyone was there at the signing... except you. I'm hoping someone will tell us what's going on."

One of Colonel Meer's aids brought in a stack of leather-bound folders and dumped them in front of Abbie. The Colonel handed her a fancy-looking pen and opened the top leather folder to reveal a document inside. He pushed it in front of her.

"What are these?" Abbie asked.

"Your first act as President. These are Executive Orders..." Colonel Meer pointed to the bottom of a document titled, *Emergency Powers Declaration.* "You sign here."

"Shouldn't I read them first?" she asked.

"That's not your job. Your job is to sign these so we can resurrect the American government quickly."

Only later did she learn that this was an Emergency Declaration giving the Executive Branch unlimited powers, until the emergency had passed. She also signed declarations which gave the Secretary of Defense immediate decision making on all military actions—if the President was not able to act, until the emergency passes; temporary new cabinet appointments; and so on.

It was a mind-numbing stack of papers, all of which she signed without reading, barely catching the titles and only a few of the words from each. All of them were already pre-done by someone or more likely several someone's who planned everything in the unlikely event that something like this might happen.

Throughout, her head was still spinning so much she felt like she had to keep one hand on the table for fear of being spun off. She tried to act "presidential" but she really didn't know what that meant for her.

When the stack was completed and then made to disappear as fast as it appeared, the Colonel found a seat and briefed everyone at the table on the state of America.

It was worse than Abbie could have imagined: millions dead and literally everything shut down, chaos on the streets and the terrorist attacks continued.

They were only minutes into their briefing, when there was a deep rumple, followed by a tremor above them. Then the lights blinked and went out. Collectively, they held their breath. When the emergency lights flickered on, they cast an eerie pale on the room.

Two radio lights flashed, and the Colonel spoke into a radio, "Yes... Okay. Thank you, Sergeant."

Then he announced, "Our bunker is under attack. But we are safe here."

Evie's hand found Abbie's and they both squeezed.

Present Day

Just as Abbie had been for nine days, her new Cabinet members were all housed in rooms off the conference room. All were protected by their bunker, from what Secretary Meer said—he no longer wished to be called Colonel, now that he was her Secretary of Defense. But they were unable to leave as they were told that they were still fighting a contingent of the enemy outside. Abbie never heard any further explosions nor gunfire after the first day, and she hadn't seen any evidence of a fight. This reporting seemed off. She still didn't even know where they were, other than some bunker on the East Coast.

The whole time she was spoon fed the smallest amounts of information about what was going on in the US and the rest of the world. But at no time was she given access to the outside world. No Internet, phones, or TV, and not even a radio. She was told none of them were usable. It seemed crazy to her that as POTUS, she had no way to communicate outside their bunker, or for others to communicate with her, except through Secretary Meer, and only from what she was told via encrypted military channels.

Then, on July 13th, Meer breezed into the conference room with his people in toe and announced that they had established a means to do national broadcasts on TV and radio.

Abbie knew if communications were established to broadcast out, then they should have a means to get communications in. But before she could ask, she was ushered to the other side of the massive room and handed a paper that was titled, "President's TV Address to a Damaged Nation."

Her heart attempted to gallop out of her chest. She looked up and saw they had set up a TV camera on a tripod, pointed at a lectern, complete with the prominent Presidential seal. All of this framed by deep blue ruffled curtains, and a set of American flags on either side...

They want me to stand there and finally address the country, she told herself.

She had a flashback to the time when she last appeared on TV. Her hair was different and so was her name. She suspected she was different as well. Not that any of it mattered, as she was President now, regardless of whether anyone recognized her or not.

She took a breath and settled herself down. She *could* act "presidential."

Pride overtook her once again.

This was the pinnacle of everything she had ever wanted, all handed to her on a silver platter. She was made President, without having to go through all the trouble of campaigning, raising money, getting picked apart with questions by the press, and the constant berating on social media. She skipped past all of this and now she was the most powerful person in what was left of the government, about to talk to a nation that wouldn't look at her negatively for anything that she had said or done in the past. They would look to her to lead their country, after the worst attack the country had ever experienced.

She ignored the comment from someone close to her about her being live in so many seconds. She wanted to pre-read her speech, which was already written for her. No doubt, it was done by one of Meer's superiors—whomever they might be—who seemed to have control over everything, including her.

Abbie was a quick reader, and even with the pressure and commotion surrounding her, she was able to speed-read the one-page statement in a few seconds.

A firm hand ushered her forward to a white X taped on the carpet, just behind the POTUS lectern.

I got this, she told herself. Better yet, she would read this one as is, because it was standard stuff: not committing to anything, but basically feel-good fluff. But before the next one, she would find out more details and she would write the address herself. She was, after all, the most powerful ruler in the free world at that moment. What could her handlers say or do at this point?

"Thirty seconds," a voice called out, as the others in the room quieted their voices and motions. All stared at her, their POTUS.

At that moment she decided. More than just reading statements from a teleprompter; she would take bold actions. Because her people would expect that of a leader. Then, she would execute the policies she had always wanted during her Presidency. She would remake America to be the country she always thought it should be.

"In ten-nine-eight-seven..."

She placed the page on the lectern, eyeballed the teleprompters to confirm they were on, then she presented herself to the camera, smiling her brightest presidential smile. It was one she had practiced in front of her mirror millions of times, just to get it right. She knew what a presidential smile should look like. Hers would shine.

"...three-two-one."

"Good afternoon, America. I am Abigail O'Neal, the President of United States."

Chapter 14
American Eagle Patriots Basecamp

Jasper crept up to them, moving slower than the soft breeze that blew against his skin. None of the dozen or so men could have heard him. Their eyes and ears were trained on the militia's camp, maybe one hundred meters away. If they looked in his direction, they weren't likely to see him in dusk's soupy darkness. He had worked his way around, putting them between him and the camp, effectively cutting off any escape. Though that wasn't his intent.

After many minutes of methodically getting into position, he still waited. He needed to be sure. When he heard them speak Arabic, he knew whose side they were on.

He whistled loud enough so they would hear him, and he turned a flashlight on himself so that he was plainly seen by them. "Asalam Alikum, my brothers." His hands were held high. The Thompson was slung around his back. Still very visible, to show he could have been, but clearly was not a threat to them.

The leader eyed him from the shadows but didn't move or say anything. Two of his men approached slowly, their eyes narrowed on Jasper, one telling him in English to hand over his weapons.

"*La!*" Jasper responded. And then he waved a paper in his free hand, telling them in Arabic to take it.

The man speaking, snatched the paper from Jasper and then ran it over to his leader, who opened and read the message.

The leader stepped from the clog of his almost twenty men and approached Jasper.

"I am Faisal, sir" he announced, returning the official document signed by Abdul Farook, telling anyone in the ICA of Imran's position. Faisal offered a bow to his superior.

"Faisal," Jasper said in a low voice. "Please stand. I'm known to these infidels as Jasper. Our Mahdi—peace be upon him—has recently instructed me to safely transport a young woman, who is in the infidel's camp now. She will be one of his wives. Tomorrow, before dawn, I will take her out of this camp. It is obvious that you intend to attack this group. You are to wait until I leave before you do so. Is that clear."

Faisal nodded, without hesitation. "Yes, sir. As you wish. We will wait and attack at dawn." Faisal offered another bow and shuffled back to his men to tell them the news.

Thomas Chase

S enator Chase gave Frank a warm smile, that was momentarily interrupted by a jolt, like from a burst of hidden pain, then the smile was fully back. His hand was extended.

Frank saw the hallmarks of a West Pointer: squared shoulders from a lifetime of drills, determined eyes and way too tall to be a grunt.

"Thank you, Major for agreeing to transport me north," Chase said, as if he were greeting a dignitary.

Frank had risen back out of his chair and immediately accepted the man's hand, returning the firm shake, but unsure what to say in return. Several questions came to mind, which he was considering how best to phrase them. "It's an honor, Senator Chase," is what came out of his mouth.

"No need for formalities. Thomas or Tom is fine, Major."

"Very well Thomas, then please call me Frank." Frank sat back down, finding it uncomfortable to stand on his bad leg, for even a short time.

"See, I knew you two would get along," Cappy offered. His voice was jovial.

Chase seemed to ignore the comment. "Being an officer and American, I know you'll understand why it's so important that I return to reestablish the American government. But first, we need to use the full force of our surviving military to kill every last one of these bastards."

There were several cheers from the militia members who had crowded around to hear what sounded like a rehearsed speech.

Frank just wanted answers.

"Senator Chase," Samuel said, in a higher pitched voice than Frank had heard earlier. "Can you tell us why the military has not done anything so far? Other than the upcoming operation, we've seen zero response to the enemy.

Chase shot a glance back at Frank, telling him he

didn't really want to answer this. But then he regathered his countenance. "Someone is holding back the military, though I don't know who it can be since nearly everyone, including the SecDef and Joint Chiefs were killed on that day. This is what concerns me."

Other militia members edged closer, some holding their hands up, their faces eager. Frank needed to ask his questions now or he'd lose his chance. "So, Senator Cha—ah, Thomas … How did you get here? You're a long way away from DC aren't y?"

"That's quite a story. Do you want the long or short version?" Chase asked.

"Why don't you give 'em the short version right now," Cappy cut in. "You'll have plenty of time to discuss the details during your trip north tomorrow." Cappy appeared to have forgotten something and stepped around the table to the radio guy, who handed him a slip of paper. He glanced at it, while returning to a position beside Chase.

"Yes, that's true. Well, I was headed to the celebratory signing on July 4th, but my plane had engine trouble and we were delayed in Daytona Beach—that's my hometown and where I spend most of my time when I wasn't in DC. We were in the hanger when the news of the attacks came. I guess we were shielded from some of the enemy's electromagnetic pulses, and far enough away from the blast in Jacksonville that my plane was still operable. By then, the repairs were done, but we remained there for a few hours to assess who had survived, how best I could help from where I was and where to go next.

"Then we heard from a commander at the Virginia National Guard to proceed there so I could be escorted to a secure location for the continuity of government.

We took off and proceeded to fly to Fort Belvoir, as we were advised. But we never reached there. Our engine exploded mid-air and we went down about twenty miles from here…" He paused and cleared his throat before continuing in a more subdued voice. "Two of my staff members, and our two-flight crew were killed. My pilot and I were the only ones who survived the crash, though he was unconscious and in bad shape. I tended to my pilot for several days, but in the end, he succumbed to his injuries. No one was coming to get us and our radios were inoperable, so I set off on foot and found my way here yesterday.

"The Captain and his militia patched me up and had been trying to arrange transport for me, when you arrived. Again, thank you."

Cappy jumped in. "We were able to make contact with the Virginia Department of Military Affairs," he waved the piece of paper he'd been handed by his radio man, who had his headphones on again. "They have just arranged an escort at the Virginia state line. All you have to do is get him there."

"And to make sure you all get there in one piece, I'm going to have Samuel lead half of our militia to accompany you."

"It would be an honor to provide protection for you, Major Cartwright and Senator Chase," Samuel added, his voice sounding more normal now.

Frank had been silent since asking his one question. Listening and assessing. It was obvious their mission to get to Mount Weather was now complicated by Thomas Chase. To say the least. They were going to Virginia anyway, so why not assist in helping the Senator get the government back up and running.

But he wanted to approach it a different way. "Don't you think it would be better to travel under the radar? Not to mention that we would make quicker time with just us three and Senator Chase, as opposed to following a group of noisy trucks that will stick out and call attention to us. Stealth would be superior with the enemy everywhere."

Cappy nodded and at the same time said, "I hear you Major. Why don't we leave that to our next President."

Chase watched and listened to each man speak. He looked up, appearing to ponder both requests before answering, "I tend to agree with Frank. The quicker the better."

Cappy nodded again. "Okay, then it's settled. You'll leave in the morning at first light and the militia will stay here. If either of you have any special requests, please let me know... Oh and Major, just before you leave, I'll give you a couple of minutes with Edgar, our radio man, to reach out to your friends."

Frank was about to thank Cappy when he caught a glimpse of Jasper, who was now standing off to one side of the tent, behind Cappy. He looked his usual dour self. No doubt he was pissed that they would be delayed once more, babysitting Chase on their way to Virginia.

"Sounds great. Thanks, Cappy."

Frank stood up and offered his chair to Chase. "Please forgive me. I just realized that you've been through more than I have. Plus, your welfare is far more important than mine at this point."

"Thanks, I'll take you up on it, Frank. Although please know that I consider us equals in every way, I have to tell you..." He grunted as he took a step toward the chair…"Between the accident, walking for a day and just being on guard 24/7 has made me exhausted." Chase fell into the chair.

Frank grimaced when he transferred his weight from his good leg to his bad and then back again. But he did this when Chase wasn't looking and did his best to hide it. When he felt able to stand for long enough, he asked, "I'm curious Thomas, why didn't you or Cappy try to reach out to Fort Belvoir again?"

Chase repositioned his slung arm so that it wasn't against the chair's armrest, before looking up. "Of course, our radio was non-operational, and I figured after the attacks that I could only get through using accepted encryption. But Edgar here did try, and he couldn't get through either. So, I suggested we follow protocol, which was to reach out to the local state office for military affairs. Virginia seemed a natural because that's where we were headed to begin with."

"So do you know who else in government lived through the DC attack?" Samuel asked.

"To my knowledge, no one. We were all going to DC for a big photo op. All part of the President's Freedom and Independence for Americans Act or FIFA program and all on our day off, July 4th. There was going to be an immense fireworks display after the signing—"

"I'd say a nuke was pretty big fireworks," said the guy who had been giving Lexi the evil eye.

"Shut up, Moondog, yah idiot," spat Gladys.

Several repeated, "Yeah, shut up Moondog."

Frank had a thought. "Wasn't there a Designated Survivor?"

Chase gave Frank a blank stare and shrugged his shoulders. "I wondered that as well. But this would have been a member of the President's cabinet... who is, someone further down the line of succession. Even more reason why I'm anxious to—"

"Wait. Quiet everyone!" hollered Edgar, the radio guy. "Listen to this." A squeal burst out of the speakers, followed by, "Good afternoon, America. I am Abbie O'Neal, the President of United States."

Chapter 15

POTUS

"So fear not, my fellow Americans, help is on the way..."

Abbie hesitated, as her pre-written speech ended with the next line, but she wanted to add something more. Something of her own.

"And I'm looking forward to bringing our country back to a place where each of us can wake up, not with worry and anxiety, but love and hope..."

She looked down to remind herself of the last line.

"Until then, may God bless you, your families and the United States of America."

She beamed at the camera. Its light went from green to red almost immediately.

The smile clung to her face, even though no one was watching. It was not because she had to, but because she felt complete confidence now. She could do this president-thing. And oh, what she could do as the President. Her mind swam with ideas of what she might do next.

"Madame President, the broadcast is over," called a familiar voice from the distance.

Abbie blinked and realized the camera had been moved

to the side and she did in fact have an audience. A group of people had assembled at the other end of the long conference table, with the chair at the end—the President's chair—empty and waiting for her to occupy it.

Sitting next to her empty chair was Evie, her Chief of Staff, and her port during this storm of the last few days. "Madame President," she said. "Please have a seat to sign some additional Executive Orders and to speak to your new cabinet."

All eyes were on her as she marched over to her seat. No longer did she feel the anxiety that she had before. She could do this.

Evie told her that there were four Executive Orders that needed her signature right away and that Secretary Meer would be back with her Joint Chiefs in a few minutes.

She sat down and accepted the first opened leather folder and pen. She started to read it when Evie tapped at the signature line. "Secretary Meer wanted you to sign these right away."

Abbie understood the point: others made these decisions for her; she was to just do what they said.

She checked again at how she was supposed to sign her name, seeing that it had her full name listed and so she scratched out her full signature.

A flash of light caused her to look up mid-signature. A dark-skinned man, with a full beard, wearing a blue jumpsuit, who was operating the camera during and after her address, was taking pictures of her signing. Just as quick, she flashed her programmed smile while her pen was still touching the document. She figured that's what she was supposed to do, but the man didn't snap another picture.

Okay, whatever, she thought and returned her focus on completing her signature on the next document which was another Emergency Declaration of some sort. She would have liked to have read it—she glanced at the middle of the document and caught "Secretary of Defense to have total authority in the event of..." There was another flash, and she ignored it. The document was pulled out from under her pen and replaced with another. She signed the other three Executive Orders handed to her, not even bothering to try and understand what she was signing. With each one, there was a camera flash.

Another man in a blue jumpsuit whisked the document folders away and hurried out of the room.

"Okay, now that that's done," Evie said to her, "Perhaps each of your Cabinet members would like to introduce themselves and tell us a little about yourselves..."

"I'll start. My name is Ramon Padilla, ma'am," a short man with a bad comb over stood up, looked at her and then the rest of the room. "I'm your Secretary of State. I've been the Ambassador to Spain and held many executive positions with multiple philanthropic organizations such as CAIR. I am happy to..."

Abbie's mind was spinning again, while Padilla went on about his bona fides. She wondered who it was that chose this cabinet for her. Wasn't it her choice?

Padilla sat down and was obviously waiting for her acknowledgment—*What was his title again?*—" Thank you Mr. Secretary," she said.

A woman, who looked to be from India, stood up next and announced herself to be the Treasury Secretary. She already forgot the woman's name, when Evie pointed to a piece of paper she had laid down before her, which said, President's Cabinet with each of the names and titles listed. She didn't even try to remember the name but scanned over the list and then looked up at each of the members along the one side of the table.

She thanked the Madam Secretary and the next person stood up.

Who really are these people? she wondered. What if their beliefs don't fit with her own? What if they disagree with her policies? If she remembered correctly, the President's Cabinet were advisers first and didn't have any authority, other than what was given to them by her as President.

She knew these people were hand-chosen for her administration and she couldn't imagine the people who put her in this position would also choose members of her cabinet who were diametrically opposed to her or her beliefs.

Do they care what you believe? That was a big question. She had made all sorts of assumptions about how everything should happen in this situation. However, this situation was entirely different than anything previous.

Still, she was President. Regardless of how she got here, she was the Commander in Chief. She may have had little control over what got her there or who put her into this position, but she was here now. And regardless of what her cabinet believed or didn't believe, she was still in charge. She would accept this cabinet for now. But they would be required to report to her and follow *her* policies as President, or she would replace every one of them.

She thanked each Secretary of Whatever, after each had said their piece. Notably absent was the Vice President. She wondered who this was. No matter. This, as well as all the other issues would come. What mattered now was that she take command of this cabinet and start proposing some of the ideas she had been thinking about since she was sworn in as President.

"Thank you, Mister and Madam Secretaries, for your introductions and kind words. It is a difficult time, for sure. But we were all put here for several reasons I think we can all agree on: To bring this country back and to help our fellow citizens." She stopped to look at each of their faces. Most seemed to be accepting of her words, only a couple grimaced at her, including her Secretary of State—*Padilla, was his name.*

She looked at her phone, which had since yesterday been keeping perfect time. It said 8:42 P.M.

"Before the military men, ahh The Joint Chiefs of Staff, return, I wanted to propose a couple of topics for discussion. The first I believe is to declare Martial Law. I believe we have all heard reports about the unlawful activities being enacted against citizens, who are using guns to steal and murder. Then there are these so-called militias. Perhaps it's time to clearly define that it is no longer acceptable for common citizens to possess firearms, at least until this emergency is over.

"What I'm proposing is..." She glanced back down at her phone because it buzzed at her. And then again. She picked it up and saw that there were messages appearing on her phone. Her phone hadn't received messages since she was put into this bunker. She opened the messages, all coming from the same sender.

It was from number 000 0000 0000.

"Ms. Khan. Do not overstep." Her eyes shot up and scanned the room.

"Sorry," she said, "Ah, I must read this. Please discuss

among yourselves."

Several of her cabinet members spoke up at once. She returned her attention to the next message on the phone, from the same non-number.

"Secretary Meer will give you an agenda when he returns. You will also have a phone meeting that you must take. And you must agree to all the terms and conditions offered. Do you understand? Just nod in the affirmative as I can see you. X"

Again, Abbie's eyes shot up and scanned the room. She snapped from person to person, studying the movements of everyone around the table to see if any of them could have texted her. Then she realized she hadn't acknowledged X, who must be watching from a camera in the room.

Looking straight ahead, she nodded slowly but decisively in the affirmative, so that X could see her submission.

She hadn't heard from him in a long time and had almost forgotten about him. She knew he must have been there, but figured it was by the proxy of others who did his bidding, as well as those who were connected to X and/or X's superiors.

Regardless, the message was received. She may have been the person listed as the President. But it was her handlers, including Mr. X who had all the power. She was nothing more than a figurehead and they were always watching to make sure she never overstepped her bounds.

Just then, Meer entered the conference room, followed by several other military generals—she assumed that was their ranks, because she really didn't know—all of whom now made up her Joint Chiefs of Staff.

Meer stopped before her, holding his tablet in one hand and a piece of paper in another. He leaned over her, the smell of his sweat was prominent, and laid the page in front of her.

"Here is your agenda for the next 90 days. The details will be given to you when it is time."

She looked at the page, which didn't have much writing on it. Barely two paragraphs. Certainly not anywhere enough to cover the next 90 days, not even a summary of them.

"But that is for later. Now you are to accompany me to a room to take the call with the leader of the terrorists who struck our country."

It was *the* phone call. X had mentioned a phone meeting that had been arranged for her and that she must agree to everything... But to the leader of the terrorists who attacked us? She couldn't imagine what she could possibly agree to or why.

She scooped up her phone and the piece of paper she had just been given and followed Meer out of the conference room as one of Meer's military men addressed the room about what each of the Cabinet members' duties would be going forward.

Chapter 16

Frank

Frank stood in his place, unmoving. He was not only stunned by what he had just heard, but he was also searching for something. For a moment, he had slipped off, away from the militia's tent, into the quiet of his own mind to find that vital piece of information he knew was there about this new POTUS, which had been stored away in one of the dusty file drawers of his memory, untouched for years. When he found it, the sensations of the world hit all at once.

The pain, the chaotic noise, but most of all, the gnawing need to do something to head off what felt like an unstoppable train, headed toward a destroyed bridge and therefore its demise. They were all on that train.

Added to the feeling in his gut that the shit was going to hit the fan soon, he now felt certain that it was all centered around what he just heard. He needed to do something about it.

Realization of two certainties struck Frank at that moment: First, his mission to Mount Weather had changed and second, he had to use his skills and what remained of his abilities to help remove the person who was occupying the office of POTUS right now so that the one person who had that right, Thomas Chase, could be properly sworn in.

As had been the case with any operation in his military career, when the orders had been clearly given, he felt the resolute need to get started and complete the operation post haste.

The tent, dense with every militia member, roared like a hundred lions all demanding to be fed some read meat. Only moments ago, each had been quietly listening to the radio broadcast, and before that Frank, Cappy and Chase's conversation. They were now firing off questions and opinions at each other and anyone who might listen. Frank ignored them all.

He wanted nothing more than to get off his bum leg. Instead, he marched—*more like wobbled*—back over to Chase. The man seemed to have slunk deep into the chair Frank had just given up to him. For a man who walked into this tent so proud and erect, Chase now looked gut shot. Only his eyes moved, seemingly studying each of his feet as if they were fascinating and unknown. Frank knew this look.

When an operation was canceled just before it was about to begin, each of his soldiers were often overwhelmed by a feeling of malaise. The moment before the operation was stopped, each had been mentally prepared to go to war, to give everything, even their lives. Then to have their purpose snatched away, what was left was as if their souls had been removed.

"Thomas," Frank belted out loud enough to draw Chase's attention. "I'm telling you now; do not worry. I will do everything in my power to get you to the place you need to be so that you can replace that fraud who is now calling herself POTUS.

Chase gave Frank a vacant stare and nodded, though still not resolutely. But he became more animated. No doubt his years of service were kicking in, instructing him to prepare for a new operation, one even more important than the previous, which lay ahead of him.

The tent was quieting down, as many of the militia members were studying Frank and Chase.

"Do you know this, Abbie O'Neal? Who is she and where did she come from?" Cappy asked.

"No, not really," Chase answered, his voice measured, not fully his own, but stronger still. "When she was appointed last year, I was having a medical procedure during the hearing... Otherwise, I may have met her once, but it was far from memorable. I don't even remember what she did before she was appointed Secretary of Education."

"Failed State Senate candidate," Frank stated resolutely. "And before that, bartender."

"Seriously?" Chase asked.

Frank nodded an, *I know.*

"You must follow politics a lot to remember her that well then?" Cappy asked.

"No. Quite the opposite. But I remembered this one because of the sound of her voice. But even more so because of what she did to lose the Texas Senate race... However, that's not important now: We have bigger fish to fry."

"Shit, Major," Cappy chimed in. "Don't leave us hanging like some indie author's cliffhanger at the end of an unfinished series. You aren't moving out until tomorrow, even if it's butt-crack-thirty."

"Fine," Frank said. Unannounced, Samuel slipped a chair behind him, and Frank fully accepted, letting himself fall into it. He mouthed, "Thanks," while rubbing his knee, which throbbed a new chorus of pain that made him wince. He didn't even try to hide it. When he looked up, he was surprised to see a sea of faces above him anxious to hear what he had to say. The tent was church-mouse quiet.

"Abbie O'Neal—she went by a different name back then—was a shoo-in for an open Texas Senate seat. And she was killing it in the polls. She was supposedly this moderate, who came out of nowhere. She looked good on camera and spoke eloquently, albeit with that grading Fran-Dresher-sounding voice.

"Anyway, no one really noticed her much until a couple of days before election day. That's when she did an interview with some backwater podcast journalist who must have put O'Neal at ease. The subject of guns came up and that's when I remembered what O'Neal said. And so did everyone else."

The crickets from his tinnitus were roaring again. Everyone else was quiet, waiting for him to continue.

"I remember her saying something to the effect of 'We already have too many guns in our military and in our police forces. We need to get rid of them all. Everywhere. She also said that it should be illegal for civilians to own guns.' When the interviewer mentioned the Second Amendment, Ms. O'Neal stated, 'Short of changing it—which is difficult—we could easily neuter it. Then gun laws could be changed around that. Then...'" Frank held a finger up, "She inferred about when she had the power to act, like being elected to higher office... *'everyone* with a gun in their possession should be locked up with all the other criminals.'"

Frank shifted in his chair. "She said some other Leftist thoughts about anyone with a million bucks should not be able to pass it to anyone but the federal government... some sort of one-hundred percent tax on the wealthy...

"Needless to say, that interview ended O'Neal's—or whatever her name was at the time—political career. She was trounced in the election. Not even close. And she was never heard from again."

"So how the hell did she become the President?" someone asked.

Chase answered. "As she said, she was the designated survivor. The problem of course is that no one knew that I was not dead."

"Well, that will all change tomorrow, when we get you safely to your meetup at the Virginia border," Frank said, looking right at Chase.

"Yes, I imagine everything will change after tomorrow," Chase responded, once again less resolute than before.

None of them had any idea how true that statement was.

Chapter 17
Mt. Weather, Virginia

Mahdi, Abdul

"The phone is ringing, sir," announced Abdul's Senior Communications Officer. The expert, Mohammad Something—he was losing track of all his close followers—handed him the phone and scurried out of the room to give him privacy. This was understandable as Abdul had left explicit instructions to everyone at Mount Weather that no one was to listen into his conversation, under penalty of immediate death.

Abdul wore a headset, waiting for the other line to pick up. He saw that the clock on the wall read 21:01. In other words, one minute after nine.

Late.

While listening, he scrutinized the device connected to his phone's headset and then the phone. Several lights flashed off and on; one blazed a bright green. Sal said this was a Voice Transformer, and insisted he use it for this and all outgoing calls. The phone was already set to encrypt his conversation, but the Transformer would make his voice sound unrecognizable to anyone on the other side of the line. It seemed wholly unnecessary, as only a few of the people alive knew his actual voice, other than all of his loyal followers. Still, he liked the idea, for the reason Sal had described. "Best for the world not to know your voice until you reveal to them that *you* are their supreme leader."

Finally, the line made a clicking sound and a strong male tongue proclaimed, "Hold for POTUS."

I have been.

"Hello?" answered a tentative female voice. "This is the President of the United States. To whom am I speaking?" She said this with more forcefulness, which was kind of surprising to Abdul.

"Madam President. It is an honor to speak with you," Abdul started, not sure because of the phone's device if the tone in which he attempted to broadcast to POTUS was as smooth as he was trying to portray it. "My name is Abdul Raheem Farook, I am the spiritual leader to millions of Muslims here and outside of the United States. And contrary to reports you may have heard; I did not attack the US."

He purposely paused for a long count to let his words sink in.

"Again, I was *not* the one who attacked your cities; nor your military and I certainly did not order the facade of having our men masquerade as own US Army, while attacking your towns. I do, however, feel complicit because I could not stop this from happening. Until now.

"You see, Madam President, my whole purpose for being was to bring together all Muslims, regardless of whether they were Shia or Sunni, so that we could collectively help to solve the world's problems, starting with the United States. My number one follower, Saleem "Sal" Hafeez took this proclamation of mine to mean attack and conquer America. He is the one who planned and then led the attacks.

"I only identified him as the leader today and I am sparing none of my considerable resources to bring him to justice. Meanwhile, all his network of followers and co-conspirators have already been apprehended and executed. When we find Saleem, he will be executed as instructed by our ways. I have also taken back command of all my armed security personnel, and they have been ordered to no longer initiate any attacks on Americans. If any of them injure another one of your citizens without cause, they too will be immediately executed. I am thankful to Allah—peace be to his name—to now proclaim that the blood shed has stopped, Madam President."

He took a quick breath and continued, not wanting POTUS to speak. Not yet. That wasn't part of his plan. "My men are now wearing the banner of ICA Peacekeepers and are charged with a dual mission: to help all of those in need, whether they be foreigner to this land or American citizen, and to ensure that Muslims are not persecuted for the crimes committed by others. I pledge all this to you, but in return I need something from you, Madam President." Again, he didn't pause.

"You must order all US military forces to stand down. There are two military operations planned for tomorrow morning. You must tell them not to proceed. Further, US authorities and military units must allow our ICA Peacekeepers to pass unmolested so that they can continue to hunt down Saleem, as well as do their jobs of giving aid to those in need and keeping fellow Muslims safe. In other words, Madam President, your forces must ensure that no further hostilities against my people are initiated. Do

I have your agreement?"

There was silence on the other line, though he could hear her heavy breaths.

"Madam President, are you still there?" he asked, knowing the answer.

"Yes, I'm sorry, Mr. Farook. Ahh, yes... I agree to your terms of... surrender."

He thought he'd misheard what she said. More so, she needed to understand who was in control and what he was demanding of the American government.

"Madam President, you misunderstood me. This is not a surrender. There is no more war. All the attackers, except the leader, have been caught. The leader will be apprehended soon and then punished swiftly, according to his crimes. We are also searching for any others potentially connected to Saleem. They, too, will be brought to justice just as Mohammad—peace be upon him—has dictated. What I am asking for immediately, is your agreement to have your own military stand down and not engage any of our ICA Peacekeepers." Barely pausing, he then added an incentive he knew would ensure the American President's submission.

"One more thing. Upon torturing several of Saleem's men before execution, I have learned that these terrorists have activated a hidden bioweapon, which is set to go off in seventy-two hours. I am told it would kill at least 50% of your population, maybe more—But as I said, we *will* catch Saleem soon and when we do, we *will* find the bioweapon and use his detached thumb to disable it long before it becomes a threat to you and your country. So no need for you to worry about this. However, for this reason alone you do not want to hamper any of my men's or my efforts to find Saleem and this weapon.

"Is everything I have said clear?"

Her breathing was even heavier. She sounded like she had just returned from a run.

"Ah… Yes sir, very clear," she said. She took several more breaths. "Of course. I agree to your terms and—"

"I'm not finished," Abdul cut her off.

"Yes, Mr. Farook," she replied. She was sounding as submissive as he wanted her.

"Finally, for the same reasons I have outlined already, you are to make sure that all private US militias or even individual US Citizens will no longer engage any of our ICA Peacekeepers."

"Wait… What? How am I supposed to do this?"

"That is not my worry. Use your power and your military if you must. But understand this, my ICA Peacekeepers will engage any hostile force. And then the blood they spill will not be on our hands; it will be on yours."

Again, there was a delay, undoubtedly, as she considered her response in fear of another outburst from him. "Very well. I understand. We will do everything in our power to stop the militias from any future hostilities… We have both lost so much. Now, my only desire is to move forward and help my fellow Americans rebuild our country from the ashes of their old one."

"Of this we are in agreement," Abdul said. "I have already sent an outline of our agreement to you. Good night, Madam President. I will be in touch soon." He hung up before she could say anything further.

He glanced at the phone and the contraption connected to it: its bright green light turned red, confirming the call's completion.

He felt satisfied with what had just happened. Everything was going exactly as he had planned.

Tomorrow was a new day and the beginning of the final phase of his plan to take over America.

Now it was time for dinner with his family, including his son, Abdul Aziz. Soon his new wife will join him when Imran has brought her and takes over as his Chief Deputy.

Chapter 18

POTUS

Almost immediately after hanging up the phone, Abbie O'Neal was hurriedly escorted back to the conference room. She was so cold inside that she trembled.

Agreeing to the demands—they couldn't be called anything else—of the leader of the group that attacked her country was almost palatable: she detested war and would do anything to stop the killing, even if it meant negotiating with terrorists. She could also almost buy the narrative argued by Farook that his second in command carried out the attacks and that Farook's ICA—now called "Peacekeepers"—was searching for him. But she found it hard to believe that this supposed leader to millions didn't know anything about the thousands of men who were brought up through America's open borders to fight a war on his behalf. Still, none of this is what caused her to shake like a leaf.

A bioweapon that could kill fifty percent of the population was out there and Farook didn't even know where it was? Surely her US Military had the means to track this down, find it and disable it before Farook could. She would have to insist that Secretary Meer allocate significant resources to this endeavor. Then she remembered.

What did Farook say, "I've sent an outline of our agreement to you?" Did her cabinet and Joint Chiefs read this already? Did Evie? Did whatever Farook sent include something about the bioweapon? Surely, they would have to work with Farook's so-called Peacekeepers to find this thing?

She was starting to calm down while thinking it through, but then she thought of the deadline... *seventy-two hours!* She shook more violently now.

At the open conference room door, she caught a glimpse of Meer. His arms were folded in front of him. He wore an impatient scowl, like some Halloween mask that he often wore. Her friend Evie sat in her usual place, possessing the same tired-of-waiting-around-for-her-look as Meer. Before them, on the conference table, was another stack of folders. No doubt more Executive Orders waiting for her rubber stamp signature. Abbie just wanted to grab Evie and talk to her in private about what had just happened. Then talk to Meer.

The moment Abbie set foot inside the doorway, and they saw her, their personas changed from impatience to excitement. It felt fake. This was not surprising for Meer, who, she suspected, looked down upon her because she was a woman and more so, unqualified to be in this position. But when Evie did it too, shining faux happiness at her, it felt shocking. Didn't she have any idea what's going on?

Every moment since she had been sworn in had felt contrived and controlled by everyone but Evie. Now, the phone call and everyone's gushing enthusiasm made her feel even more unsettled.

Get a grip, Abbie. Evie is your friend! her mind demanded.

"Abbie, I heard your phone call went well," said Evie.

What? How could Evie know... and still act this way? She wanted to ask, but instead stood, facing Evie, utterly dumbstruck.

"Madam President," Meer boomed, please sit. I have the newest Executive Orders for you to sign, regarding the agreements you have made with the leader of the ICA Peacekeepers."

She couldn't help herself. "How could you possibly know this, much less have these already drawn up, based on a phone call I had just hung up on not less than five minutes ago?"

Evie's smile wilted for half a second, like she had forgotten to hold it up, but then it snapped back.

"Madam President, the ICA leader had already sent an outline of his requests. Besides, your conversation was monitored by our intelligence agencies' AI program, which immediately drafted a summary of the points you agreed to and the Executive Orders that were needed to carry them out. They were reviewed and accepted before they were handed to me for your signature."

She forced herself to think logically about this. It did have a ring of truth to it. She'd seen AI create an entire book almost instantly. Of course, they heard her phone call: all those who were making decisions for her had been monitoring her... It just felt so suspicious.

But what about the bioweapon?

Meer held out the first of the stack of Executive Orders he was intending for her to sign.

She didn't accept it. "Wait Mr. Secretary, what about the bioweapon? Isn't that the priority here? If everything

Farook says is correct, don't we need to at least work with his Peacekeepers to find the weapon, before the seventy-two-hour clock en—"

"—Madame President!" Secretary Meer barked. "Leave the hard decisions to the men. By this time, you should have realized that you are nothing more than a figure-head. That's it. All branches of the military have already been notified. And when you can stop wasting my time with these inane questions and do your job by signing these EO's, then we can do our jobs and remove the threat. Now sign this!"

He shoved the EO folder into her chest, stinging her more than his words.

She glared at him; her rattled brain offered no clever words of rebuke. So, she took the folder from him and opened it.

This time, she sped-read the whole thing.

"Like the others, you do not need to read it; just sign here." Meer pounded the signature line with his forefinger.

"I understand English"—she read further— "and I'm going to read it," Abbie spat at him. Less than five seconds later, she scratched her signature to what was a demand by the Executive Branch to all branches of the US Military to cease any combat actions and operational plans scheduled against the ICA. Further, that the US Military's sole actions going forward on US soil, would be to offer citizens and non-citizens with aid and comfort and assist ICA Peacekeepers with their mission, including finding other terrorists and weapons which may pose a threat to the United States.

"Next!" She handed back the first folder as a second

one was laid out before her. This one stated, among other things, that "no adverse actions" were to be made against Muslims in the US. And if there were (adverse actions), the violator would incur "the most severe hate crime penalties available." She signed her name before the Colonel could point it out to her.

So far, she had been in nearly full agreement with both Executive Orders. She probably could have written something similar herself...

...even though I'm just a figurehead.

"Next!" she stated.

The third one instructed all US authorities and civilians to take no violent actions against anyone wearing the ICA Peacekeeper flag. That was also part of the agreement and made sense. She signed this and shoved the folder back at him.

"Next!"

The fourth and final document she had to reread twice. Not because she disagreed with it, but because she agreed with it absolutely.

Civilians who were not active members of the US Military or law enforcement were no longer, during this time of an emergency, allowed to possess any firearm. They were to surrender them immediately upon request by any federal, state, or local US authority. Further, any citizen caught with a firearm after an official request to surrender it, would be subject to treason charges.

"No shit," Abbie said, shaking her head in the affirmative. She signed the document and handed it back to Meer, who added it to his pile and left with them in a hurry.

She still wanted to punch that pompous man in his

sanctimonious mouth. But there was no point in this thinking. She was, as he said, just a figurehead. That much was made plain to her by X and now restated by Meer.

"Fine," she huffed under her breath. Despite Meer's attitude and her concerns about everything, they did seem to be on top of all of these maters. Surely, they would not let a bioweapon go off.

She would comply for now. But she would bide her time until she could step in and use the power given to her when she could.

"Alright Madam President," Evie said, startling Abbie from her thoughts. Evie's smile was big as she had seen it before, "Now, you get to record a few words for the American public on radio and TV." She handed Abbie a two-page script. "You'll record each now and they will be broadcast multiple times, to each appropriate audience, starting early tomorrow morning."

Abbie was escorted back toward the microphone on top of the Presidential lectern, while the same man in the blue jumpsuit set up the camera again.

She read the script as she approached the lectern and smiled.

Chapter 19

Travis

A different armed guard let Travis out of his cell—Uncle Abdul called it an apartment—and escorted him to "see your father."

He couldn't wait.

Travis wore a traditional thobe outfit, tailored just for him for "special occasions" such as this one. It was all black, with floppy slacks. But the outfit's best feature were the long sleeves which perfectly hid the homemade knife he had fashioned just for this moment.

He wondered if his sister Lexi was as nervous as he was now, when she had planned to kill Abdul. He was so anxious; he could puke toenails right on the spot.

Focus on the mission, he told himself, while breathing out a sigh. That's what Frank would do. Yes, he would concentrate on the mission, he'd be strong, and he would not show fear. He would do this, just like his godfather, but it wasn't for himself. He was doing this for his murdered parents and his sister.

As his soft foot falls echoed down the outstretched hallway, his mind's eye played out how he would get to Abdul. He would have to be patient for the right opportunity.

Patience was the key. Then, when it was time, he would—.

"Move faster, kid," said the guard.

Travis picked up his pace and flashed an automatic smile at the guard. "Sorry," he said and returned to thinking about how he would stab his uncle to death.

"Abdul Aziz," whispered a man, dressed just like him, standing before a double door, titled Manager. A clone—same outfit, beard and height—stood on the other side of the door. Two bookends to a horrific story he had no interest in opening, though he knew he had to.

"Your father will see you now," Clone One said to Travis, then to the guard who had just walked him from his jail cell, "Thank you Muhammad." He hadn't remembered the guard's name, but knew he had a fifty percent chance of getting this one right.

Muhammad nodded and walked away, leaving Travis to the Clone Brothers and his uncle/faux father, Abdul.

Clone One stepped in front of Travis. "You are to do what your father says and not argue with him or any of Mahdi Abdul's men. Do you understand me?"

"Yes, sir," Travis responded and then flashed his forced smile.

Clone One glared at him, as if he had said something far less submissive than he should have. One thing Travis had learned in the short time he'd been in and around Abdul and/or his goons. It's all about submission: submission to Allah, submission to the Mahdi or an endless number of imams, and submission to just about everything else the leaders wanted him to submit to.

Clone One opened the door and Travis wanted to say to Clone Two, "Thanks for the conversation" or something similar. Instead, he bit his tongue and stepped through the doorway.

That's when his whole plan was dashed to bits.

There are too many people here, all watching me!

In his surprise, he jostled the knife free from where it had been strapped to the underside of his wrist, using the sawed-off top of one of his socks. It had been tight enough to hold the knife under his wrist, but loose enough to pull it out when he reached for it with his other hand. But when he reacted to all the eyes on him, his jostling dislodged the knife, now sliding down his arm, toward his elbow. It's almost out of reach.

In a moment of desperation, he whipped his knife arm around his back, feeling the knife stop its slide and movement in the other direction. He reached back with his free hand and clasped it around the outside of the knife arm, stopping the knife's progression.

While inching the knife's blade back up his wrist, he trained his forced smile on all of Abdul's wives and children sitting in the room's center, and then at the others. Surrounding the giant room lined with carpets and pillows where servants who watched everyone's movements. It seemed impossible that he could get a chance at his uncle with all this attention... Assuming, he hadn't already blown it with his jittery agitations.

Feeling like it was the right excuse for his arms being folded behind his back, he slowly bowed forward. All his powers of concentration were laser focused on moving the knife back to his wrist, and under the flap of elastic sock material. When he rose back up, he had the knife back in its resting place. He might not get a chance at his uncle here, but at least the knife wouldn't fall out.

"Abdul Aziz, come here," commanded one of Abdul's

wives. She was the oldest one with the perpetually bad attitude—*Sarti is her name*, he thought.

"Yes, Sarti," he said, once again revealing his teeth for show.

He shuffled over to the big carpet covering most of the middle of the room's floor where the family was congregated.

Sarti pointed to one of two empty spots with a cushion like the one she was sitting on, about five feet away from her. The other children were sitting on their pillows, quietly waiting for what he could only guess.

In one motion, he moved his arms back around to his front, careful not to lose the knife out of his sleeve, while sitting on his designated pad. He slid his free hand into the sleeve and got a firm grip of the knife, not so much to use it but to make sure it didn't go anywhere. He no longer trusted his system.

Travis didn't have to wait long, because Abdul arrived through a different door, just behind him.

He knew it was Abdul because everyone rose and bowed toward the door. Only Abdul would command such supplication. So, he, too, began bowing, while turning to face him. His eyes were thrust downward to avoid making contact.

Out of his periphery, Travis could see Abdul having a word with one of his servants. After some hushed words, Abdul marched in and took his place in between Travis and Sarti...

Abdul is sitting right next to you!

You're going to do this!

Abdul lowered himself onto his cushioned seat, and everyone followed.

With the knife now firmly in hand, but still covered by the sleeve, Travis quietly smiled in Abdul's direction. His uncle's attention was elsewhere; some sort of greeting to his two wives.

Abdul clapped his hands, causing Travis' heart to thunderously stop in his chest.

All of the servants descended upon them with plates full of food and Jasmine tea.

He slid the knife a little further out, just inside the sleeve, when Abdul turned his attention on him.

"Tell me Abdul Aziz," he said, his face as stern as he had ever seen. "What does the 32nd Hadith say?"

Oh shit-oh shit, was that part of my studies?

He looked upward for answers. "Ahhh…" The verse was coming to him. "No harming… I mean, there should not be harming nor reciprocating harm." Only after he spat it out, did the words hit him. He flashed a panicked glance at Abdul.

At the same time, Abdul clamped down on the outside of Travis' sleeves, squeezing painfully on both hands and the sharp knife in between them. Abdul made a show of twisting, causing Travis' blade, sharpened for just his uncle, to cut into skin. The bones of his hand felt like they might snap.

Travis convulsed in pain, but Abdul held on.

"So, what does that mean, Abdul Aziz?" Abdul demanded, his face emotionless.

Blood began dripping from Travis' sleeve. But the pain was so intense, he didn't notice, much less answer Abdul's question, even though he understood exactly why he brought up *this* Hadith.

"I'll answer you. It means you should never try to harm

a fellow Muslim, and certainly not your adopted father."
Abdul twisted further and Travis yelped. The knife fell out
of his sleeve and clanged off the floor.

Abdul released Travis, who yanked his arm back and
writhed in agony. "I'm sorry," he whimpered.

"It also means," Abdul continued, taking a silk handkerchief, and wiping a spot of Travis' blood from his own
hand. "I will not reciprocate harm to you in spite of your
actions. In fact, I look at this as a learning experience for
you. You now comprehend that you cannot kill me, and
you finally understand that I know everything you do and
think before you do it. That's because I am your father
and your Mahdi. And you will respect me and submit to
my will. Is that clear?"

"Yes, sir," Travis responded.

Chapter 20

Jasper

His thumb played with the Thompson's safety, flicking it from Fire to Safe and back. Over and over again. All night long, *click-click-click... click-click-click*. When Jasper waved at Frank for the third time, he decided he'd waited long enough. He would grab her now.

Again, Frank had been checking on Lexi, before saying once more, "going to try and sleep." This wasn't what really made Jasper nervous.

For the last couple of hours, militia members had moved about the camp, and just before Frank's last visit, a large group marched with purpose to the northern perimeter of the camp. It was the same place Jasper had intended to go. But he couldn't let that dissuade him.

All night Jasper had remained hidden, while watching and waiting for the right moment to spring into action. After Frank had left for the third time, and the movement around the camp appeared to be as quiet as it had ever been, he figured this was his chance.

He slung the Thompson to his back and made a B-line for Lexi's tent. Once there, he first poked his head in to make sure she was still unconscious. She was, but he knew it would not be for long. The drug he had given her was supposed to completely wear off in twelve hours.

Once in, he peeled back her sleeping bag, unsure what manner of dress or undress he would find her in... She still had last night's T-shirt, camo pants and boots on. Stopping there to look at her, he tried to decide if he was disappointed or pleased with this. He would at least relieve her of her pistol.

Pulling it out of her holster, he discarded it on the tent floor. Scooping her up in his arms, he left all her belongings, except what she wore, behind. He would give her new clothes where he was taking her.

Compared to other young women her age, he suspected Lexi weighed very little. Yet carrying her along with his pack and Thompson felt a bigger struggle than he'd considered. Repressing a grunt, he rapidly marched forward with her in his arms, cradling her head on a shoulder. For just a flash, he let his imagination go, wondering what it would be like to take Lexi as his own wife rather than doing what his Mahdi requested of him. He didn't have to decide just yet. He still had a little time. He might even have her decide.

There was movement in front of him and he slowed.

It was the militia's young leader. The one he should have put down earlier, though he couldn't remember the kid's name.

Slum... Slim?

"Hey, Jasper," the kid said in a low voice, examining him and then Lexi. "Are you all heading out... *now*?"

Jasper chewed on his response as he kept walking. "Not quite." He passed Slim, while still talking. "Frank just wanted to get everything ready, including getting his goddaughter into the truck."

"Wow, she's still out of it? Hadn't seen anyone this out of it since a friend of mine took a roofie... Hey, would you like help? She looks heavy."

"I'm good," Jasper said, not slowing down.

The black Hummer came into view.

Just in time, he thought.

"Samuel, is that you?" Lexi asked from a dream, batting her eyes, and trying to fix her glare on Jasper as if he were the young kid—*Samuel was the kid's name!*

At first her face was that of an angel's: happy in the belief it was Samuel who was carrying her away in some dream infused reality, and not a much older Jasper. Then her brow twisted, her mouth opened wide as if caught in a scream and she breathlessly heaved out the word "Abdul." Her body writhed spasmodically in his arms.

"Settle down, Lexi. It's Jasper."

Instantly, she released her tension.

"Can you stand?" He asked, he pulled up to the middle of the truck.

Not waiting for an answer, he chanced it, planting her feet down on the ground. He guided her hands to the truck's back passenger-side door handle hoping she'd grab it to hold herself up. She mostly did, but was otherwise just glaring at him, her head lolling forward.

He opened the front door and threw his stuff inside. Then he unclamped her hands from the rear door handle and guided her into the front seat. Putting his body into it, he slammed the door at the same time he heard four successive gunshots.

That was Faisal's alert to attack the camp.

"The fool. You're too early!" He muttered and trotted

around the front of the truck to the driver's seat.

I must leave now before that idiot's fighters mistaken me for one of the infidels.

Frank

It was no use. There was no turning off his brain tonight, much less catching a wink of sleep. That gnawing sense that he had missed something; that whatever crisis was about to strike, would occur because he failed to see something so obvious. He wished he knew what it was.

It was his third unsuccessful attempt at sleep. Each time he was more fatigued but less able to let go of the multitude of potential issues that lay before them. He decided then it was time to go. Even if it was still dark. He'd rouse Chase and Lexi and get Cappy to give him his radio time now. Then they'd bug out of this place and head to Virginia before whatever boogiemen infecting his gut and imagination would catch up with them.

Lexi was good for now. Last time he looked, she was still out of it. Plus, she remained under the watchful eye—at a distance—of Jasper. After securing his pack, and double-checking his AK and Glock, he headed to Chase's tent.

At Chase's tent flap, he asked not too loud, "Thomas, are you—"

"No worries, Frank. I'm up and ready to go. Is it time?"

He popped out of his tent, fully dressed, with a small

satchel around his shoulder. He had discarded his sling and head bandage.

Frank couldn't repress a bit of a grin. He liked Chase more and more.

"Thought we'd get a jump on things. Would you head to the truck? I'm going to see if I can use Cappy's radio. Then I'll wake Lexi from her slumber, and we'll join you." His damned gut gurgled out another warning. "You'd better take this. You know, just in case."

He handed Chase his AK. "You familiar with an AK?"

As a show, Chase tossed the rifle's sling over his head, pulled the charging handle back half-way and checked the chamber for a round and then said, "Yes, sir. See you at the rendezvous point."

"Roger that," Frank said.

Yep, Chase is my kind of people, he thought.

Chase took off North, toward the location where Cappy had shown them where they'd find their transport: a black Hummer. Frank headed toward the main tent, keeping his eyes open for Cappy.

Just before the main tent, Frank found Cappy giving directions to one of his youngest militia members. It was the red-headed kid who enthusiastically chatted with him about Gladys. Everyone called him Pimples, even though he had a clear complexion.

Pimples ran off in a hurry, carrying a Ruger mini rifle as if it were heavy.

"Morning, Major. You Oscar Mike?" Cappy asked.

"Always. Life starts pretty early around here."

"That and after your sharing your gut feelings with me last night, I increased our perimeter defense. Can't be too careful, right?"

"Indeed. I thought it would be good if we left a little early. Any chance I could grab that minute of radio time you promised?"

"Good plan, Major. No problem on the radio. Let's go see if—"

There were four rapid gun shots, less than a hundred meters away.

Both men jumped into action. Cappy unslung his AR pistol, aiming it in the direction of the gunfire. Frank yanked his Glock from his holster, and then cinched down his knee brace, getting ready to bolt.

Another gunshot, only this one to their east.

Two separate rifles; both shooting AK rounds.

"Skip the radio," Frank said. "Thanks for everything." He extended out his free left hand.

Cappy reciprocated with his own lefthand. "Pleasure, Major. So you know, I sent Samuel ahead in case you needed help with your exit. Stay frosty."

"Thanks. You as well."

Frank darted one tent over to Lexi's, while Cappy dashed south and out of sight.

"Get up now, Lexi," he yelled toward the open flap and then not waiting, he ducked in.

She's gone.

"God, I sure hope you're with Jasper," he muttered, while scanning the tent.

All her belongings were still there. "Shit."

He collected her AK, pack and revolver and bounded out of the tent.

Even with his limp and the added weight of two packs, he was jogging at a pretty good clip. With two more gunshots in front of him, he did what he always ended up doing in battles: he sped up and headed into the line of fire.

Faisal

Faisal wasn't happy about Imran's demand on behalf of Mahdi Abdul. Still, he had agreed to wait for Imran to take the girl out of the camp and leave before the attack. But Imran said nothing about letting any of the infidels leave.

Long before Imran's planned exit, Faisal had his eighteen men surround the camp. They all waited for Faisal's signal to begin their attack before sunrise, whether Imran left or not. And as soon as he could confirm Imran's leaving with the girl, he could begin. Faisal would lead the attack from the south, followed by a couple of his men on each side of him, with all three pushing north. This would force the infidels north to their only road access and therefore the only place to escape with their equipment and supplies. But they would be cut off from all other sides. It would be a killing field, with half of his men waiting for them. While the other half would be squeezing them from all sides, exterminating every man or woman who attempted to flee like the dogs they were. All he had to do was wait for Imran to leave.

And yet each passing minute, as more and more of these infidels moved around the camp, many making their way to the northern part of the camp, where their vehicles were parked... *As if they knew what was coming.*

Faisal decided then that Imran was in fact a traitor. So, he fired off the signal of four successive shots from his AK and began marching forward. This told his men the attack was beginning now.

He no longer believed what that traitor said: the Mahdi was *not* waiting for a wife from this camp. That was Imran's *al-taqiya* or concealing his intent. But Faisal didn't care.

Unlike his unit commander, who let these infidels win the last battle, he would now bring honor back to his unit. Because of his quick thinking, Faisal was able to save his men. Now with patience and expert planning, he alone would secure a victory. He would make sure that his Mahdi knew it was he who secured this glory.

Two of Faisal's men flanked him wide on each side, marching at the same pace as him, as the three of them moved toward the camp's main tent area.

One of his men fired a shot from the east, followed by several shots in the north. The victory would soon be theirs.

Closest to him, just under the tent, a man was attempting to call for help on a radio.

Faisal smiled, aimed, and fired.

Then he saw an older man coming from the other side of the tent. This one looked like their leader.

Faisal lifted his rifle and took aim.

Chapter 21

Frank

Shots thundered everywhere around him. Mostly AK's.

Frank maintained a running limp at a controlled pace, keeping low until he saw the Hummer.

Oddly, it was already moving and coming right at him.

Once at the west shoulder of the camp's exit route, he stood up high to be seen by the Hummer's driver, at the same time attempting to figure out the driver's intent.

The Hummer accelerated into its turn, kicking up loose dirt until its tires met the hardpack of the small road, then it straightened. It didn't look like it was going to stop for him, much less slow.

Ahead of the Hummer, only a few yards away from Frank, standing in the middle of the road was Chase. He had the AK Frank had given him pointed at the oncoming Hummer.

Frank automatically did the same, pointing Lexi's AK at the driver even though he knew it would do no good. The low light made it hard to see well inside the cab, but the driver looked like Jasper. He couldn't see Lexi.

"Isn't he one of us?" Chase hollered.

"Thought so," Frank responded.

When the Hummer was almost upon him, Frank sucked in a breath, but held back pulling the trigger. At the last second, Jasper braked hard and slid the dark vehicle to within a few inches of him.

At this point, Frank didn't know if Jasper stopped because he planned to or because they were aiming their AKs at him. He also wondered if Jasper had not heard Cappy tell them that the Hummer was his only hardened vehicle, and that it could withstand most everything fired at it, except an RPG.

The driver's side window slid down, revealing Jasper who beckoned them with a hand and one word, "Inside." Frank jumped into the back seat from the driver's side, and almost at the same time, Chase joined him from the passenger side. Once in, Frank could see Lexi slumped over, but belted into the front seat, yawning.

"Glad you got here when you did," Jasper said. He stomped on the gas pedal, lunging the vehicle forward before Chase had a chance to close his door. "Did you hear the gunshots?"

The muffled gunfire was now all around, though most of it seemed to be behind them.

Several pings rattled off the vehicle's front grill and two off the windshield, drawing everyone's attention.

Jasper laid off the accelerator and huffed, "Oh, it's bulletproof?"

He gassed it, aiming the vehicle at the Jihadi standing at the curve in the road, in the middle of their path, firing off his weapon at them. Each round did little more than blemish the vehicle's exterior.

Just then, another Jihadi appeared near the first, this one was holding something long and tube-like. When the Jihadi planted his feet and pointed the tube in their direction, Frank yelled out, "RPG!"

Cappy

The shot was close. Cappy ran toward the meeting tent, to where he had heard it. Before he could get there, Pimples collided with him.

"Whoa there, Pimples. Aren't you supposed to be with Samuel?"

The boy was frantic, tears welled up in his eyes.

"He's dead, Cappy." The boy's eyes now leaked.

Cappy swallowed a lump. "What? My son is dead?"

"No-no, not Slim." Pimples' eyes darted from one side to the other, frantic. "It's Edgar. They shot him, sir. I le-left my gun in my tent. Came back to get it, and-and..." The kid tried to run off like a cat stuck in a room full of rocking chairs.

Cappy had seen enough boys in battle to know that this one was in shock and not thinking straight. But he didn't have time for this. He grabbed both of the boy's shoulders, gave him a shake, and then pushed his face into the boy's. "Pimples, where-is-my-son?"

Pimples gave up resistance and glanced back. "I think I saw him ga-go to the vehicles... Yeah, he had Grandma, Hotshot and others with him."

He held tight to the boy, even though he was no longer

attempting to get away. Earlier, Cappy had told Samuel to ignore Chase and Frank's request for back up. Samuel was to take Gladys, Mike, and Pimples with him. They would hang back in several vehicles and follow Frank's vehicle without their knowing. That way, if they came upon an ICA unit or some other resistance, they'd have enough guns to mount a fight. Their mission felt even more important than before.

He assumed they were all there now, helping Frank get Chase out of the camp. He knew he should trust Samuel to execute his wishes and that his own job was to protect the rest of their militia at their camp, but...

"Dammit! Alright Pimples, you follow behind me. Keep your head d—

A thundering shot. Pimples shuddered violently and grunted. Then he went limp. Wetness blossomed below his chin.

The boy had caught a round in the chest.

A figure was dashing right at them, firing an AK in his direction. Cappy dropped Pimples. While falling to a knee, he slid out his Colt 1911, acquired a good sight picture and fired three shots at his target's center of mass. The figure tilted sideways and fell over.

Cappy holstered his 1911 and unslung his AR. Turning on his night sight, he scanned around where much of the gunfire seemed to be focused: the North end of their camp, where Samuel should be; where Chase and Frank were attempting to escape.

Then he ran toward the gunfire.

Frank

The fighter with the RPG had them dead to rights.

They weren't far enough away nor going fast enough to evasively avoid the shot. Instead, Jasper did something completely unexpected. He turned on his brights, blinding both fighters and gassed the engine.

Shots pinged the truck's body and windshield, marking it up, but still not getting through. One of their headlights shattered and went black, just as the other fighter appeared to reposition his RPG and fire.

Jasper yanked at the wheel, jigging them to the left so hard, Frank tumbled into Chase in the seat beside him. The rocket sailed toward them and then flew past, exploding not too far behind them.

Little trees and bushes slapped at their vehicle as Jasper tried to right them back onto the road, but he couldn't avoid the dip. All of them shot upward from their seats and then sling-shotted forward, their bodies punching hard into the seat backs or dashboard as the truck slammed head on into a berm, stopping them dead.

Jasper did a quick reverse, then drove them forward, twirling the wheel to send them up and out of the ditch and back toward the road. But they were now broadside the two fighters, the first one's rifle rounds already pinging Frank and Jasper's windows. Then the shots stopped.

The other fighter was loading another rocket, and the gunman was changing his magazine. Jasper straightened the wheel and corrected their vehicle so that they were pointed right at the Jihadi's position, now with the headlights off. Either they were both shot out or he had turned the functional one off. Frank wasn't sure if they were stopped either because Jasper didn't know what else to do or because he thought the RPG couldn't hurt them.

Frank was going to yell "Go!" when his attention was drawn to the woods.

Several headlights flashed on from various positions around them through the trees. Momentarily, he thought that the enemy had them surrounded, until Frank realized it was their new friends from the militia.

"They're ours," Frank stated, for his benefit as much as the others.

Even with their blinding headlights on, and just the low light from a sunrise still ten minutes away, Frank could make out some of the players.

To their right, Samuel's brother, Mike was in the bed of a full-sized pickup, with his rifle benched against the rear panel of the truck. Samuel was in the driver's seat yelling something to his brother.

Mike fired and the gunman who had been uselessly shooting at them fell to his knees. But almost immediately he was getting back up. The other fighter with the reloaded RPG now turned his rocket toward Samuel's pick up.

Jasper couldn't get to them in time even if he tried.

Frank blinked and almost missed what came next.

Another truck appeared from their left, bound in front of them and was gunning for the two fighters. In the moment it took to recognize what was happening, the truck struck both fighters at once. But the RPG was already on its way.

The truck didn't slow, driving through and over the fighters, and seemingly followed the rocket's trajectory... right for Samuel's truck.

Frank caught sight of Samuel attempting to do what they had done and accelerate the truck out of the rocket's path.

It was too late.

The rocket caught the truck's tailgate. A fireball lifted the extended cab from behind, sending it upward and over.

Jasper must have seen an opening, because he once again put them into gear, gassed them forward, depositing them back along the little road previously occupied by the Jihadis. It supposedly would take them to the high-way.

"Was that Samuel's truck?" a groggy Lexi asked from the front seat.

"'fraid so," Frank responded.

As Jasper steered them slowly around a curve in the road, before the trees took out their view, they glared out the Hummer's side windows and took in one last glimpse of the American Eagle Patriot's battle with the unknown Jihadis who attacked them. Frank caught two separate battles simultaneously.

In the first, the truck that had run over the two fight-ers, slowed enough to pick up the driver of the pickup that was RPG'd. He hoped it was Samuel. Unfortunately, there was no scenario Frank could have imagined where Samuel's brother Mike survived the explosion. The pickup barely slowed and then moved away from the wreckage, confirming this thought.

In the second battle, further away, a figure who looked like Cappy was surrounded and firing at several fighters converging on both sides of him. "Fu…" Frank muttered, when he saw Cappy get hit twice and appear to go down.

Then their view of the camp was gone.

Other than the roar of the Hummer's beefy engine accelerating down the dirt road and the sounds of their hitching breaths, the cab of their truck was silent. Jasper guided them, with their lights still off, toward the highway.

In the rearview mirror, Frank caught movement and then the forms of three other trucks appearing one by one behind them. None of them had their lights on. He spun in his seat and checked the back window. One truck looked like the large four-door truck which had picked up Samuel. All three matched their speed and followed from a distance.

Frank turned back to face forward, feeling hateful guilt for not doing anything further to save their new friends. Instead, they drove off. He threw his AK onto the floor and muttered an Arabic swear word he hadn't recalled since his time in Iraq.

Yet, he knew what his current mission was, and as much as he hated what happened, they were doing what they needed to. Other than keeping Lexi safe, finding Travis, and then killing Abdul, their mission now included getting Chase to the Virginia border. "Stick to the mission, Frank," he whispered to himself.

The mission was all that mattered right now, he repeated to himself over and over, as his mind simultaneously replayed their losses.

In front of them, the sun peaked over the horizon, blinding them to what no doubt lay ahead for them all.

The Final Phase

Chapter 22
Outside of Fort Rucker, Alabama

Porter

July 14th

Lieutenant, John Miles would lead the first wave of their operation. His Seal team was to be the tip of the spear, supported by Ares Company from the 2-29 out of Fort Benning, who more than anyone else wanted to return the favor of their base getting sarin gassed. Finally, the third wave, if needed, was composed of multiple Army and National Guard Units.

Porter and Wallace were part of the third wave of the operation, or what Wallace called, "the end of the spear." Their function was mostly advisory and back up. As Miles stated, his Seal team was a well-oiled machine, and he didn't want anyone outside of their team to "gum up the works."

From what all of them were told, Operation American Freedom was to be the first military operation led on US soil against a foreign enemy since World War II. None of the participants cared about its name or its place in history, only that it was happening. Lieutenant Miles' expressed their common sentiments when he announced to them in the operational briefing, "I'm pissed off that it took so damned long for payback."

As many of their fellow service men and women had expressed, it had been ten long days after the 'sonofabitches' killed over a million of their country's men, women and children. But what incensed all of them was that the terrorist assholes were using two of their Air Force bases to attack and kill their own military and still no action was demanded by their military superiors. Even after a group of them, led by Major Cartwright, unsuccessfully tried on their own to take back the base. Nothing.

Yeah, Porter thought, *it was time for some payback.*

Porter also caught wind that another operation was being carried out simultaneously at a separate Air Force base out west. He could have guessed which one, but everything was hush-hush, including even their immediate operation. So he didn't articulate this to anyone, not even Wallace. He suspected that few in his immediate chain of command knew of the second operation, much less any of its details. They were focused enough on this one.

However, time was not on their side.

Besides the enemy seeming to have gone quiet at their target, all were concerned that the enemy would catch wind of either operation before it was executed. Still, neither military operation could commence until after final approval had come from the very top.

So, they all waited in their positions for the "Go!" command, to come directly from their new Commander in Chief. Already, their start time was delayed. They were supposed to invade at dawn and the sun had been up for an hour.

Porter sighed again and Wallace wiped another layer of Alabama sweat from her forehead.

"If we wait long enough, perhaps the enemy will invite us in for tea," Wallace quipped, while eyeballing the east perimeter of Fort Rucker with her binoculars.

"Cucumber sandwiches? Scones? I'm in for that!" Porter replied mimicking a British accent and with equal sarcasm. He wiped an eye with the end of his *shemagh*. "Or we could just crash the party ourselves and throw them some pineapples?"

"Pipe down there," demanded Lieutenant Bingham, the commanding officer of their unit. Bingham had been snippy the moment he'd been assigned Porter and Wallace.

"Sir, I'm getting something from command," barked the skinny private who had been manning their radio.

"Are we a go, private?" begged Bingham.

The private was silent. His lower lip fell as he glared at his CO rather than answering.

"Spit it out, son."

The private handed Bingham his headphones, while shaking his head in the negative.

Just as quick as Bingham put on the headphones, he spat out a mouthful of obscenities.

He tossed the headphones back to the private, who put them back on and continued to listen.

Bingham exited the tent and marched toward the large platoon of men and women assembled nearby. He cracked a quick whistle at them to get their attention. It was unnecessary as all were watching him. "We are negative on go. Repeat, Operation American Freedom has been terminated indefinitely. We are ordered to return to our FOB for further orders and under no circumstance, are we to engage the enemy."

Daleville High School

They returned to their temporary Forward Operating Base at the high school gymnasium as if they had just lost a battle. In every way, it felt like they did.

A low mumble of a multitude of voices shuffled into the gymnasium. One-by-one, the proud men and women of multiple branches of the US Military filed in slowly, each of their shoulders slumped as if they carried more weight than after completing a ruck march. Most took the same seats they had when they had assembled last evening. Then, they were sitting tall after receiving the details of the operation. Now they slouched in their seats, looking defeated.

Once more, they had to wait for their orders. Only this time, without the excited expectation.

"Do you suppose they're just going to bomb those bastards and that's why they wanted us out of there?" Porter asked as he sat down in a seat.

"Shit if I know," Wallace snapped at him, "I'm a damned grunt like you in this non-operation."

"What the hell is taking them so long?" Porter asked rhetorically.

Wallace flashed Porter that look that he had grown to understand: "Stop asking your stupid questions!"

But Porter couldn't help it. He was tired, hot and sopping wet from perspiration. And not a damned thing to show for the fatigue.

Bingham trotted to the microphone and the din of voices quieted.

He leaned into it. "I'm" —a high pitched feedback tone sounded and then was gone— "I'm told that we have a recorded broadcast for us from the President of United States. Please remain as you were."

Bingham stepped away from the microphone and off the dais.

A few voices uttered some vulgar and satirical rants, followed immediately by "Shhhs" or "Quiet!" Porter watched Bingham march toward a table where their skinny private was busily working the knobs on multiple transceivers. Another tapped away a the keyboard of a mobile SINC-GARS.

Then there was a crackle and a female voice broadcast over a public address system.

"Greetings men and women of the United State Armed Forces. My name is Abbie O'Neal, the President of the United States.

"I know you want revenge against the enemy that has caused so much death and injury to this country. I assure you, that has already happened.

"I'm happy to announce that we will soon have apprehended the head of the terrorist organization that attacked us and have already apprehended many of his followers. The leader will be tried and punished publicly, while his followers who were the other instigators in this tragedy have already been executed."

There were several "Cheers" and "Hallelujahs," once again followed by "Shhh"s. Porter wondered what this meant about Abdul, but he kept his thoughts to himself.

"I am also happy to announce that my administration has reached a cease fire agreement with the organization known as the ICA. From this point forward, we have been promised that any ICA troops still in our country will take on the role of peacekeepers and will no longer violently engage civilians or our military."

"Say what?" escaped from Porter's lips before he could stop it. He wasn't the only one.

"As part of this ceasefire agreement, our military is no longer authorized to engage in combat with the ICA's members. If you see any of them, you are to let them pass by you peacefully, so they can return to their families and do their intended work to ensure that American Muslims, regardless of immigration status, will be protected against any hate crimes or xenophobia."

"That's such bullshit," Wallace spat, obviously not caring that her words were heard by most of the audience, including their superior officers. She looked like she could eat metal and spit nails.

There was another crackle in the speakers, as if they too were expressing displeasure at Wallace's comment, before POTUS continued in a softer voice. "Peace is a fragile thing. So it will be important for you, our military, just like our law enforcement officials to assist us in maintaining this peace process... However, our peaceful goals are currently being uprooted by civilians, who have taken it upon themselves to violently engage ICA Peacekeepers. This-must-stop!"

POTUS took a breath and then spoke in a less emotional tone. "To this end, my administration has signed into law an Emergency Weapons Ban. The EWB will take effect at noon, Eastern Time, today, and it shall remain in effect until this national emergency has abated."

Porter and Wallace turned their heads and flashed a look at each other. Porter felt a chill run up his spine.

"Soon you will receive your new orders, which will outline the specific rules of the EWB, and what you'll be expected to do to enforce them."

POTUS paused once again, and when she spoke, her voice was thick with emotion, like an actress auditioning for a theatric play.

"I am speaking to you now as a fellow American and not just as your Commander in Chief. I think you'll agree that these are critical times, and because of this, we must all make sacrifices for the benefit of our country as a whole. The rights and privileges that we once enjoyed before our country was attacked, must now be set aside as we attempt to protect the vulnerable from the unruly during this emergency. To do this, you will be called upon to do things which once would be considered unacceptable, but now must be required. I have faith in each and every one of you to do your job for your country.

"And when the crisis has passed, we can reexamine what is best for our country moving forward.

"Thank you for your service. May God or Allah, whomever you believe in, bless you and this country."

When the broadcast stopped, the gymnasium was stunned into silence.

Porter shivered.

Chapter 23

Abdul

While POTUS' pre-recorded words were broadcast to the military throughout the US on encrypted channels, a separate public broadcast was transmitted over several VHS television stations and multiple short-wave radio channels. The public message was to be re-broadcast multiple times throughout the day. Abdul was waiting when the first broadcast began.

He did not even attempt to restrain his grin. One foot was propped on top of the desk cluttered by the former Chief Administrator of the Mount Weather facility. Abdul hadn't bothered having the personal effects cleaned away after executing the administrator, because he preferred the daily reminder of his conquest. Now, tilting back in a comfy leather chair, he consumed the glorious words coming from the female President.

A part of him wanted to cheer out loud while listening, as if he'd won a great battle. Better, it was a portend to his soon winning the war. But as a Mahdi, he would not celebrate audibly. Restraint was necessary, even when he was alone.

He clenched a fist and mouthed the word "Yes!" when

POTUS pontificated about how the US Military had already begun working with ICA Peacekeepers. They would assist those in need and hunt down any additional responsible terrorists, including their leader.

But when POTUS began to speak about how Americans' rights must be abridged during emergencies, such as this one, Abdul sat up in his seat to pay strict attention to her next words.

"... and that is why I have taken several proactive steps to protect the welfare of all of our country's current residents.

"First, I have signed into law, the Redefinition of Militias Act. Effective immediately, civilians will no longer be allowed to gather privately as militias. All private militias are effectively disbanded, and it will be unlawful for any civilian to be a member of one.

"I have also signed into law an Emergency Weapons Ban, which will take effect at noon, Eastern Time today. As part of the EWB, no civilian will be allowed to possess military assault weapons, which our ATF has defined as any pistol or rifle having the ability to fire more than one round of ammunition.

"The only exceptions to this rule are active members of the US Military or law enforcement, who are excluded from this.

"Therefore, all civilians, who are not active members of the US Military or law enforcement, who are in possession of any military assault weapons, must surrender them by twelve noon today. If any civilian, again who is not an active member of the US Military or law enforcement, is caught by an officer charged by the US government with an assault weapon, they will be required to surrender it immediately after noon today. Any resistance to comply with this rule will result in an immediate arrest. Anyone failing to submit, will be subject to the US Military's and law enforcement's authority to use all means necessary to ensure compliance..."

Abdul couldn't resist any further: he leapt from his seat and pumped his clenched fist in the air.

What he had just accomplished in a few days, was something that other American politicians had been unable to achieve after decades of attempts: he had neutered the Second Amendment. And with that primary constitutional right—which protected the others—gone, every other American right would bend to his will.

He only needed to maintain control for a few more days, and his plans would be fully realized.

If the Administration and military would buy his threats for a few more days, he would complete his takeover of America.

All I need is a few more days, he thought.

He would not worry about any of this though. As Allah had taught him, he would be thankful for everything that was already provided to him and trust that in the fullness of time, everything else he needed would come to him.

There was a knock at his door and Abdul glanced back up at the TV. The broadcast was over, and the TV was blank except for a static symbol announcing the station was having broadcast difficulties. This was another added bonus of his knocking out the grid. It gave him control over social media and now most amplified broadcast signals. No longer were there talking heads appearing after a President's broadcast, dissecting the meaning of her words and then telling their American followers what they should believe was the real message.

Another knock at the door.

Abdul sat back down. "Enter," he said, still having difficulty masking his smile.

"Sir," said Ali Baig. One of his many bootlickers, but Ali was an important one right now. "I was told to wait until the President's broadcast was concluded."

"Thank you. What is it?"

"You wanted an update on how your troops are performing under their new role."

"Yes, please come in and report to me what you have learned."

Ali shuffled in, holding his yellow pad. Once in front of Abdul's desk, he searched through the first few pages and then found the page he was searching for. "Okay sir," he looked up at Abdul and then returned his eyes to the page. "We have multiple reports from all over that your troops have all converted their patches and signs into that of ICA Peacekeepers and it appears that most of them are in place and ready for further orders from you."

"Thank you, Ali. Any word yet of problems with them being accepted by the Americans as Peacekeepers or is it too early to tell?"

"Yes, I'm afraid there still are..." Ali was counting places on his page, and then several on the next page. "Twelve reports so far of violence committed against your Peacekeepers by various civilians, many of whom claim to be part of an American militia. So far, fifty-six casualties have been counted. But a nearly equal number of infidels—" Ali's head shot up, as he realized his faux paus, though too late— "I mean, American civilians were also killed. I am sorry sir." Ali's head drooped forward and his shoulders sagged.

Abdul expected continued losses to his Peacekeepers, at least for another day or two. He was prepared for this news to continue for another day or two. He just hadn't expected this delivery.

Ali, like all of Abdul's followers had been advised to no longer speak about American civilians as infidels, at least until after they had completed their takeover of the country. At that time, it wouldn't matter. Until then, each should always speak resoundingly about their faith and continue to live under the rules of Sharia. But they are to not speak negatively about those who do not share their specific Muslim beliefs as it would not help their cause until such time as their Mahdi tells them to do otherwise.

Abdul let his smile show again. "Ali, my faithful servant, I appreciate your concern to get this correct. You are forgiven. Was there anything more to your report?"

Ali's face appeared less dire at once, although it was obvious, he would not dare smile back. The man snapped back to attention and checked his notes once more before looking back up. "No sir, that is all."

"Excellent. Now please tell me have we heard anything from Imran?"

Ali's face turned grave again. "No, my Mahdi. Imran has not yet contacted us. We have one worker whose only job is to monitor for Imran's call."

Abdul's smile was gone.

This bugged him. He was impatient to make Imran his Chief Deputy, and to officially have him take over from Sal. Until then, Ali was acting as his temporary replacement, although not as well as he had hoped. He missed Sal, who had a sense for how everything should work.

Abdul once again regretted this part of his plan. It was a sacrifice Sal would be willing to take for him; Abdul just didn't like the sacrifice he was having to make, waiting for a competent second in command to follow up on all the details.

"Please tell me Ali, how is Mr. Hafeez?"

Ali momentarily stared at Abdul, his face a blank canvas, as if he were asked what the square root of Pi was. Then he nodded and again referred to his notes, before looking back up and pausing to deliver an answer. The man must have taken special measure to be careful about what he said next, because he paused before delivering what his notes told him. "I have a report from the head of the prison. He tells me that Saleem Hafeez, AKA Sal is, and I quote," —Ali took in a gulp of air— "very angry about being locked up and he..." Ali glance up from his notes again, and held onto Abdul's gaze, *"demanded*, that he be told what he is being charged with."

At that moment, Ali's face resembled some of Sal's followers, just before they were executed: like death.

Abdul did not mind executing them: they were in fact planning a coup and were caught discussing their plans after Sal had left them. He would still search for any others who had allegiances to Sal and didn't appear to be on his side. No doubt, Ali was feeling this and the pressure of his new responsibilities. It was likely a job few of his followers wanted.

Abdul gave an accepting nod. "Do not worry Ali. I understand. Please tell the Prison Chief that I will be over to speak with Sal soon."

Abdul hesitated before asking for his next update. "Very good. Any news about my son?"

Ali didn't refer to his notes this time.

"He's very quiet, sir. Ravi Abdalla checks on him approximately once per hour and makes sure that he no longer possesses any contraband. The boy has been respectful and observant of Mr. Abdalla's requests."

"Very good, Ali. Thank you for all your reports. Please return to me in the next hour with updates or sooner if you hear from Imran."

"Yes, sir," Ali answered, turned on a heal and shuffled out the door of Abdul's office.

Abdul returned to view the television, which was already rebroadcasting The President's address to the nation. He enjoyed it too much to not watch it once more.

Chapter 24

Travis

For the second time this morning, Hairy Ravi, one of Abdul's henchmen entered and then left Travis' unit after searching for what he called "contraband."

"So stupid," Travis mumbled under his breath. Why not just say "weapons" or something more obvious. Instead, Hairy Ravi—Travis thought of him this way, because Ravi's face, neck and arms were carpeted with thick black hair—entered, and then repeated the same dumb question from his last visit, "Abdul-Aziz, do you have any contraband in your possession?"

As if Travis would have then responded, "You got me Hairy Ravi; now that you ask, here's my RPG. I never liked the thing anyway..." He was going to do his inspection regardless of his answer. So why ask this at all?"

Travis rolled his eyes and shook his head at the insipid nature of the whole exercise. But he dare not say or even hint at anything after last night's epic failure to take out his uncle. He could pretend to be good.

He stood up, feeling the giggles bubble up from an image that came to mind. It was a better feeling than the anxious nervousness that swept over him since being caught by his uncle and then being unceremoniously deposited in this cell after dinner. Feeling better, he embraced the image of his sister and relived that moment in his mind.

It was when she described... "Your nether region" to him that his giggles turned into snorts. Like now.

Lexi was teaching him how to hide things on his body. She said there was one place they would never dare search you... When he asked her honestly where that was, she pointed to her crotch and said, "your nether regions, silly." The first time she said this, he turned as red as a cherry lollipop—*I sure miss those,* he thought.

Lexi had explained how to put whatever he was hiding, if it was small, in his underpants.

Later, his uncle Frank taught him about picking locks using paper clips. At that time, Travis wondered why such a skill would be important, though he studied it just the same. That was before Abdul's thugs kept abducting him and his sister.

Travis pulled on the elastic of his waistband to reveal one of his hidden paper clips. This one had been turned into a tension wrench before he was abducted. On the other side of his briefs, he pulled a second clip, bent at the end with a single hook pick. He had just made that one using a pin-sized hole in the concrete wall.

In a mocking voice, barely above a whisper, Travis asked the door, "Would *these* qualify as contraband?" He offered the picks in the open palm of his unmutilated hand as if he were presenting them to Hairy Ravi as proof of their ineffectual search methods.

"Dummies!" Travis huffed.

Leaning forward, he put an ear to the door and listened

for any of Abdul's thugs who might be on the other side. If it was just Hairy Ravi, he could at least confirm that the man had marched off as he usually did a couple of minutes after his search.

There were heavy footsteps which sounded as if they were disappearing down one of the hallways.

Like clockwork, he thought.

But he couldn't be sure Hairy or anyone else was there, about to enter, unless he looked.

The next exercise was probably unnecessary. But he didn't want to risk someone in the general area walking in now. Just a quick look. At the same time, he'd confirm his directions as well as how far each hallway stretched. He had tried to memorize these facts, but after failing so miserably last night, he found himself questioning his abilities and memory.

Go! he told himself.

At that moment, Travis started a mental timer and turned his attention to the door lock with his makeshift picks. His record on any lock was twenty-eight seconds. But that was when he had all ten fingers, and it wasn't a double cylinder lock like this one. It would be a little more difficult and therefore require more time. He would try to be patient.

After eight minutes, when his nine remaining digits began to hurt as much as his missing one, the lock clicked open.

Slowly he twisted the handle and pulled the door open.

No one was there.

He quickly checked in both directions to make sure nobody was coming his way. The only activity was some distance away to his right.

Check.

To his left was undiscovered territory as he hadn't been down there and had only seen one door opened and that was opposite his. The hallway was not nearly as long as the one to his right, ending at a left angle barely twenty feet away. He didn't recall seeing anyone down that hallway and no one was there now. If he had to guess, these were unused offices or storage closets like his. Though he hadn't intended to go that way.

Check.

Back to his right, the hall led to the only places he had been, and the only direction he intended to go. About fifty feet away, the main hallway broke off in two directions: one way led to where Abdul and most of his men seemed to go and the other direction seemed to also be heavily trafficked, though not only by the thobe-covered men. Travis wasn't going in either direction.

He focused further down the long hallway, to where he had first arrived at the complex. He was hooded then, so he couldn't see much detail. But the hood was porous enough that he could see through it somewhat. Plus, he had counted his steps then.

To the right was his way out and he now confirmed how impossibly far he would have to go without being seen, based on the number of tiles to his exit.

Check.

He closed the door and gave a quick glance around the room to see if he had forgotten to do something. There was nothing in this unit that mattered to him, other than his father's medal which he now wore on the outside of his shirt.

After what happened last night, he decided to leave

this place. He had resigned himself to not being able to kill his uncle. So, he settled on the next best thing, even though it meant his own death. He would hurt his uncle and put questions into his uncle's followers. After Travis was done, they would all question how a Mahdi who knew everything could have allowed his newly adopted son to resist and cause so much trouble.

Travis remained inside his unit for several long breaths, not bothering to go through the time of relocking the door. Instead, he pulled his study desk from the next wall, cringing as the loud screech-sounds it made across the concrete floor. He left it in front of the door. It wouldn't stop anyone, but it would give Hairy Ravi a struggle. And when the man entered, he would see what Travis had done.

The next thing he had planned was even better. He knew he wasn't supposed to find such a thing funny. This time, he didn't even try to suppress the giggle that took hold of him.

Hairy Ravi

Less than five minutes later, Hairy Ravi returned to Travis' unit.

It wasn't that Ravi had forgotten to do what he was commanded to do by Ali Baig, the Mahdi's new Deputy... "To search Abdul Aziz and his room to make sure the boy was not hiding contraband on his person." The orders were clear enough.

Ravi just thought it was a little too personal to have a ten-year old boy strip down and search him, especially since it was the Mahdi's son. He resisted the orders, only asking the boy if he had any contraband, and searching the boy's unit. He didn't dare go any further and search his person. But after almost returning to Ali Baig to give him his update, he decided it was better to follow orders explicitly and search the boy, no matter how embarrassing it was for the boy.

Immediately upon slipping his key into the lock, he noticed that it had turned too easily, as if he had forgotten to lock it in the first place. He spat out a muffled epithet at the door, while twisting its handle and pushing inward. But it only opened a crack, as if something were behind it keeping it in place.

Hesitating at first, and then resolving it was a trick by the boy, Ravi put his shoulder into it, pushing the door open further and causing a loud squealing sound. That's when an object hit him on the head.

"Abdul-Aziz, this behavior will not be tolerated," he yelled, while sliding his rotund body inside the kid's dwelling.

He stepped on something and glanced down to see what it was, guessing whatever it was, the kid must have thrown it at him and hid under his bed.

When he saw it was the kid's copy of the Koran, anger consumed him. Playing tricks with the door or hiding something were both unacceptable, but forgivable to a point.

This was intolerable.

He gingerly picked up the lovingly worn copy of the Koran from off the floor, ready to release a tirade of fury at the boy. But what he witnessed next froze him in his boots.

In fact, he couldn't move for a moment or two as the big man was consumed by both revulsion and fear.

When he did move, he was cheetah like. Spinning on a heel, Ravi dashed out the door, running as hard as his plump legs would carry him. He had to report what he just witnessed, no matter how impossible it was.

Chapter 25

Grimes

Gunny Aimes practically tumbled into Grime's radio shack, a former spare upstairs bedroom, which was now AFN's headquarters.

Aimes gulped in several breaths of air, then bellowed, "Turn on the TV."

Grimes, sitting in his usual chair, pointed to the wall-mounted flatscreen, already playing the only broadcast on American TV since the attacks ten days ago. A pretty woman, with a swarthy complexion, wearing a white business suit, was speaking from behind a podium made miniature juxtaposed to its giant Presidential seal.

"Just started again," Grimes stated, "moments ago." He pulled the spare desk chair next to him, knowing his friend limp-ran all the way from his house and up the stairs to get here. Aimes fell into it with a groan.

The two men remained transfixed for the broadcast's entire seven minutes. Grimes busily scribbled notes in a notebook, while Aimes muttered several F-bombs in between his hitching breaths.

When the video stopped, it was replaced by a static image neither of them had seen in a long time: the test pattern screen with the overlay words "PLEASE STAND BY." Both men turned in their seats to face each other open mouthed.

They remained silent for a long few seconds until Aimes spoke first. "Did you hear what I just heard?"

"You mean that the Commies have somehow taken over and they're coming for our guns? Yeah, I heard that."

"How..." Aimes asked but didn't finish his question.

Grimes finished Aimes open ended question with several of his own. "How did this happen? How is it possible for our government to do this? How the hell did we get here?"

"Yes, all of those."

"You know as much as I do, buddy. I have a better question: Do you remember when Frank told us about the Leftist state politician who had said she would take everyone's guns if elected, but then lost and disappeared from the public?"

Aimes scratched at his head, probably trying to consider what Grimes said, but also because he was trying to relieve the itch around where the bullet had grazed his scalp. "Yeah, I do remember the Major mentioning something about a Senator wannabe with an annoying voice who admitted in an interview—wait, you think this is her? How would *she* have become President?"

"By some stroke of our misfortune, also known as the presidential line of succession. You know the Designated Survivor and all that? Anyway, the questions of how or why we got here aren't important. What we do now is what matters."

Aimes' face tightened, his eyebrows met on his forehead, and he took in an enormous breath. His face began turning a bright crimson, as if he were damming up the words he wanted to say until he couldn't keep them back any longer.

"Yeah, I know. But..." The dam burst. "—it fricking kills me that somehow these Lefties have wrestled control of the government and are using the attacks and subsequent war against the Jihadis to take our rights from us. And to grind salt into our open wounds, they've made peace with the terrorists, who have so far kicked our asses with *zero* retaliation by our military... Dammit!" Aimes beat the armrest of the chair he was sitting in with a balled fist."

"Feeling better?" Grimes asked.

"No!" Aimes took in another long breath, but this time he spoke calmly. "You're right, we need to warn everybody. But what exactly is the warning?"

"That the US Military and local law enforcement are coming for you and your guns." Grimes spat back.

Aimes shot his friend a look of incredulity. "And so our message to all gun owners is that they then claim they lost all of their guns in separate boating accidents?" It was the common joke that 2nd Amendment advocates said they would use if the Feds one day showed up at their door asking about the status of their firearms.

Grimes could see Aimes wasn't done with his point. "Seriously, the faux-President has just told everyone, very plainly, that someone in authority will be visiting every gun owner in America to confiscate their guns. What could we possibly say as an additional warning?"

Grimes was silent for a moment, scouring his notes for something.

Then a thought came to mind.

He spun his wooden desk chair around, while flipping over the scribbled page to reveal a clean one. Using the desk surface rather than his lap, he started to write rapidly on the spiral-bound notebook.

"What are you thinking, Lu—" Aimes began to ask, but cut himself short when Grimes held up a forefinger.

Grimes continued writing for close to five minutes. Then he stopped, put his pen down and handed Aimes the notebook. "Tell me what you think of this."

Aimes took it, glanced at the text, and then looked back up at Grimes. "Okay, I think I get what you're saying. Let me re-read it again, this time slowly." He didn't look up while his finger traced through it line by line.

Handing it back to Grimes, Aimes pointed to one part of the message that he thought could be even stronger. He offered several suggestions, even quoting US Military law.

Thirty minutes of back and forth, they came up with their broadcast text.

After Grimes read the final copy out loud, Aimes nodded and then said, "Okay, this might actually work. Except—and it's a big except..." Grimes was now nodding an affirmation believing that he knew what Aimes was going to ask, but he let Aimes continue his thoughts. "So how do we get the word out there, to all our fellow militia men and women? In spite of the so-called-President transmitting without any interference from her bunker—which is interesting in itself—I assume the damned terrorists still have control of Mount Weather and will jam every short-wave signal of ours. So how do we get this out?"

Grimes responded immediately. "Same way we've been asking militias to recruit: the two-meter—which by the way, I've found many more repeaters now"—Grimes held up a different spiral bound notebook with a hand-written page titled Working Repeaters. "So we'll broadcast on those two-meter channels and hope they get repeated far enough to be heard over a wide area. And we'll keep rebroadcasting the message. At the same time, we'll get on the CB and ask that our message be repeated, word for word, to others all over the US."

A grin that had been creeping up Aimes' face faded. "I think Frank, wherever he is, would approve."

"So do I. Just wished to hell we knew that Frank and his niece were okay."

"Yeah, and I'm dying to know if his Florida friend was able to reach them?"

Jonah

They idled past the bodies of soldiers. But it was immediately obvious they were not American military, despite their familiar looking vehicles. The dead were strewn around several old Army trucks, some of which looked as if they had been kicked and stomped on by a vindictive giant. It was hardly a mystery.

The spray-painted eagle told them of the roused giant who had won this battle.

Up ahead was a roadblock and tell tail signs of a trap that had already been sprung. The lifeless ICA fighters and their trucks blocked the purposeful detour.

Still Jonah Price and Randall White rubbernecked, feeling an unease about even stopping to properly take in the sight.

"Looks like our side threw them a curve ball," Randall said.

"They struck 'em all out," Jonah mused. Regardless of Randall's baseball metaphor, one thing was for sure, the Jihadis were the clear losers of this odd match-up.

Randall eyeballed the roadblock and barked out a warning, "Hey, Jonah, don't you think—"

Before Randall could finish, Jonah punched the Vette's gas pedal and spun the wheel, executing a quick U-turn. "We're going around this, to the other side." Jonah added as an afterthought. He wished now he had driven his truck with the push bars: he could have gone through, rather than the long way around. When they left at midnight, he was thinking of speed over brawn.

He babied the Vette through I-95's median and then up the south bound entrance ramp, taking them parallel to the highway, but on the opposite side of the unpassable overpass.

"You think your buddy Cartwright was part of this?" Randall asked.

"Doubt it. At first, I would have said it was the military, but based on the Wolverine-like spray-painting..."

"Wolverine?" Randall asked, turning back to catch another glance of the eagle drawing on the side of the truck.

"Never mind, the point I'm making is that this was a local militia, led by someone with military experience."

"Nice!" Randall said while pumping a fist up into the *whooshing* wind overhead.

They were silent again, listening to the blasts of air rushing through the convertible's cockpit, as they raced back onto the highway. Each man continued to scour the road up ahead and on each side for any sign of a Plymouth Fury on or off the pavement. It was the same highway Frank said he would take all the way up to Virginia. But with what they had seen, Jonah would not have been surprised if Frank had altered his plans. That was even assuming Jasper hadn't already taken out Frank and Lexi or they weren't hurt or killed by all the crazies they'd encountered taking pot shots as they drove bye.

Adding to the surreal nature of their nearly impossible mission, was the new President's announcement on their emergency radio that nearly all guns and militias were now illegal...

It just made them ever more frantic to get to Frank before they were too late.

"Hey Randy, why don't you see if you can get anything on the CB, since we've heard nothing on the 2-meter."

All morning they had been trying several channels on the 2-meter, hoping against hope, that they could reach Frank and Lexi. Grimes, suggested if they connected with Frank on the radio, they should tell him to, "Watch out for Brutus," in case Jasper was listening too. But they hadn't heard a peep on the radio, much less any evidence that they were catching up to Frank or even if they were matching his same route.

Randal clicked on the CB radio, already pre-tuned to channel 9. A southern voice crackled through the small speaker.

"... after I-95, mile marker 180, at the state line. There are at least a dozen vehicles there. Most look like military.

At least some aren't ours. Those have black and white flags with ICA on them. So there's no way to get through the border without being stopped—"

Jonah stomped on the gas pedal. The two-hundred-ten horsepower motor pushed both back into their seats, its throaty engine drowned out the radio.

"What are you doing?" Randal asked, his head following the highway mile-marker 154 sign as it flew by.

"We have another reason to hurry: Assuming he's still going this direction, we need to catch Frank before he gets to the state line and gets arrested."

Chapter 26

Lexi

"I'm sorry about your friends," Senator Chase said, breaking the silence and startling everyone inside the Hummer's cab. No one had said a word since they had left the encampment.

"Thanks," Lexi responded, before Frank could.

"How you feeling?" Frank asked, momentarily focusing his attention on Lexi.

"Not like I should after drinking *only* two beers."

Frank turned around and glanced again out the back, barely catching the glints off of the windshields of the trucks still following behind.

He wasn't ignoring her. Lexi's words troubled him as he was convinced that someone had drugged her beer. Worse, there were only two suspects who could have done it, and neither choice made any sense. But something else troubled Frank even more. And the logic of what that might mean rattled around in his head ever since meeting and speaking with Chase.

When Chase was regaling his story about crash landing in his private jet, before finding Cappy's militia, one huge alarm bell rang out.

"Excuse me, Thomas." Frank chose his words carefully because he didn't want to color the answer.

Chase turned to address him. "Yes, Frank."

"Just curious about something... Before your jet's engine exploded, did you feel anything or see anything that seemed... out of the ordinary?"

Chase replied almost immediately. "Yes. In fact, when I heard the explosion, I looked out my window to check out the source of the noise. Besides the ruined engine, I caught what looked like a trail of smoke coming from the East and leading up to the engine. At the time, I thought it was a piece of exploding debris. I gave it no further thought because I was sure we were all going to die. But now... Why are you asking?"

"I'm pretty sure that your plane was shot down, and probably by a ground-to-air missile." Frank was saying this, while staring forward. Jasper was glaring at him through the rearview. Lexi had turned in her seat, with her seatbelt still attached and gave him a confused look.

"Okay..." Chase said, "I had considered this while we were uselessly waiting our rescue. But how does that help our situation now?"

"Only that it seemed suspicious that the Jihadis back there attacked us out of the blue and that Cappy had so easily secured a handoff point for you to continue your path to the same bunker you were headed to when you were shot down." Frank was now examining Chase.

"Wait, don't you... Sorry, didn't you trust Cappy?" Chase's face had become darker, even though the cab was awash in light from the rising sun.

"Yes, I do—did. But I don't believe in coincidences, and I am suspicious of anything going smoothly, ever since the

Jihadi's apocalyptic attacks."

He turned his attention back up to Jasper, who was still scowling at him. Jasper cleared his throat and said, "Each of these points can be easily explained. The group that attacked you could have been part of that convoy that your militia friends ambushed. And Cappy used an encrypted radio, which is not so easy for civilians or invading terrorists to hack so as to fool someone on the other end."

Frank studied Jasper.

A couple of alarm bells had gone off based on what he had said. But Frank countered this with how hypersensitive he was about anything out of the ordinary—it seemed like everything was—and his suspicions of everyone. Jasper was the most likely candidate to drug Lexi. Frank just couldn't figure out what the man's motives could be, assuming his thinking was at all correct.

Most likely, the reality of this was his gut feelings leading him astray. Maybe his conscious mind was lying to him, just as he had been to others. He looked at his knee as if he expected it to answer.

It did. A fireball of pain erupted there, sending shock waves throughout his body. He almost couldn't manage the pain anymore. Perhaps his malady was already spreading as fast as the lies he used to cover up what was really happening to him.

He put his head back and closed his eyes, mentally counting down from ten.

"Are you alright?" Lexi almost begged from the front seat. She reached down to detach her belt while she attempted to prop herself up onto the seat with her knees.

"Did you get hit during the fighting?" Chase asked, also sounding genuinely concerned.

Frank opened his eyes and focused on Lexi. "I'm alright. Just tired and I hurt like hell from all the previous battles. Jasper's probably right. I'm just overly sensitive about shit right now."

The Hummer slowed down enough that each of them lurched forward in their seats. Jasper's head bobbed around, and he pulled them off the highway, onto the shoulder. He yanked his Thompson from the floor and put it onto his lap, while he spoke to the rearview mirror. "Several vehicles have been following us for a while. They just sped up and are now flashing their lights at us."

Samuel

Since leaving the camp, Gladys continued to guide their convoy of three vehicles just out of sight from the Hummer, not more than a half mile behind them. Samuel confirmed it with his binoculars, before returning them to his lap.

His other hand pressed a feminine napkin against his forehead to stem the bleeding from the deep gash he had received from the blast. He glared out the window, staring at nothing, while his ears endlessly rang like church bells on Sunday. His mind unceasingly replayed a loop of the final minutes before they had left. Each time, the conclusion brought tears.

"It's not your fault, Slim," Gladys bellowed this once

more. "Sorry to yell, Slim," she said, "But you're not hearing for shit since the blast."

A minute or so passed before he responded. Samuel was pretty sure Gladys was referring to the loss of his brother Mike, who was killed instantly by the Jihadi's rocket blast. Somehow Samuel didn't die from this, but his brother did. Yet, as hard and raw as that loss was, he could accept this. As his father said, this was war and "there are no runners up in war." Mike knew this too. That wasn't what got to him.

It was leaving his father and the rest of his militia to die. At the time, when everything was coming at him at once, he couldn't think of anything he could do to save them. But now, after reliving those moments over and over, he felt sure he could have saved his father, and maybe some of the rest of his militia. Instead, he left them to die. *Like a coward.*

Just before they left, Gladys insisted that the battle was over: this group of terrorists caught them by surprise. They needed to escape with their lives and fight another day. Right after, she reminded him that his father tasked Samuel and Gladys to personally look after Chase by providing Frank and his friends whatever back up they needed until they reached safety. As Gladys said, "We couldn't very well do this if we remained in camp."

The loss of so many friends just gnawed on him like rats had earlier done to their supplies. Out of a camp of thirty, only twelve of them escaped. It was a gut-shot and it ached in his belly. *Twelve!*

He punched the dash and spat out a flurry of the same colorful epitaphs his father usually used when he was angry at the world, which had been often.

Now he's dead, he mused and felt the tears threatening to come back. "Screw it - Can't do shit about it now!" He wiped his eyes with the back of his free hand, still keeping pressure on his wound with the other.

"Have they seen us?" he asked Gladys.

"They haven't acted like it," she said. "But since you're back, I had a thought."

"What's that?" For the first time Samuel looked behind him and noticed that both Double-Tap Tommy and Jimmy the Axe were in the extra cab of the truck, silently watching them. Samuel guessed he must have checked out for the last twenty minutes or so.

"I'm thinking we should tell them we're here and come up with a plan."

Samuel didn't have to consider this too strongly. She was right. If one of the ICA convoys came through right now or if there was a blockade like the one they had erected, they'd be caught flat footed. They really should have a plan. They're simply hanging back and jumping into action if the Senator, the Major, or Lexi needed them was not a plan. And whether Major Frank or Senator Chase liked it or not, they were going to remain attached to them like glue until the Senator was delivered. Better to be on the same page.

Two radios pinged, followed by a crackle. "Slim, you there man?"

Samuel clicked the button. "I'm here."

"Thank God! Thought you bought it, man."

"I'm alive. What's up, Moondog?" Samuel was a little annoyed at the interruption.

"Oh right. Well, Leftie has been monitoring the CB and there's all sorts of shit going down. Have you been listening?"

"No, Moondog..." Samuel caught Gladys glaring at him, while also rolling her eyes to mock the man. Moondog was the worst conspiracy theorist of their group, arguing such gems as the Apollo moon landings were faked—it was how he got his name; the Earth was flat, and with that, Australia didn't exist; and then his daily warnings that they were all going to be invaded by radical Muslim groups... *Well, even a dead clock is right twice per day*, his father used to say.

Samuel suspected Moondog's next conspiracy theory was probably partially true and so he should listen to it, but hoped he'd be done quickly this time. "Okay, what sort of shit is going down?"

He had no idea what was coming next.

"The President announced that all militias are illegal, they're coming for our guns, also illegal... Oh, and there's a blockade up ahead, near the border, full of Jihadis, working together with... get this, our military."

Samuel and Gladys flashed looks of surprise at each other. "Hit it. Let's catch up and pull them over. Now!"

She had already punched the gas at "Hit it!"

He glanced up ahead on I-95, seeing the 5-mile sign to the Virginia border and sub-consciously mashed his own foot into the floorboards, trying to will them to go faster.

Chapter 27

Hairy Ravi

Ravi Abdall was beside himself. As he ran down the long hallway, looking for his superior, he felt a flood of emotion he hadn't felt in a long time. It wasn't the shock and then terror he first felt, upon seeing the boy's apartment. Now it was exciting wonderment.

What else could he experience, but a comforting joy: the boy, who was their Mahdi's son, had disappeared into thin air. It was impossible for any mortal to do this, especially a short ten-year-old. Therefore, the only explanation was that the Mahdi's son was in fact a Jinn.

Raised as a Sufi, but living now as someone who follows the leader of an orthodox practice of Islam, he had kept his spiritual beliefs to himself. But confirming now that the Mahdi's son was a Jinn was a big deal and he couldn't restrain himself. He had to tell his Mahdi right this instant of this revelation. Naturally, he couldn't help letting others know along the way.

As Ravi came upon one or more of the many of the Mahdi's followers or regular laborers, now populating the hallways of this complex, he'd announce, "Abdul-Aziz is a Jinn. I must tell Mahdi Abdul or Ali Baig. Where are they?"

It was easy to ignore the jeers from those who didn't believe it. He never cared that many of them called him an *Ahmaq*. They may call him a *simpleton* now, but they weren't there. They didn't see the boy's magic with their own eyes as he did.

At Abdul Mahdi's office, he arrived just as Ali Baig was coming out and appeared to be startled that Ravi was there at the same time.

Before Ravi could excitedly regurgitate the entire story to him, the Mahdi called from behind the door for both men to enter so they could talk in a more private setting.

Ravi was there less than a minute, describing what he had done and what he had witnessed, before Mahdi Abdul arose abruptly from his desk chair and was out the office door, leaving the two men behind, while Ravi continued to babble. Before the door shut, Abdul mumbled only two words, which silenced Ravi.

Just then, Ravi's joy was replaced by fear.

Even Ali stepped away from Ravi, as if he had been cursed by those two words. In a way he was. Because Hassan Sabbah—the two words uttered by Abdul—was the name of a cold-blooded killer, who was a curse upon whomever he was tasked to kill.

Hassan Sabbah

"**L**eave this place," Hassan Sabbah barked at the men who had swarmed outside and inside of the boy's unit.

Like rats fleeing a fire, all of them scurried away from the area, many fearing to even make the slightest eye contact with Hassan.

Not that he cared what they did or didn't do, just as long as they would leave him in peace to do his work... He caught a glimpse of a boot print on a piece of paper on the floor. "And had not *trampled* on all of the clues which would abbreviate my finding Abdul-Aziz's whereabouts," he huffed at the rats, causing a few of the stragglers to quicken their rushed steps away.

In the end, it would not matter. He was sure to find the boy. As with any task the Mahdi set before him, he would be quick about it. Everyone he hunted, he found. Without exception. This boy would be no different. He was, after all, a child and had been gone for only fifteen minutes.

It certainly made no difference what Ravi, that bumbling *Ahmaq* said. There was no magic surrounding the boy's disappearance. The boy may have fooled Rafi; he would not fool Hassan.

When the hallway was finally quiet, Hassan approached the open doorway, paying attention to every detail. Anything out of place was noticed. And at first glance, he guessed this mystery would be figured out within the first two minutes.

It took less.

The desk in front of the door was the key. It wasn't so much as Ravi described it, "a way to keep him out." It was a means to an end, and when Hassan pushed through, he saw the boy's path out right away.

On top of the desk was the boy's footprint and a chair. Hassan eyeballed the area right above it and nodded.

He blasted a whistle with the curl of his tongue, generating the near instant response he expected: multiple footfalls sounded off down the hallway, approaching quickly. With that, he drew his *Jambiya* from its bedazzled wooden *Asib* or sheath. It was gift from a Saudi Prince for his work back then on a reporter who got too close to one of the prince's many secrets. He preferred the longer-bladed *Jambiya* that he often wore in fights to this one's four-inch double-blade, but it was perfect for what he needed to do next.

Ali Baig bolted inside first, his eyes instantly stretching wide when he saw Hassan's knife.

Hassan turned away from Ali. His submissiveness was purposeful. "You need to tell Mahdi Abdul that I have found where the boy has gone," He removed the chair from the desk. "But I need to know if I am authorized to do as I please after I collect the boy?"

"I have already spoken to the Mahdi..." Ali referred to his notepad. "He said to tell you—and I quote—this boy has caused too much trouble; Hassan is to bring him back dead or alive. The choice is his."

Hassan nodded at this. "Very well, go now and tell Mahdi Abdul I shall give the boy an honorable death and I will bring his body back within the hour."

With that, Hassan hopped on top of the desk, with the agility of someone half his age. His face was level with the AC's vent cover.

It was the fact that the cover lacked screws that gave away the boy's location. With the *Jambiya's* small blade clasped now between his teeth, Hassan pulled the vent cover off and tossed it onto the bed.

He gave Ali a snarling glare that told the man to stop loitering and report now to Mahdi Abdul. The man did and Hassan pulled himself into the AC ducting, his mind already savoring what he would do to the boy when he caught him.

Travis

Travis made his movements lizard-like to travel through the ductwork: pushing one knee and opposite hand forward, and then repeating this with the alternate knee and hand. That's at least how the lizards moved in his yard in Tucson. Though lizards didn't make swishing sounds—from his pant legs sliding over the metal ducting—like he did, and he wasn't near as fast as the lizards at home. But he didn't need to move fast to get where he was going in time.

Looking ahead, he saw it was maybe twenty feet more until his turn. It would be a right turn and then another hundred feet or so to his exit. Though he wasn't sure about that part. At least he knew he had his directions correct, thanks to the map.

When he was first drug through the main hallway, he noticed an escape map on the wall titled, "In Case of Emergency." His kidnappers had stopped there long enough for him to study it through the wide weave of his hood. The map showed regular pedestrian exits, which he would avoid. That would be where Abdul's men would begin their search for him when they found he was missing. They might even think to check the HVAC ductwork when they figured out that he had exited his room that way. But they certainly wouldn't think of the route he had planned out of this bunker complex...

Well, they might when they realized that he messed with the AC system, he thought and smiled.

As if the HVAC system itself had a mind of its own and knew what he was up to, a giant blower fan kicked on, sending a dusty blast of refrigerated air against his face, stinging his eyes, and buffeting him enough to slow him down. This happened each time the system kicked on, which seemed pretty often. "Not much longer will you kick me around," he taunted the system.

At the turn he stopped and looked. This branch was another stretch of ducting that shot off the main one at a ninety-degree angle and went for a long distance. It was too dark to see its end, though he knew how far it was.

For his subterfuge to fully work, on the off chance that they had someone short enough to crawl after him through the ductwork, he had planned a diversion. The gale force winds of the blower fan stopped. It was his invitation.

He quickly lizarded his way forward through the main passage, only getting wisps of air and dim light, every twenty feet or so, from smaller T-branches in the ducting. It was just enough to show him the way, until he had to stop abruptly.

It was almost a disastrous miscalculation, which would have sent him down a long shaft. He wasn't sure how far it went down, but it was his destination and all a necessary part of his deception.

He had to stretch to grab the toe of one of his socks and yank it off. Then with the other hand he pulled off the other. Both he tossed into the abyss, smiling at this. Hopefully they would find it at some point.

The blower kicked on and another blast of air hit again. He backed up, now making thumping sounds after several swishes, as his toes painfully caught hold of the ribbing of the metal ducting. At the next T-branch openings, he turned around and with the wind behind him this time, he moved faster.

Almost lizard fast!

At each T-branch, breaking to the left and right, leading to the next set of offices, he passed by without looking. Just before the last branch, the one before his actual turn off, he would leave his next clue. This one was a big one.

He pulled from his overshirt his father's Purple Heart. He read in the journal, that Lexi had discovered, that he earned it for saving a captain from an explosion by using a Hummer's blown off door. His father went partially deaf, and carried pain the rest of his short life, but at least he received some recognition for what he did.

Travis cherished this memento of his father's and hated to give it up. But it's the kind of sacrifice his father would have made for his family, so why not? Besides, something this important to Travis would only be left behind unconsciously. It would convince Uncle Abdul and the others that he had lost it while continuing all the way through the conduit, to the drop-off, which is why he would not put it at one of the branches. At minimum, it would be enough of a diversion to buy him the added time he needed to figure out how to create some mayhem and then finally escape for good.

Making sure there was enough light so that it was obvious to someone coming in this direction, he laid it against some of the ribbing. Then purposely tried to avoid kneeling on it or kicking it by doing a slow lizard-walked around it and back toward his junction twenty feet away.

He turned left, down the long dark passage, trying to keep a mental count of how far he would be traveling before he came to his exit point. At the same time, he tried to think through his plan.

If he figured correctly, he would end up just inside the big systems room that held the condensers and pumps for the AC system. He figured all he would have to do is destroy a pump or take out a pipe and that would take out their air conditioning. Then while they were all getting mighty uncomfortable, he would find the air in-take duct and scale his way up the forty or so feet to the exit outside. Once he was outside, he'd have no problem escaping the compound, wherever this place was.

It was a solid plan. That is if he could execute it correctly. He couldn't wait to tell Frank about what he did. He was sure his godfather would be proud of him. Maybe his sister would be proud of him too.

Travis looked up and stopped not a moment too soon.

One more step and once again, he would have tumbled down a score of ductwork that went straight down. "Whew, that was close," he said to the eerie darkness he couldn't see, but felt it, below him.

"Pay attention dude!" he admonished himself. Then he backed up to the last two branches. One went to the right and one to the left. At that moment, he couldn't remember which one to go to. He lost his bearings because he turned around more than once.

"Shoot!" he cursed much too loudly. "Shoot," he whispered.

Well, he couldn't stay there all day. So, he chose right.

After only a few feet he was at the register. Glancing through, he could barely see that he was seven or so feet above and at the end of a long dark room. Not quite what he imagined, but without ever seeing a room like the one he was headed to, he knew no difference. To cement his resolve, he smelled something like cigarette smoke, which he figured must be how a machine room, operated by sweaty machinists, must smell like.

After carefully listening and watching, he decided the area closest to his opening was empty. Doing a careful roll backwards, banging his head on the top of the ducting, he ended up with his feet pointed at the register. He inched a few feet forward placing his feet against the register. Then with all his might, he pulled his feet back and then mule-kicked it, sending the register into the room.

Easier than I thought.

He backed up into the room, spinning around so that he could lower himself down. Letting go, he landed feet first on a hard carpet.

That was unexpected.

He figured the floors would be concrete. When he spun around to take in the dark room, he knew for sure he had ended up in the wrong place.

This was an office of some sort. It was long with an empty conference table in the middle of it, with devices that he guessed were office telephones blinking different color lights on top of it. The room would have been black were it not for the phones' lights and an exit sign above him.

He straightened his clothes out, which were bunched up in places. Then he stopped stiff as a board when he saw the unmistakable red glow of a cigarette being smoked in front of him.

He wasn't alone.

Chapter 28

Lexi

The convoy of four trucks, led by Gladys and Samuel, pulled off I-95, onto NC 46 and into Oakgrove Baptist Church's parking lot. The Senator had described it as "a pretty little church, right off the highway." Apparently he was familiar with the area, telling them that he owned a "tiny place nearby."

Only when Jasper pulled them onto the church's broken asphalt did they see that the building's interior had been gutted by fire, leaving only its red brick facade as a testament to some unknown lost battle. Lexi's attention was only on the pickup in front of them.

The moment all four vehicles halted, and Samuel exited his truck, Lexi burst out of the vehicle. Overwhelmed by some unknown need to get to him, she embraced him with a full-on bear hug. Immediately, she felt embarrassed. She backed away, while studying his blue eyes cast in a dirt encrusted face. They were an angry red and looked to be holding back an insurmountable flood of sorrow.

"Samuel, I'm so sorry about your brother and your dad. But I am very glad to see you are sa…" Only then did she notice his holding an odd-shaped bloody-bandage to his head. "Are you okay?"

The thumb of his free hand went up and he said, "Just a cut."

Not believing this, she again stepped toward him, her hands finding the bandage. She pulled back on an edge releasing fresh blood. "You need stitches," she said, laying a hand over his and demonstrating the pressure he needed to maintain on his wound.

Samuel grimaced and gave her another nod. "Yeah, later." Just then, he appeared to become aware that others were watching him. He squared his shoulders and stood more erect. Frank was talking to Chase about the burned-out church but clammed up when they caught Samuel's gaze.

Samuel cleared his throat. "Ah, the reason why we pulled you over is there's either a roadblock or checkpoint up ahead at the Virginia border."

"Plus," Gladys added, readjusting her AR pistol on her shoulder, "if an ICA truck were to come by, we need to be on the same page about what we are supposed to do."

An agitated man, sporting a long beard and bushy eyebrows, pulled up behind Samuel. She recognized this man from the camp as the one who gave her the evil eye for her earlier comments.

"I know we agreed on no escort, but after what just happened, I'm glad you're here." Senator Chase chimed in, next to Lexi. "And I too am sorry for your loss, Samuel. Both Captain Horton and Mike were obviously good men and patriots. And I will forever remember them fondly."

Samuel teared up and turned his head away from them.

"Well." Gladys stepped closer. "Cappy was the one who

had us follow you. But when the attack happened, he directed us to help you get out. So..."

Samuel returned his attention to the Senator, his eyes a little redder. "Our mission is your mission: to get you to your destination. But in light of this new information, we really need—."

Bushy Eyebrows pushed past him and then turned around to face Samuel. "Did you forget the broadcast from the gun grabbing POTUS? Don't you think that's more important *new information*."

"We haven't confirmed this yet, Moondog," Gladys snapped.

Moondog's eyebrows furrowed, and he spat some chaw or something equally disgusting on the asphalt in her direction. Gladys balled her fists, looking like she was about to dare the man to try it again. They obviously didn't like each other.

"Listen to the damned radio yourself. She's on the radio," Moondog said, backing away.

"Did any of you hear the President's newest broadcast?" Samuel asked, no doubt trying to mitigate the rising tension between them.

Heads turned, each person checking the other, but no one nodded.

"Other than the broadcast yesterday, I don't think any of us heard anything," Frank said. He was propped up against the Hummer's front bumper a few feet away. He grimaced and then rubbed his knee. As she witnessed in the Hummer earlier, it was one of the first times she remembered seeing him outwardly show that he was in pain.

Leading a noisy cloud of dust, a black Chevy pickup,

coated with more rust than paint, pulled off the road near the church's entrance. It slowed, its driver eye-balling the group meeting in front of the church out his open window. As soon as they stared at him, he sped away.

That's a "red flag," she thought.

"This is too exposed," Frank said, pushing off the bumper with a low grunt.

"I have a place," Chase said. "It's just a few miles from here. We can go there, tend to our wounds, get some supplies and adjust our plan based on this new intel."

"Great. You lead," said Samuel.

Jonah

A new sign announced, "Border Station Ahead." Jonah slowed.

In the past, there had never been anything more than a sign to announce the state's border was coming. Certainly no warning. It wasn't like it was his first time on this road. He had driven this route numerous times, sometimes as far as Bangor. Up ahead the signs were even more ominous.

Cones diverted traffic into the rest stop, which appeared to now be the "Border Station." Just before the turnoff, the Welcome to Virginia sign was covered over with a hand-written message, "Be prepared to be searched." Almost a dozen military trucks were parked all around the rest stop, indicating their seriousness.

"Did we make a wrong turn and end up in some other country?"

Jonah knew Randall's rhetorical question wasn't meant to be funny. He had the same feeling. Adding to this surreal scene were the ICA vehicles. Three older Army trucks, with ICA Peacekeeper emblems on their sides and flags on their antennae. At least those were back from the line.

"What the hell are they doing here?"

"Have no idea, but I don't like it," Jonah said.

There were so few working vehicles on the road these days, having a border stop, for whatever valid reason seemed ludicrous. And so far on this trip from Florida, they could count the number of functional vehicles they saw on one hand.

Yet, at this new border stop, two vehicles were pulled over and now were being searched. The first vehicle's occupants were standing around as members of a National Guard Unit were pulling out seats. The second's occupants appeared to be handcuffed and kneeling to the side of their vehicle. On the roof was a hunting rifle. Jonah could only assume it belonged to one of the occupants.

Jonah's vet was idling in the middle of the highway, with only one direction to go: to the border crossing. Based on what they were seeing, they didn't want to go there. Besides the fact that they both possessed firearms, which they had no intension of giving up, their purpose was solely to track down Frank, Lexi and that traitor, Jasper.

They could go no further. If Frank and Lexi had gotten this far, they would have already been arrested and there was nothing they could do. They could only hope they hadn't crossed yet. So they had to catch them before this crossing point, if they were still okay.

One of the Guard members seemed to have noticed them and was now waving them forward.

Jonah turned in his seat and peered out his back and then forward.

"You're not going forward, right?" Randall asked.

"Nope."

The guard whistled at them and started stepping in their direction.

Jonah put the car in reverse and tapped on the gas.

The guard stopped where he was, and then unslung his rifle.

That's the only sign Jonah needed. He stopped, shifted and punched the gas while yanking the wheel. He drove them through the one and only pass-through in the guard rail, separating the highway's two lanes. They went through the median, and onto the south bound lane. Neither of them heard gunfire, nor did they look back to confirm whether or not they were going to be pursued.

"Now what?" Randell asked.

"The radio," Jonah hollered.

Randell unclipped the microphone and began once again calling to Frank.

Lexi

"Tiny place, huh?" Lexi mused, speaking the only words expressed by anyone since they left the church parking lot. She wasn't expecting an answer, only chiding the Senator to lighten the mood all of them felt after what they just heard. In front of them was a palatial home, which seemed to grow even bigger as they approached from the home's private road.

"It's been in the family for three generations," Chase said, looking slightly embarrassed. Lexi sure everyone else had the same thought after seeing his house.

"I had considered retiring from the Senate multiple times and settling here. But with my wife gone and my kids on their own, I feared I'd just rattle around in the damned place, all alone. And every time I reconsidered those thoughts, something or someone would urge me to remain for reasons that escape me now. Guess it was good I lasted this long—you can pull up and park in front." The Senator pointed from the backseat, behind Lexi, to a long-curbed area. A walkway leading to the front door intersected at the end of the circular drive.

After Frank parked there, Senator Chase hopped out, directing the others to park behind their Hummer.

It certainly was private as the Senator had said. His private drive was surrounded by thick trees and an expansive green pasture with no other visible structures.

"Come on in," Chase said, after pulling out a key from under the front door's Welcome mat. *Lame hiding place for a key,* Lexi thought.

After he unlocked the door, he put the key back under the mat and marched inside leaving the door open for everyone to follow.

Frank entered first, his limp more pronounced than

ever before, followed by Lexi. When she stepped in, she was mesmerized.

Through the entry, past an expansive living area, beyond a giant fireplace and an endless glass wall on both sides, a picturesque lawn was bounded by a lake that sparkled like diamonds. That flash of peaceful tranquility lasted only as long as she gasped to take in the view.

"Damn, it must suck being you," Moondog hollered from behind them. Like a slap, it broke the spell and brought her back to a reality that seemed more inescapable by the minute. First it was a group of well-organized terrorists constantly attacking her and everyone she knew, and now it was her own government. Right then, she felt sure that neither she nor any American would soon experience a day where relaxation by a lake or an ocean was possible. Instead, each day would be spent worrying about being in constant peril. *This is my life now.*

With that revelation, Lexi felt an overwhelming feeling of hopelessness.

"Let's all sit here, the Senator ushered them to a dining room table that could seat thirty, while he moved into the kitchen.

She followed him, trying to refocus on something she could control.

"Sorry to bother you, Senator, but would you have a bowl of water and towel? I'd like to sew up Samuel's head." Just then she realized the house had power.

She gaped at the open refrigerator, interior light blaring, clouds of condensation billowing out from inside. Her mouth must have been askew, because he smiled and responded, "Solar power, keeps the refrigerator and other essentials going. He snatched out an unopened twelve pack of Stella Artois and handed it to Lexi. "Give everyone one and I'll be back with what you need."

Even though a black wave of despondency weighed on her more than the heavy pack and rifle she still had slung around her back, she felt a little like Santa about to dole out gifts at Christmas.

Even better, when the others saw what she was bringing them, they acted like children about to be given what was the number one item on their wish list.

"Fricking hell, these things are cold," Samuel said after she passed him one.

Because Frank, Gladys and she declined to drink, there was one left for the Senator, who was just returning with the bowel and towel Lexi had requested. In his other hand was a package of bottled waters. Under his pit, an old Rand McNally map book.

"Thank you," she said to the Senator, handing him a beer in exchange for what she needed. *"Focus on what you can control,* she told herself again and turned to address Samuel.

"What are those for," Samuel asked as she laid the bowl and towel on the table in front of him. She sat down and opened her pack, pulling out the emergency med kit. "I'm going to mend your gash," she said. "Now don't be a baby." She attempted humor, in part because her emotions were so topsy turvy at the moment. But she was also serious. She really needed him to be strong, although she didn't know why.

She took a swig from a bottled water and then poured some on the towel. Then she got to work on Samuel's head as Senator Chase stood at the head of the table, holding open the map book and hesitating before he spoke.

"Frank, you sure you don't want one?" He held up the white can.

"I do, more than you can imagine," Frank licked his lips. "It's one of my favorites. But I'll wait until after our victory."

"Here's to that and to all of you," Chase said while lifting the can in the air. After studying each of the militia members, he took a sip.

The others did the same, except Moondog, who had finished his in one messy gulp.

The Senator put his can down. "Okay, I believe we all listened to and heard the broadcast as Moonbeam mention—"

"Dog. It's Moondog. That's what everyone calls me, and thanks for the beer, man." Moondog smashed his empty can between his palms, and he probably smiled, though it was hard to see with all his unkempt beard hair.

"Sorry. Just as Moon-Dog said, the newly appointed President has taken it upon herself to go after your militia and any citizen carrying a gun, in direct opposition to the Second Amendment."

"How is that possible, sir?" one of Samuel's men asked. Lexi eyed Samuel, who was squirming as she cleaned his wound. But he was otherwise silent, which seemed to silence the blackness she'd felt moments ago.

"It appears that she's using the Emergency Powers Act, which was butchered after 9/11, and then by every subsequent president since then." Chase remained standing, hovering over the map book.

"She's just a fake President anyway. Nothing she says holds any wat—." Moondog belched the rest of his statement, which elicited a couple of chortles by Samuel's people.

"Shit, that hurts," Samuel whined. Lexi smiled.

"No, the President is not fake; just prematurely appointed," Senator Chase continued. "All the more reason why I need to get to my rendezvous with Colonel Wilkins at the border.

"And to that point, I don't expect any of you to risk yourselves any further on my behalf. You've lost enough already, and I appreciate everything you've done. I can go it alone. But before I go, I wanted to show you on this map—"

"Forgive me Senator Chase for interrupting," Frank rose from his seat near the Senator, both palms planted on the table's surface. Lexi recognized that Frank was about to say something not only to the Senator, but everyone else. "You're not going to do this alone. Even if Colonel Wilkins is real and waiting for you at the border, it's likely that ICA may take some action when they see you. But assuming they will do nothing or they're not there, you have to consider that, whatever government officials are manning the border may likely try to stop you on some trumped up charge."

"Thank you, Frank for your selfless offer. And yes, I have considered all of that, but I believe that the contact made by Cappy with Colonel Wilkins was legit and I really need to try and reclaim this government before it's too late. I need to go. But I am open to any suggestions you may have, to give me the best chance of success."

Everyone agreed that they were going to escort Senator Chase to the border. Next, they formulated a plan. But they needed more intel.

So, per Samuel's suggestion, two men were sent ahead to the border to see how the border checkpoint was set up and then report back. They all agreed this was best and the two men left, while those remaining refined their plan.

Chapter 29

Travis

Travis wasn't sure if he should run out the door and take his chances or what. So, he just held his breath and stared at the dark form in front of him.

After a moment, the outline of the person smoking a cigarette and the tilt-back chair they were sitting in became more obvious.

He breathed out a small sigh of relief because he could see it was a woman, and she wasn't wearing a Burka. He reasoned if the woman was breaking Abdul's rules, by not wearing proper Muslim clothing and smoking in public, he might be able to get away with his infractions.

The woman leaned forward in her chair, allowing enough of her face to be illuminated by the red glare of the room's exit sign so that he could mostly see what she looked like. She was attractive and she smiled at him before blowing a puff of smoke in another direction.

"Hi young man," she said. She looked like Lexi might look if she were older. Most importantly, he confirmed, unlike all the other woman he had seen in this place, this one wasn't dressed in traditional Muslim clothes. She wore a business suit. He reasoned that she must work in the bunker, but she also must be breaking rules by being here smoking and not being covered.

"Hi, to you," Travis' nerves twinged when he reasoned if she worked there, it must be for his uncle. But he also guessed she wouldn't know him directly as he had lots of employees, many of them with families of their own here. He took his shot.

"Um, please don't say anything, but I'm hiding from my uncle, who works here." The white lies were coming out as easy as breathing now. He playfully held up his finger to his lips, as if it were all a game of hide and seek.

She reciprocated, putting her finger against her pretty pursed lips. "Okay," she whispered. "It will be our little secret."

Travis figured he was probably good, as this woman couldn't know who he was, or which uncle was his. Regardless, time was his enemy. Once they found him missing from his room, they would probably search from room to room, throughout the whole complex. They must have found he had given them the slip by now. He figured he needed to step up his pace.

"Sorry I don't have anything to offer you," she said, with a smile. "I'm taking a cigarette break here. They would frown on me smoking. You know, all their strict rules..."

"That, too, will be our secret," Travis said with his own smile, though he didn't think she could see his face in the room's low light.

Feeling she was no longer a threat, Travis turned to address the door, ignoring the woman's additional ramblings about her smoking habit. If he was correct, the room he had meant to end up in would be across the hall.

He cracked open the door, just enough to reveal a

chaotic hallway with men running past in both directions. Some looked panicked. "Damn," he whispered, not liking his prospects of making it across without being seen. Then he noticed the sign beside the door on the other side. It read, *E16 - Systems*. That had to be it. Yet how could he get there without being seen?

Travis ducked back in, closing the door behind him. The woman was asking him something, but his mind was busy calculating options.

He had an idea, though he wasn't sure how he would convince her to do what he wanted.

He smiled wide and this time he turned his head so that she could see it. Then he said, "Beautiful lady, could you do me a big favor?"

Abdul

Abdul stepped into the largest of the five jail cells and sat beside the accused, on the edge of his cot. Sal had been mostly loyal to him, and for longer than anyone. For this reason alone, the man deserved to hear from Abdul himself about why he was here.

"Can I have something brought to you, Sal?" Abdul asked, putting a hand on Sal's shoulder.

Sal remained mannequin like since Abdul had entered the cell, with his shoulders slumped and his head stoically downcast. Finally, Sal turned to look directly at his Mahdi, his jet-black eyes almost unreadable. Abdul had expected anger, but these eyes looked... remorseful. "How did you know?" he asked.

"You mean how did I know that you were meeting behind my back and planning to take over, all because I would not reveal everything to you?"

Sal's stare barely faltered and if it did, it was only one or two facial ticks. Any other man except Abdul would have missed the slight movements in his lip and cheek. Abdul wasn't most men. It wasn't just that he was Mahdi. No one knew Sal better than he did.

"Of course, I knew. I know all that is happening here. Besides being your Mahdi, I know you so well.

"But I forgive you for this. In fact, your actions are the root of why you have been my Number One all this time: you question and scrutinize everything. This quality has always been buttressed by your fortitude to follow your instincts, without any fear nor regard for your own self.

"For all these reasons and so many more, you will be so dearly missed, my brother."

"What are your intentions for me?" Sal asked, offering no hint of emotions.

This was Sal, dealing with absolute certainties. He knew he was not going to get out of this alive. Long before this episode, he had resolved that he would die for the cause, even if it meant being disruptive.

Abdul rose, while turning to face Sal, keeping his hand on the man's shoulder. He went to his knees so that he could address Sal with the respect his former Deputy Director and closest advisor deserved. Sal's eyes were locked onto his. "My brother, you will be publicly hung for the crimes you have committed against the Great Satin.

You will die a martyr and you will be beloved by a billion Muslims, who will believe you to be the instigator of our attacks against America. Then, while our enemy is seeking peace and every opportunity to resume its sloth ways, I will complete the takeover and set up the promised caliphate, where Sharia will reign. All of this will occur because Allah deemed you to die for the benefit of us all."

Sal's face crinkled just enough, and his eyes became glossy, as if he were going to get emotional. Abdul didn't want to witness to this.

Abdul stood up, turned and left Sal in his place, walking out of his cell and then the small jail without hesitation. He no longer wished to see this man in this way: a captive, forced to submit to other men. He would remember him the way he had been, a lion who would stand up to anything and anyone, only submitting to Allah or his Mahdi. Abdul would probably have to attend the public hanging—and he won't like it—but he would forever keep in his mind this picture of Sal.

He even ignored Sal's last plea from behind the door, "But wait..." That wasn't the Sal he knew or would remember.

Upon exiting the jail, Ali approached him. But he said nothing, waiting instead for Abdul to invite him to report. "Please Speak," Abdul offered, not really wanting to hear what his temporary Chief Deputy had to say.

"I've been waiting to give you an update on Abdul-Aziz," the man said, out of breath from either running or anxiety or both.

Abdul already missed Sal. "Go ahead."

"Hassan has found where the boy is hiding."

"Great. Let me know after the boy has been captured

and killed. Now leave." It was one more bit of housekeeping he didn't want to dwell on.

Ali first flashed a look of shock, either at the "killed" comment or his being excused so abruptly. Abdul didn't care. But then Ali collected himself and scurried off

As he watched the man race away, Abdul did in fact begin to dwell about his son. One more emotional distraction he wanted to avoid. He considered Abdul-Aziz's tenacity, feeling almost a sense of pride for the boy keeping out of Hassan's clutches for this long. Perhaps he was too hasty in giving Hassan the kill order. The boy was tough and could have made a great leader someday. He could have been someone who would have garnered respect, and maybe even have taken over for him one day... *Perhaps I could put a stop to it,* he thought to himself.

Only then did Abdul realize the buzz of activity surrounding him.

Two men raced down the hallway, pausing just long enough to bow to their Mahdi, before then racing away and continuing their conversation.

"The Mahdi's son is in the ducting," one said.

"But Hassan is in there too, on his trail. He will certainly..."

The two men turned down a junction in the hallway. And they and their voices disappeared.

A deep sadness crept up into Abdul's heart. He no longer wanted to kill the boy. But he knew Hassan would be unreachable at this point. More so, the man would not stop until after he had tracked down the boy and killed him. The boy was as good as dead already.

Travis

"Excuse me, sir," the fully covered woman said to a guard who had just been racing down the hallway. "Where are you going unaccompanied by a man?" demanded a gruff voice that Travis could barely hear through all the thick clothing.

He could feel her stiffening up. But there was nothing he could do under the woman's Burka, except hold on and hope she didn't mess up. This was all Travis' idea and he felt really embarrassed to even suggest it. But she was very supportive and said it was a good idea. Only now, she was putting herself in danger for him.

He decided to give her a squeeze to remind her that she had this and he was there... Not that she could forget his presence, as he was firmly pressed against her back, his arms wrapped around her sweaty belly.

She took in a breath to speak. "I am under orders to check in this room for the runaway boy. May I pass now, sir?"

Oh-oh, she already knew who I was, Travis thought. Now he stiffened his hold onto her.

"Whose orders?" the gruff man spat back. The woman was almost shaking now, as if she were cold, even though they were both perspiring from their mutual body heat. He held on tighter, though he wanted to release her and remove his nose from the stink of her soap, sweat and cigarettes.

"Ali Baig, by way the way of Mahdi Abdul. I will wait here, potentially letting the boy slip through your fingers, if you wish to first confirm what I am saying with Mahdi Abdul?"

She's really good at this.

Several long seconds passed, and the woman was doing her best to suppress her breaths. She definitely reminded him of his sister Lexi. They were equally brave.

"Okay, you may pass," the man bellowed, obviously not happy with a woman taking such an assertive stance against a man. "But next time, you must be accompanied by a man."

To her credit, she said nothing. Instead, she bowed, and her legs started moving right away. Travis did his best to keep up, but her stride was much longer than his.

She stopped as abruptly as she had started, and her arm reached out. A door clicked open. Hopefully *his* door.

Travis matched her steps through the doorway, the sounds of loud machinery dulled all other sounds.

She turned and the door clicked closed. Just as quickly, she pulled up her Burka, exposing him to the satisfyingly fresh aroma of oil. "Okay, it's safe," she said.

He shuffled away and eyed the expansive room of machines, pipes and wires, as she fully stepped out of her Burka. He was very appreciative of her help, but he hoped that she wasn't going to stay. He had work to do, and very little time to get it done.

"What are you planning next?" she asked in a way that was not nosy, but genuinely interested.

Travis looked her over: sweat poured down her cheeks smearing her makeup and mascara. Even so, she was beautiful.

"Perhaps it's better you didn't know. You nearly got yourself into trouble for me already."

"Oh, *that* was fun. I don't care for these people, but they give me what I want. Anyway, I was on a long break. But I will be missed soon. So, I better get back."

She sighed and then put the Burka back over her head and around her.

By this and her facial expression, he could see she didn't care for the thing. "At least you won't be as hot with me underneath." He beamed at her.

"I didn't mind, Travis. As I said, that was fun. Plus, it felt nice to have a handsome young man hug me so hard."

For reasons unknown to Travis, he felt at once unsteady on his feet and he was so hot, he thought he might pass out. He was glad there was little light in this room as he was sure his face was as red as the giant bottle of liquid just behind her.

"Well... Ah, thank you for your help," he said... "Hey, what do I call you?"

"You can call me, Lynn." She held out her hand.

He took hold of hers—soft tingles blossomed up his and. He shook and released her. She exited the door and was gone, like she had never been there.

Travis kept checking out the bottle of red liquid, licking his chops. He could sure use a drink of something. He looked around to make sure no one else was there, including the owner of the bottle of liquid. The vacuous room was full of machines but empty of people. So he marched over to the two-liter bottle, sitting on a workbench.

It was cool, like it had only just been abandoned and

there were drops of perspiration on it, indicating that its temperature was less than that of the humid room. But he had to be sure it wasn't something caustic. He screwed off the top and gave it whiff. It smelled like strawberry Hawaiian Punch. Searching his mind for chemicals that were red and smelled like berries, he had nothing.

Travis took a little sip, getting ready to spit it out... *Amazing!* He wanted to scream, but just thought it and took several gulps.

Now satiated, he turned to face his project. He searched for something, anything that would tell him what he should do next. He had no idea what he would do, only... Finally, he saw it.

He knew now exactly what he would do. And when he was done, he would make everyone in this complex utterly miserable.

Grabbing a large wrench off the same bench with his free hand, Travis marched to the largest sound brandishing a smile, feeling confident in his mission.

Chapter 30

Lexi

While waiting for a report from the Virginia border, a discussion about their next move started with Frank questioning why they were even considering crossing at a border with a military checkpoint.

"For only one reason, Frank," Senator Chase stated. "That's where my Army escort is waiting."

Frank nodded from the wingback chair he occupied beside the Senator, just off the dining room table where everyone else sat. "What I mean is this, why not cross into Virginia on a small road and stay entirely off the highway? Then we will drive you directly to where you need to go. This avoids any possible confrontations at a patrolled border."

"I appreciate the offer. But I'm not even sure where exactly I'm going: I was told it's hush-hush for my protection and that of the few others who survived the attacks. Besides, and I mean no disrespect to all of you," he glanced first at Frank and then the rest of the militia members. "I'd rather have the Army as my escort. Like all of you, they will do whatever is necessary to get me to my destination. But they have nearly limitless resources to do this."

Frank drilled his eyes into the Senator's. "But can you trust them, Thomas?"

He responded immediately. "I must Frank. If we cannot trust the US Army to do what they are legally charged to do, then in my mind we don't have a country anymore."

"It's not so much trust in the Army; it's my lack of trust in the Army's orders, which have come from an unelected government that has made friends with an enemy which laid waste to our country and killed millions."

"All the more reason why I need to be the engine that changes all of this. There has always been a threat of this happening when a government's representatives are decided by any means except legal elections."

Frank rustled around in his chair, his face refusing to hide his discomfort. Samuel and the rest were silent, listening carefully to the two senior statesman debate. Even Moondog, who apparently argued with everyone, was sitting on his hands. "With any luck, this will be an enlightening discussion, but for another day. I just want you to be certain the Army will do what they're supposed to do."

"I am."

"Okay then, what about the Guard? They may not let us get through the border to wherever the Army is waiting, assuming we can even easily find your Army Colonel contact."

The Senator momentarily glanced at the others and then back to Frank. "Let us wait to hear what Samuel's volunteers have to report first, before we make that judgment."

Frank stood up, with a throaty groan and stepped toward Senator Chase. "Very well. Until then, could I trouble you for a yellow pad and a place to write?"

Frank

Frank sat at a small Louis XV writing desk, just outside the dining room. Though he could see and hear them chattering about politics and their next steps, he was there to complete a more important task.

It was something he had been putting off for the last couple of days. But he feared he wouldn't get another chance, with his gut screaming out constant warnings of their pending doom. He forced himself to sit, with the gifted yellow pad, pen poised on paper, getting ready to do something he rarely did: write a letter. It was perhaps the last one he'd ever do.

She needed to know what he suspected was going to happen next and where to go if it did. She would be given the details in preparation for the worst-case scenario. With any luck, it wouldn't be that bad and was just his conspiracy theories gone wild.

He was already so proud of her and of how quickly she had grown into a tough young woman and in such a short time. He was even more thankful that over these past few days, he had the honor of getting to know her and help her down a sane path during this crazy time.

She was obviously struggling with the upcoming show-down with Abdul. Frank was about to place upon her an even greater burden: saving her country.

He was hesitant to tell all, as it was against his nature. But in the end, he decided to come clean, starting with his cancer... "Dear Lexi," he finally wrote.

For the next several minutes, Frank scribbled away furiously, while at the same time being aware of everyone in and out of the room. He had to finish before Samuel's men returned or called in a report from the border. That's when their time was up, and they'd have to jump into action.

A border reconnaissance trip before Abdul's attacks would have only afforded him twenty minutes, at the most. He hoped for much longer to get everything onto paper.

Midway through, he teared up. He snapped his gaze at Lexi to tamper down on his emotional upsurge so he could target what had to be written next. When he left her, she would need more help, even if his primary resource was available.

She had stepped outside with Samual and both were now sitting on a bench beside each other. They looked good together; like a couple that had been through much over a long time, even though it had been less than a day. Conflict and death did that to couples. She would need to lean on Samuel. He added this to his letter.

But she would need much more support than just Samuel's.

He glanced at Jasper, who had returned to his seat in the back corner of the living room, after disappearing out front for a few minutes. Frank wished he could fully trust the man. But he was pretty sure Jasper was the one who had drugged Lexi. It made no sense considering

Jasper had made it his mission to look after her. Frank's final resolution—the only one that made any sense—was that Jasper must have had a similar feeling to his; that something was coming, and it was the only way he could get her to leave without her putting herself back into harm's way. However, until Frank confronted Jasper, or she received his letter, he would make sure Jasper wasn't alone with Lexi.

Assuming the best, but articulating his concerns, Frank included something about Jasper too. Still she would need more assistance.

Gladys was certainly the most competent of the militia members. As Frank scrutinized her, she returned his look and gave him a nod. If he had more time, he would have liked to have talked to her.

Other than Moondog, the remnants of Samuel's militia might all be called upon to help Lexi too, if Frank wasn't there. He made notes of this as well.

He wished they still had contact with Endurance or Stowell. She could keep checking her portable on the off chance a signal might get through. He added this too.

Finally, he finished his letter, scratched his name at the bottom, folded it into thirds and slipped into an envelope that he had already personalized.

The ornate chair he'd been sitting in, creaked like his old bones when he pushed himself up. He intended to surreptitiously slide the letter into Lexi's bag, before Lexi and Samuel returned.

But they were already headed in.

They held hands and shared concerned faces, as they entered through the slider. The couple of others who had been out back followed close behind. At the same time,

Chase entered the living room carrying what looked like a heavy leather briefcase.

"We just heard from our men at the border," Samuel announced. "We need to talk."

Lexi

"T he intel is not good," Samuel announced from Senator Chase's dining room.

All eyes were on Samuel, except Frank, who seemed to be focusing all his attention on Lexi, like he was displeased with her. Though she didn't know why.

"It's just as the President was saying on the radio: The National Guard is in fact stopping everyone trying to cross the state border on I-95. Each vehicle is inspected, and it appears that anyone in possession of a weapon is being arrested."

"Damned Commies!" Moondog huffed under his breath. Samuel paused as more than one threatened Moondog with bodily injury if he didn't hush.

"After the National Guard were several vehicles sporting ICA flags and armed ICA troops, all standing and appearing to be waiting outside their vehicles."

"Did it appear to them that the ICA vehicles were blocking the path through the border, after getting past the Guard?" Chase asked. He looked as if he were late for a meeting, as a soft leather bag was slung around his shoulder and matching valise temporarily parked against his ankle.

"It would appear so, Senator," Samuel answered. "My men said that the ICA troops hadn't interacted with the Guard or the occupants of the two vehicles which were being inspected. But they seemed to be waiting for whichever vehicle was first released by the Guard. One of my men thought the ICA were watching for someone specific..." —Samuel caught Lexi glancing hurriedly at Frank and Frank back at her— "but my man couldn't guess who this might be during the short time they were observing..." Samuel paused again, eyeing Lexi.

"Continue Slim," Gladys said.

"Well... behind the ICA troops, further away, was a small contingent of the US Army. They did not appear to be taking an active role in the border stops. Also sighted was a full-bird Colonel, who fit the description of the Senator's point of contact."

"Okay, that settles it," Senator Chase stated, still standing in place, halfway between the dining room and the front door. "I'm going to go there myself, unarmed, driving my Bronco. I'll demand the Guard turn me over to Army Colonel Wilkins."

"With all due respect, Senator," Frank said, now limping in the Senator's direction, a stuffed white envelope in his hand. "Whether you go it alone or we're there with you, what makes you think the Guard will let you through?"

"They will have to let me through once I identify myself."

Frank stopped at the wingback he'd been occupying earlier, a few feet from the Senator, and leaned on the back rest's ornate top. "But what if they don't?"

Gladys raised her hand. "Excuse me, but aren't you

forgetting the elephant in the room?"

"Meaning?" the Senator asked.

"I think she's talking about the ICA troops, blocking the way through to the Army," Frank stated.

"Yep. Your faith in the US Military is admirable, but why would you have faith in our enemy letting you through? And isn't it too risky to find out?"

"I have an idea!" Jasper popped up from his chair while speaking. "It may be risky, but less risky than your going it alone..."

All eyes were now on Jasper, who stepped out of a corner of the dining area carrying something he had pulled from his satchel.

It was an ICA flag, which he stretched out with both hands. "If Frank, the Senator, Lexi and I dress up as ICA, with this ICA flag on our vehicle, we'll be let through to the ICA troops who are waiting. Once there, we can announce that we have business with the Army. Frank speaks perfect Arabic, so he can command them to let us pass."

Several voices erupted at once, asking questions.

Frank whistled for silence and turned to face Jasper. "Okay, Jasper. I get why you, me and the Senator go in his vehicle. But why Lexi?"

"We'll use her as bait to get by the National Guard."

"Bait?" Gladys asked.

"Yes, we'll just tell them the truth: that Lexi is Abdul Farook's promised wife."

For a millisecond, it was as if all sound was somehow vacuumed out of the room. Everyone sucked in their breath. With their eyes bulging fire, each practically burning holes in Lexi with their dirty looks.

Then like a tidal wave of movement, they all reacted: Moondog went crazy spitting, "I knew it! She's a damned terrorist;" Samual stepped away from Lexi as if she were radioactive; and Gladys raised her weapon, training it in Lexi's direction.

Chapter 31

Abdul

Abdul collapsed into a high-tech chair in Mount Weather's primary Communications room, huffing and puffing after having run to get there.

Too many actions were taking place at once: The search for Abdul-Aziz continued, at the same time as Abdul was trying to get word to his hitman not to kill the boy; they were monitoring multiple encrypted communications with the US Military, all concerning the President's new directives; they were getting reports from their troops positioning themselves alongside the Americans; and they had just received word from Imran. This is what brought Abdul to Communications in a huff.

His Deputy, Ali, had told him that Imran had just called in and said he would call again soon with instructions. Abdul wanted to be there for that call.

"Yes, my Mahdi," Mohammad his Senior Communications Officer continued. "As you directed, because you were having trouble receiving Imran on your satellite phone, we monitored your channel. Imran called fifteen minutes ago and said he would call again very soon with further instructions.

"He said he was with Suhaimah, but also several of the enemy. They were only a few miles from the Virgina border, where the road I-95 crosses. He said that they would be traveling that route today, maybe within an hour, and would need help there."

"Good work... Mohammad. Have you notified our commander at that border station?"

"Yes, we have. They were already looking for her. But now they know she is coming through that crossing.

Abdul rubbed his hands together and closed his eyes, causing others in the large room to also bow their heads in respect to their Mahdi, whom they thought was praying.

He wasn't. He was imagining taking his new wife and killing those who made him wait so long. It would all happen today.

Frank

"Whoa-whoa-whoa! Settle down, friends," Frank begged, hands held up high, limping forward so that he positioned himself in between Gladys' weapon and Lexi.

Gladys backed away from where Jasper stood, keeping eyes on him, Frank and Lexi. "One of you better explain fast what he's talking about."

"People, we don't have time for this," Thomas hollered,

seemingly unconcerned by the revelation.

Frank turned toward Thomas. "Please be patient, Thomas. I promise I will be brief."

Senator Chase half-nodded.

Frank kept his hands up. "As you know already, Lexi is my goddaughter. Lexi, by no fault of her own, other than birth, happened to be Abdul Farook's niece."

No one said a word, but their eyes were still screaming profanities.

"What you also don't know is that before Abdul attacked America, he murdered Lexi's father and mother and then later abducted Travis, my godson and Lexi's brother. Abdul had callously left Lexi instructions: if she didn't come directly to him so that he could marry her, Abdul would murder Travis. To prove his intent, he had cut off the boy's finger and left it with the note."

Lexi had begun to sob.

"We were headed—when your militia knocked us off the road—to Mount Weather, Virginia, where Abdul is currently holed up. After we hand off the Senator, we still intend to head to Mount Weather, kill this degenerate psychopath once and for all and retrieve the boy."

"Is this true?" Samuel implored; his eyes were now full of compassion instead of wide-eyed shock.

"Ye-yes," Lexi said through her hands. "Bu-but, I'm not sure he can be killed. I stabbed hi-him once and he li-lived through that..."

Samuel marched toward her, opening his arms to receive her.

"Bu-but it's the only way to save my bro—" she buried her head into the crook of his neck, no longer holding back her wailing.

"Sounds like a bunch of BS, if you ask m—"

"Shut up, Moondog!" Gladys hollered; her gun pointed down now.

"I had no idea, my dear," Thomas offered. "But it's not your fault. You cannot choose your relatives."

"And *this* is why we said nothing..." Frank lowered his hands. "So can we finalize our plan on getting the Senator to his destination safely so that Lexi and I can then go on to kill the head terrorist?"

"Please, Frank," Thomas stated.

Frank let out a sigh and then really considered Jasper's suggestion. He was going to reject it at first, because it seemed foolish to put her in harm's way. But this idea had merit and may be safer than his own idea to have her travel with Jasper—because he wasn't bound to let her out of his sight—in the bullet-proof Hummer.

"Okay Jasper, let's get back to why you're suggesting Lexi would be safe in the first vehicle going through the border stop?"

"Because once the ICA knows that Abdul's promised wife is in the vehicle, they will not fire on it, for fear of hitting her. You can then drive right over to the Army and deliver the Senator."

The agreement was subdued, but unanimous.

Just like that, they put together their plan of attack. Everyone, knowing their roles, moved rapidly. This was good for Chase, who grew more antsy by the minute. They all shared the sense of urgency of getting the Senator into the right hands as quickly as possible.

Before they left Chase's home, Frank whispered a message to Samuel, who looked perplexed at first and then after staring at Lexi for many seconds, nodded in agreement. Then Frank turned his attention to Lexi.

"Here," he said to Lexi. "Put this in your bugout bag, but read it later, when you need to."

"What is it?" she asked, while accepting the envelope with "LEXI" carefully written in block letters on it.

"Instructions for what to do if any of us get separated or run into trouble. It's just in case of an emergency."

As he explained this, she slipped the envelope into her bag without looking at it further. Understandably, her mind was on what was ahead of them.

She watched him sling his rifle over his shoulder and hurriedly limp out the front door, behind Chase.

"Come on everyone," Chase announced.

Frank waited out front, barking off reminders of everyone's place, and thanking each for participating.

Moondog was the second to the last to exit, mumbling something about not getting, "one for the road."

Before Thomas could lock up, Jasper came bounding out the door. By his manner of dress and beard, he looked exactly like a member of the ICA, just like Frank and Thomas. Frank had wondered where Jasper had been. He had disappeared right after the meeting had broken up.

"He said he needed the toilet," Chase answered as he locked the door, slipped the key under the Welcome mat and marched to the front passenger seat of the Bronco, already parked out front. Jasper had already taken residence behind the driver's seat, beside Lexi.

It was agreed that two vehicles would take the lead to the border: Frank driving the Chase's older model Bronco, with Chase, Lexi and Jasper inside. Then Samuel would follow behind in the Hummer, with Gladys and four of his trusted men sitting down low inside. The other three vehicles would hold back and not cross, but would be on the ready if there was any trouble. All vehicles would keep in contact via radio.

Once they were all inside their vehicles, Frank radioed, "Alright, let's go."

He pulled them out of Chase's drive, followed by Samuel behind the Hummer's wheel.

Chapter 32

Travis

When Hassan had finally figured out where Travis had gone, the HVAC system began blowing a warm noxious smell, stopping everyone in their tracks.

At that same moment, Travis giggled at his handywork, imagining what everyone who worked and lived below ground at Mount Weather would look like when they caught a whiff of the poop-smell blowing everywhere. "Take that Uncle Abdul," he said, pumping a fist in the air.

He had figured out how to stop the cooling pump from pumping cold water to the blowers, thus halting the air conditioning. At the same time, he broke open a sewer pipe and was able to jerry-rig a new conduit, using spare pipe into the blowers. So now the blowers were blowing sewer gas instead of A/C into every office, workspace or living area of the bunker complex. He only felt bad for Lynn, who was so kind to him. But everyone else in this place...

The same work bench on which he had found the two-litre bottle of Hawaiian Punch, also had all of the tools he needed to do this.

But when he accidentally took in a deep breath of the

stench, his smile evaporated. That stink provided him an even more urgent need to escape before they found him.

He snatched his pilfered bottle of punch back off the workbench, still three quarters full, and shuffled toward a vent register that he had found leading up towards his freedom.

The giant intake fan was already turned off. He did this so that no fresh air would be pulled in from the outside, lessening the pungentness of the sewer air.

He removed the vent register and stuck his head in to make sure the fan was definitely off so he could climb up the vent without any fear of being sucked in and chopped into little Travis bits. He laughed at this until he looked straight up.

"Dang!" he responded to the faint light calling to him from so far away. He forgot how high four stories looked up close and personal. "Yesseri, snowflake," he castigated himself. "It's just over fifty feet. So no dawdling."

It really wasn't that bad, because he could stop every twelve feet at the next floor up, where a T-intersection of venting extended in each direction.

He slipped the bottle of punch into his long-sleeve shirt rucksack. It had been removed when he got hot and tied the arms of the shirt together. Looping it over his shoulder, he had figured it would be of use to carry any supplies he could take on his way out.

There was a pounding sound from the entrance door that he had locked up. This was his sign to leave now.

He stepped inside the vent and reconnected the register so that his exit wasn't visible from the other side.

"Poof, I vanished again," he said, marveling now at the echoey sound of his voice. "Again-again-again," he mocked.

Reaching up and pulling with one hand while simultaneously pushing up with one foot, he mounted the first couple of feet of the vent.

"Two feet down; forty-eight to go."

Hassan

Hassan bounded up the stairs, with the Mahdi's foreman in toe and one thought on his mind: what he'd do to the boy when he finally caught him. He would make this little dog pay for making him look bad.

He had followed the boy through the ventilation system, sure he had him when the boy appeared to be sloppy and dropped his father's war medal. It was logical, when he found the boy's socks to focus his search on the G floor, two floors below E, the complex's main floor. They first searched every room with ventilation access, then every other possible hiding place on that floor, but found no sign of the little dog. It was a giant fool's errand. And he was made a fool.

Just before the cooling system started blowing in sewer gas, one of his men reported seeing a woman in the main hallway, in front of Room E16. Hassan demanded that the women be tracked down again and be made to talk, but when he smelled the stink in the air, it was explicit confirmation of the little dog's handiwork and location.

But by then the damage was done.

Hassan would surely pay with his own life for not catching the boy before this. Several men had just informed him that his Mahdi was trying to reach him. But he would wait until he did what he promised his Mahdi: capture and kill the boy.

When he arrived at Room E16, a clog of men was standing before the room's broken open door... waiting.

"What are you waiting for? Get the boy!" Hassan bellowed.

Still, they barely budged until Hassan bounded through the Systems room door.

Just inside the vacuous space, he commanded, "Search everywhere." Finally, all the Mahdi's sycophants scattered by him like a stream's current flowed around a large boulder. Each worked at staying out of the reach of his wrath, which grew by the second. He might have to kill one of them to just to quell some of his anger.

Oh, when I catch that little dog, he thought.

He needed to concentrate.

Hassan closed his eyes and quieted his mind. He needed to see what the boy saw; feel what the boy felt when he entered this place. Only then would he find the clues that would lead him to the boy.

After slowly breathing in and out several times and feeling much more at ease, he opened his eyes and looked. Really looked.

The foreman was busy searching around his workbench for something "Hawaiian." He had left his station abruptly when the command came for everyone in the complex to search for the boy.

His tool belt and his tools.

"The boy has them," Hassan said in a measured voice.

The foreman grumbled something to himself. Then he nodded acceptance, gathered the few loose tools on the bench and ran off to what Hassan assumed was wherever he had to go to fix the damage the boy had caused. Hassan wasn't interested in what the boy had done or how he did it; only what the boy did after his destructive actions.

On the way over to E16, the foreman had explained to Hassan what the boy must have done and how ingenious it was for a ten-year old. It also helped Hassan to understand that the boy was indeed very smart and shouldn't be so easily discounted as he had previously. He would not make that mistake again.

Hassan first guessed that the boy would have created the damage and then hidden himself somewhere until he could feel safe enough to wait out their searching for him.

"No, you went to an escape route out of the complex," Hassan whispered under his breath.

There were only so many ways to escape from this room and he would find the one the boy used. First, he would eliminate all the possible escape routes. Then, if he was wrong, they would look for all the hiding places.

No matter. They would find him soon enough. And when they did, he would take the greatest pleasure in ending this smart ten-year-old's life, slowly and painfully.

Chapter 33
Virginia Border

Frank

The National Guard unit policing the border hit him as wrong. But seeing the enemy, still armed, casually waiting around protectively surrounded by the Guard and a small contingent of US Army personnel... *that* made his blood boil.

"What the hell has become of our country?" Chase begged the question he was thinking.

Frank navigated Chase's Bronco up to the point where a National Guardsman was directing them. Chase was in the front passenger seat, ready to exit, while Lexi and Jasper were in back quietly watching.

A glance in the rearview, confirmed to Frank that Samuel was still following closely behind them in the Hummer. Gladys was no longer riding shotgun and had slipped out of sight. The other four trucks were not visible, hopefully perched somewhere, but keeping an eye out for them through their binoculars.

Frank glanced over to Chase, who like him and Jasper wore traditional-looking Muslim clothes. All three of them wore *shemaghs* covering all but their eyes. It was all part of the plan. "Everyone ready?" he asked.

They confirmed they were.

When they came to a complete stop, Frank noticed the guard immediately take note of their clothing.

"Everyone out for inspection," commanded the captain.

Frank pointed to the ICA flag flapping on top of their antenna. The Hummer, behind them, had a similar one.

Attempting his best rendition of a natural Arabic speaker, using broken English, Frank hollered at the captain, "We are ICA. Do you not see the flag? We will only report to ICA. I have woman that ICA leader wants." Frank pointed with a thumb back at Lexi.

Frank glanced at Lexi through the rearview. She wore a scarf that covered her hair, but her face was exposed so she could be seen. Lexi seemed unsure how she was supposed to look at the , who was now eyeing her. She furtively looked up and then down and forced a half-smile.

The captain refixed his gaze on Frank, then Chase... and then the AK rifle that Chase had a hand on, only partially hidden by his legs. At once, the captain became ridged, his face flashed concern, but then changed to its normal sternness.

"Okay, we are at peace with you people now. So, you can pass and meet up with your people at the ICA truck up ahead."

The captain took a step back and waved them through the check point.

Frank inched them past and then let out a sigh. Besides feeling momentary relief, he felt utter incredulity that the captain's unit were pulling over and arresting US citizens, but letting through what he obviously saw were fully armed—with fully automatic weapons to boot—foreign terrorists, illegally trespassing on US soil. Besides breaking so many US laws, it was against everything the US Military was founded upon.

"Now the hard part," Chase emoted, also breathing out a sigh. He was once again examining the weapon he had his hand on and Frank's AK, perhaps making sure they were easily within reach. Each was less than two seconds away from being able to grab their weapon and take a shot if they needed. If the Senator was at all nervous, it didn't show.

Chase had earlier stressed his reticence at firing upon any American service man or woman, regardless of how screwed up their orders were from their new Commander in Chief. Chase was more than happy to shoot at the enemy, he just didn't yet want to consider any of his countrymen the enemy, much less fire upon them. Frank had counseled him that he might not get the choice; that everyone must choose a side in this battle and then live or die with that decision.

"Did you catch the logo?" Frank asked.

"Does that really say… Peacekeepers on it?" Lexi asked from the back seat, sounding equally dubious.

"Seriously?" Chase said, "They may be pretending to be like the UN, but they are still the damned enemy."

"Exactly," Frank stated.

He inched them closer to the ICA truck, its terrorist members now actively jumping into a predetermined formation.

All four sets of eyeballs in the Bronco were so focused on the upcoming ICA troops, no one seemed to notice that the Hummer backing them up was no longer following behind. It had been stopped by the same Guard captain.

Samuel

The Guardsman held up a palm demanding that they come to a stop.

"We're with them," Samuel stated almost yelling, while pointing a forefinger at the enemy flag attached to their antenna.

"You don't look like them," the guard said, scrutinizing the scores of bullet marks carpeting the vehicle. Then he attempted to examine the inside of the vehicle but couldn't see through the side windows. It was a good thing he couldn't see that Gladys was pointing her AR pistol in his direction... *Or could he?*

As if receiving a stiff shock, the guard hopped a step back and put both hands on his M16, his eyes falling on Samuel's AK rifle, resting on the floorboard. "I'm going to have to ask you to step outside of your vehicle and surrender the weapon."

Shit-shit-shit, Samuel shouted in his head, already regretting his going along with Jasper's plan of using the ICA flags to get through the Guard checkpoint. The man seemed strange the first time he met him and he wished he would have offered more resistance before he agreed to this stupid plan. Now it was too late. He had to roll with it.

The nervous guard continued. "We are under orders, by the President of United States to confiscate all assault weapons, and that—he pointed with his M16—certainly qualifies as it can shoot more than one round of ammunition."

The Guardsman then whistled to two other National Guard members, in an attempt to gain their attention from under a canopy erected off to the side. They had been talking to a man who was kneeling and handcuffed.

When the other Guardsmen noticed they were being summoned, they each grabbed their weapons and shuffled toward their Hummer.

We need to do something right now, Samual thought.

He glanced in his rearview at Gladys, intending to signal her, but her attention was up ahead.

Not more than forty feet in front of them, the Bronco had stopped, and an ICA soldier appeared to be talking to Frank through his side window. Suddenly, the Bronco's passenger door popped open, which was not part of the plan, any more than his having to argue with the Guardsman.

"Wait, what's going on there," Samuel asked, pointing at the Bronco, momentarily forgetting the agitated Guardsman.

Jasper had jumped out of the Bronco, and he pulled out Lexi with him. She was yelling something, which was alarming the ICA guards.

The Guardsman had had enough of being ignored. He raised the barrel of his M16 and pointed it at Samuel. "I'm not going to ask again. Get out of the truck," he ordered.

Samuel did two things at once: he huffed "Go-time!" under his breath and he stomped his foot on the Hummer's gas pedal, snapping them forward and past the Guardsman.

They accelerated right at the ICA guards, all crowded on Frank's side, pointing their rifles at Frank, Jasper and Lexi.

"Fubar," was all Gladys said.

Lexi

It had started just as they planned, with Frank speaking Arabic—he had told the ICA guards exactly what he said he would, using his Army translator skills. "Peace be upon you, brother. I have a prisoner for Mahdi Abdul; it's his wife, Suhaimah, who has been waiting for her— "

But while Frank was doing what he was supposed to do, Jasper did something Lexi hadn't expected: he pointed his Thompson machine gun at her. She could see his finger was uncomfortably close to the trigger. Then he put a finger to his lips, demanding her silence.

This was not part of the plan, she wanted to yell.

Jasper further complicated their plan when he briskly opened his door, made like he was about to jump out and in one abrupt motion, he yanked her too. She almost fell out of the Bronco. That's when she verbally let loose on him.

"What the hell are you doing, Jasper?"

A thought occurred to her, maybe he was improvising and acting, because his personality had changed dramatically.

That thought disappeared at once.

In what sounded like Arabic, Jasper howled something to the ICA guards.

It was then that Lexi knew that this guy, who pretended to be her father's friend and her sworn protector, was in fact one of Abdul's ICA terrorists the whole time.

Frank

When Frank's rehearsed demand appeared to fall on deaf ears, Jasper jumped out with Lexi, in what looked like an ad-libbed moment that was both puzzling and frightening. But at the instant Jasper began hollering Arabic—a language he said he didn't know—it all became clear: Jasper was an ICA mole and all of Frank's concerns about the man became reality.

"I have Suhaimah, Mahdi Abdul's new wife. Shoot these infidels and then take us to my Mahdi right away," Jasper shrieked in perfect Arabic.

The words cut like a rusty blade across his jugular: Jasper had never been a friend; he was planted at the house across from the Broadmoor's by Abdul; Jasper's whole job was to get Lexi to Abdul; to keep her safe for Abdul.

Lexi screamed and gunshots rang out behind them as both Frank and Chase snapped their weapons up from the floor and brought them to bear on the ICA guards. But their enemy's attention and weapons were no longer on them.

All eyes were on the oncoming Hummer, racing from behind, headed right at them.

The National Guard troops were firing, as now were the ICA troops.

Just as they had planned, the Hummer took a jig to their right and zoomed past them, as the ICA guards brought their weapons around. Frank fired a burst from his rifle, bringing down all four.

"Move, little girl," demanded Jasper, who was tugging on one hand, as she held onto the truck with the other.

The Hummer spun a U-turn in front of them.

Frank leapt out of his seat but was tugged back by the AK's sling getting snagged on his belt. Frank craned his neck to see if Lexi was all right, while attempting to free his rifle.

Lexi let go of the truck, and with her hand free, round-house punched Jasper in the ear.

She was free but didn't run away.

Lexi planted her feet, and just as Frank had taught her, drove her open palm into Jasper's nose, generating a cracking sound and sending him backwards. At the same time, Frank let go of the AK and sprang out of the truck.

The National Guard captain and his troops had stopped firing, and now had their backs to them. Frank kept his eyes on Lexi, who had lost her balance after her blow and was falling toward the ground.

Upon landing, she spat out some Arabic obscenity even he had forgotten.

Frank set his gaze upon Jasper.

"Prepare for death," Frank growled at the traitor, who looked up, still stunned, nose bleeding, and saw Frank barreling at him.

Jasper struggled with his Thompson, attempting to turn it on him. Frank didn't care. Without a weapon, but his two hands and his tortured body screaming of pain, Frank went right at the man, who was back peddling away.

There was other gunfire and the roar of an engine, but Frank ignored it all. Every bit of anger and hatred that he possessed was directed on this agent of Abdul, whom he intended to rip apart.

Jasper continued his retreat, losing ground to Frank, while regaining command of his Thompson. He swung it in Frank's direction, but the rumble of a powerful engine and a louder volley of shots distracted him.

The *rattatat* of the Thompson was cut off by a blur of something red that whooshed by Frank, just before he could reach Jasper.

In a blink, Jasper was gone.

Stumbling to a stop, Frank turned toward the screeching brake-sounds.

It was a Corvette, sliding to a halt, yards away.

The mangled corpse of Jasper lay in a heap, halfway between the Vette and Frank.

The Hummer pulled in front of Frank and turned itself to provide a shield between them and the National Guard unit that had ceased firing. A door burst open. "Get in," called Samuel to Lexi.

She looked up at Frank for confirmation, as she pushed herself up off the ground. Frank smiled and then shot a glance at the US Army truck.

The five Army soldiers, one of whom could have been

a Colonel and maybe their contact, were taking cover from the gunfight that had apparently concluded, at least temporarily.

Maybe Chase was right about them.

Frank returned his gaze to Lexi, who was now poised by the Hummer's open passenger door. Frank nodded and said, "Go!"

When the Hummer's door slammed shut, he returned his attention to the Bronco. Chase had remained in his seat as he had asked, reminding the Senator that he needed to stay out of harm's way.

"Let's go," Frank said, and he hopped back into the Bronco and dropped it into gear.

The Vette, despite its disfigured front end, revved its engines and screeched forward, pulling up alongside the Bronco.

"You alright?" shouted Jonah's familiar voice. In the passenger seat was a dark-skinned man, wearing a smile—*Randell Something, the baseball player from Endurance*, he remembered.

"Yes, thanks to you. Follow the Hummer out. We have an appointment." Frank gunned the accelerator, moving them toward their destiny.

From the side mirror, Frank could see the Hummer shoot forward, heading back for the border. The Vette, shedding some of its fiberglass front end, followed behind. This time, the Guardsman didn't shoot, appearing to be giving them a wide berth, as if conceding that their bullets would do nothing to stop them.

Most importantly, Lexi was safe.

Frank turned his attention to the oncoming Army truck.

Chapter 34
Daleville High School - Ft. Rutker, FOB

Porter

Direct from HQ, General Daily addressed the group. General Brown the Southern Command commander was gone, with no explanation given. So was Lieutenant Bingham. Rumors were already circulating that Lieutenant Bingham was arrested for telling the brass to shove their new orders up their "fat Leftist asses."

The audience had changed too. Same men and women; different demeanor. Yesterday, it was a group of well-disciplined military units, ready to engage an enemy. Everyone expressed jubilation at being able to fight. Now, the three hundred or so men and women appeared to be more akin to an angry mob, ready to riot.

Porter couldn't blame them. He felt a disquieting rage roaring inside of him.

They went from taking back Fort Rutker and killing the damned terrorists who attacked them, to making peace and acquiescing to this enemy. Worse, they were now setting their sights on American citizens under the guise of unconstitutional proclamations by an unelected President to take away their rights to assemble and possess a weapon. Essentially, regular gun-owning Americans had become the enemy.

But what Porter feared the most was what he suspected was coming next: that the US Military would become a federal police force, being charged to arrest those who didn't comply with these new rules.

It felt like some surreal nightmare. He still couldn't believe this was happening.

But to drive home the new reality, they were all threatened by the general.

They were told if they followed their new orders, their families would be properly cared for during this "time of crisis." That included receiving food rations and medical care. However, if they did not follow these new orders, they would essentially be considered traitors. They and their families would be cut off from all government assistance and they would be arrested by MPs.

That's when every mouth in that room expressed their discontent.

Besides being ludicrously unconstitutional, as sworn members of the US Military, they could not accept these orders.

"Silence or I will have you all shot!" Daily yelled, spraying spittle onto his mic.

The room went dead.

"You have heard your new General Orders. Next, each of you will receive your individual Special Orders.

"Line up at one of two tables at the back of the room to receive your Special Orders..." He stared back into the furious crowd, his mouth opening, as if he intended to say something more.

Then he stated, without emotion, "No more smart-ass comments. Get your asses up and proceed to one of the two lines forming in back, on the double."

He turned away from the microphone and walked off the stage.

"Come-on," Wallace insisted. "Let's find out how many laws they really expect us to break."

She marched off to the back of the room.

Secretary Meer

The Honorable Ryan Meer stood at the head of the table, about to address his handpicked, Joint Chiefs of Staff. To each man present, the purpose of this meeting was to simply deliver their verbal reports. But to Meer, this was to be his victory lap. The doors were sealed, protected from entry by Marines. Even POTUS was locked in her chamber under armed guard. After all, assuming absolute power over one's country was never a public event.

Taking over was not part of the original plan. But Meer was more opportunist than pragmatist. And an opportunity like this, forged over many years, much by his heavy hand, was not something anyone could pass up, least of all him.

The whole plan was begun by his predecessor, over twenty years ago.

It was uncomplicated by design: give absolute power over all military decisions to the Executive Branch, by removing power from the citizens. Too often he had witnessed President after President have their executive powers hamstrung by an unruly population. Voting for representatives was one thing. He was all for a democratic process, within limits. The problem was all the other rights given to them, especially those enumerated in the First and Second Amendments of the Constitution. These rights have been the Achilles' heel of previous administrations since the Civil War. Add to this Congressional oversight and it was a wonder Presidents ever accomplished anything.

His predecessor envisioned their country, where POTUS had full control over the world's strongest military, without interference from the public or their representatives in Congress. Whereby the US Military would follow POTUS' every command without question.

But to do that required two major changes fueled by some careful chess-like moves.

The first major change started over a decade ago by his predecessor—who was forced to step down for trumped-up charges—was completed by Meer, after he took over as National Security Advisor. Simply, they changed the face of the US Military one general and admiral at a time. Using the politically popular concept of diversity without regard to ability, they were able to place the most malleable men and women into positions of power, ready to do the President's and SecDef's bidding.

With control over the military, they only needed to wait for an event to usher in the second major change to complete their plan: a national crisis. Farook's terrorists provided this crisis, from which Meer and his chosen people could take care of the second and final change:

remove power from the citizens.

Using a national emergency to enact Emergency Powers, and the actions of previous Administrations, the rest was easy.

First Amendment rights had effectively been destroyed after the attacks, when the Internet and television broadcasting were taken down. These were the public's largest mouthpieces. Farook's command over the radio waves meant no further public discourse. Then, with one Executive Order, they eliminated the public's right to assemble.

That left the removal of the cornerstone of all other rights and the true power of the people: the ability to fight back with weapons.

The Second Amendment had always been a thorn in every administration's quest for power. Without that bulwark, countries like Australia, Great Britain, China and before that, Nazi Germany, had been able to easily confiscate weapons from their citizens, allowing them to use authoritarian rule—which is necessary at times—to take control of its population.

They could no longer afford the risk of a revolution, which would pit an over one-hundred-million-strong gun owning populace against a million-man military. Attempts in the past to confiscate certain types of guns had failed.

Politicians never had the stomach to take this issue head on, calling it the "third rail of politics." They used ATF fiats to ban commonly used weapons by declaring them as "Assault weapons," or reclassifying a common rifle as a more regulated "Short Barreled Rifle." But all those attempts were thrown out by the Supreme Court, again buttressed by the stalwart Second Amendment.

Now, with a declared National Emergency and his suggested reclassification of all weapons that shoot more than one round of ammunition as a military assault weapon, they would be able to easily sidestep the Second Amendment. They would only need to forcibly divest the public of their weapons.

Check, Meer thought.

He puffed up his chest as he began to consider himself akin to a chess Grandmaster.

But the ultimate move; the one that gave Meer the opportunity to take total power came when he was alerted to Farook's attack plans. As the President's National Security Advisor, he pulled a few levers in the government's machinery that were already in place to make sure that every leader in all three branches of government was in DC on signing day, except for their prechosen President Designated Survivor. And when this was threatened by the delay in the VP's and President Pro Tem's planes, he made sure neither ever made it.

Checkmate.

So why then cede control over to the new proxy Administration that he could continue to control per his wishes? No, he would assume all power. Yes, it was true he would have to deal with Farook—who was no more than a knight on his chessboard—and the threat Farook wielded over the new Administration to achieve his own means. But there could only be one king on this chessboard.

Once they had neutered the public's ability to fight back, Meer could use the full strength of the US Military to do anything he wanted. No one person or their army, much less any other country could stand in their way to rebuild America in the way he saw fit.

He was momentarily startled, catching the quiet gaze of every man in the room. The room had come to order without him even having to say so. They all looked up at their true boss, who had brought them all together for this, anticipating his next words.

On the inside, Meer was grinning from ear to ear. But he would not give any hint of his excitement at reaching this point. Just knowing this was enough of a celebration for him. "Thank you, gentlemen. In a moment, I will ask for reports from each Chief about the readiness of each branch to carry out your new orders to address the national emergency at hand."

Meer stood tall, with as much pride as he had ever felt for his country and his military. He looked at each man, starting with the Chairman of the Joint Chiefs, Vice Chairman and then each of his Joint Chiefs of Staff.

"Okay, starting with the Chief of Staff of the Army, each of you report as to how your troops are complying with their new orders."

Porter

The queue wasn't very long. But each step felt like a death march.

Wallace had no interest in receiving her special orders, and neither did Porter. They had little choice, as articulated by the general.

Without saying it out loud they had agreed to what they would do if their orders were as they suspected. The process of waiting for the inevitable felt like watching a train about to career over into a ravine after its bridge was knocked out. They both watched with dread as their line shrank until Wallace was next. Each of them was called by a different superior seated side-by-side at a long table.

"State your full name, rank and current unit," the Army Sergeant demanded, not even looking up at Porter. Wallace was asked the same question by another, a National Guard corporal.

"Grimes, Porter, PFC, currently an adviser to Lieutenant Bingham, Sergeant."

The Sergeant looked up and then down at what appeared to be a long list of printed names.

Then he pulled a single sheet from a stack of preprinted pages. "Private, you are now part of the Southwest Enforcement Unit. Here are your orders." He handed Porter the piece of paper. "Lieutenant Bingham has been reassigned. You will now report to Lieutenant Ben Arnold at thirteen hundred hours to carry out your new orders. Next."

Porter stepped out of the line and glared at the words on the piece of paper he had just been handed. They were supposed to be orders, but they read like a George Orwell novel.

The din in the hall grew louder than before, but Porter didn't hear any of it while he prepared himself to taste this vile medicine. Instead, he gagged at the taste of each unsavory word. His rage returned just reading the Action title...

"Creation of Military Units to Enforce the New Emergency Weapons Ban (EWB) and Disbursement of Civilian Militias (DCM) Rules," then he skipped down to order details.

"All US Military service personnel have been given the same orders as you. You are hereby ordered to stand down from any efforts to engage any group or member claiming to be members of the Islamic Caliphate of America or ICA. They are no longer your enemy.

"The new enemy of America are unorganized militias, fueled by right-wing extremists and their illegal weapons.

"Your CO will assign you to a unit which will be given a list of suspected locations of US militias. Your orders are to confiscate all weapons, disband the militias and arrest anyone who does not comply.

"Some units will be sent to state borders to stop all vehicles and check for weapons.

"Some units will be assigned to a FEMA Food Distribution Center to enforce the EWD.

"Finally, other units will be dispatched to neighborhoods, going to homes suspected of hiding illegal weapons."

Porter turned over the paper and saw the Order #, Order Name and two boxes, one with "Accept" printed beside it and the other with "Reject." Below this was a signature line.

He looked up at Wallace, who was standing next to him, stiff-clutching her crinkled orders, while spitting several rapid-fire profanities under her breath.

She made eye contact with him.

"What are you planning?" Porter asked. His question was rhetorical.

"To do what Bingham did, but literally: I'm going to shove these illegal orders up our new CO's ass. Are you with me?"

"Damned straight. I've never been in a military prison. I hear the food's pretty good."

She didn't say anything, but instead marched directly to their new CO, who was standing against a wall in the corner of the gymnasium. Several others, with the same orders in hand, were already barking questions at him.

It was still a few minutes before thirteen hundred. But Porter followed Wallace to report to Arnold, just not for duty.

When they arrived, Wallace pushed through the rapidly building crowd in front of Arnold. She stood directly opposite him and demanded, "Your pen, Lieutenant."

"It's not thirteen hundred, Lieutenant," Arnold said, handing her a pen.

Wallace overtly marked the "Reject" box and signed her name and then handed the document and pen to Arnold. He glanced at her written rejection and then at her.

She stood at attention. "Lieutenant," she said loud enough to be heard by many, but not loud enough to be yelling. "Our oath is to "Preserve, protect and defend the Constitution of the United States, against all enemies, foreign and domestic. These orders clearly go against the Constitution *you* are sworn to protect and consequently, it is an unlawful order.

Therefore, empowered by the Uniform Code of Military Justice, I am doing my duty to disobey by rejecting these orders. And lieutenant, I would respectfully ask that you do the same."

"Sir," Porter chimed in immediately, "I am doing the

same."
Many others parroted his words.

Chapter 35

Frank

Anticipating a reaction at any second from the National Guard unit, Frank stomped on the gas to get them to their appointment with the Army Colonel quicker. They barreled toward the Army truck, as two Army Privates drew their weapons.

"Get down," he commanded Chase, who was still sitting high in his seat, his rifle in his lap. "We exit with our hands up and no weapons."

Frank slid them to a stop in front of the Army Hummer. The two Privates swung around their vehicle, taking positions on each side of their Bronco, their weapons aimed at Frank and Chase.

In response, they thrust their arms in the air, each slowly opening their doors from the outside so the Privates could see they weren't trying anything funny.

Frank stated, "We're here to meet a Colonel Wilkins. I have Senator Thomas Chase, the next President of the United States with me."

He methodically exited the vehicle and so did Chase.

From out of the front passenger seat stepped a man wearing the stripes and eagle insignia of a Colonel. He marched around the Army vehicle and walked toward Frank.

"Hello, Colonel Wilkins. I'm Major Franklin Cartwright, retired. I'm here with President Pro Tempore, Thomas Chase. We spoke to you on the rad—"

The Colonel held up his hand to silence Frank. Then he said, "Privates, arrest these two men for subversion, treason, hate crimes, the murder of four ICA Peacekeepers, resisting arrest, and for the unlawful transport of weapons."

The privates marched forward, as Chase flashed Frank a look that said many things: "You were right; I can't believe this; and are you kidding me?"

They weren't kidding.

Lexi

"They're arresting them?" Lexi begged, almost ululating.

She handed the binoculars back to Gladys, who then took another look.

Samuel put a hand of comfort on Lexi's shoulder, who was fighting back a combination of anger and a need to cry.

She could hardly believe that in the span of a few short days, Frank, Lexi and every member of the US militia, had gone from celebrated freedom fighters to outlaws.

Their government should be focused on vanquishing a common enemy and providing aid to its citizens. Instead, it has made peace with the enemy and is now arresting those who were the only ones standing up against the evil plague her uncle Abdul had brought to her country.

It was all absolutely mind numbing.

"We have a problem," someone hollered from one of the other vehicles in their group, which had pulled off the road, on a hill, under a thick bramble of trees.

"Report," said Samuel from his radio, keeping his hand on Lexi's shoulder. She hoped he wouldn't remove it.

"We have activity coming from the border," the radio responded back.

"Yes, have a look," Gladys said, handing her binoculars over to Samuel. He removed his hand from Lexi's shoulder and pulled them to his eyes, immediately training them on the border and then giving them to Lexi.

Another National Guard truck came down the road from the Virginia side. This was separate from the small detachment posted at the border that had shot at them.

"We need to leave ASAP," hollered the radio.

They all felt the urgency.

"Let's go back to Senator Chase's residence," Lexi said. "We can figure out what to do next there."

They didn't need any further coaxing.

The group of six vehicles, now including Jonah's banged up Vette, headed back in complete radio silence toward Senator Chase's lake-side residence.

Chapter 36

Hassan

Two minutes! That was all it took for Hassan to find the boy's exit point.

Once more it was a vent register without any screws. That told him where the boy went.

Hassan pulled at the register, but it didn't let go. He whistled for the foreman, pulling him away from his attempt to fix the broken AC system. Hassan was more interested in his prey than this trivial inconvenience to everyone's olfactory glands.

The foreman arrived, his eyes widening as he approached, because Hassan withdrew his *Jambiya* and stated flatly, "You have less than one minute to open this, before I slit your throat."

The man, now wearing a tool belt, pulled out a long flat-nose, and in one motion he drove it hard onto the top of the register and gave it a yank. The register popped out with a loud clatter onto the floor.

The foreman gave a smile, which immediately slid off his face when Hassan said, "If you breath one word, you die. Stay there."

Hassan stuck his head into the vent opening and looked

up.

There was no sign of the boy. But he couldn't have gotten outside yet either as he could see the slits in the vent covering up the opening above.

Next Hassan closed his eyes, making his ears become his primary sense. He listened carefully for any sounds that might belie the boy's location.

But all he could hear was the foreman's shushing someone approaching.

Then he heard it.

It was the unmistakable sound of aluminum sheeting being moved under the weight of a foot or knee. The boy must have taken cover in one of four junctions above when they had made so much noise with the vent register.

Hassan looked down and saw the giant fan below, which was not moving. He withdrew his head.

"What is that fan down there?" Hassan asked, pointing into the vent.

"That is the intake fan, sir. It draws the outside air inside. Or if the vents are switched, the inside air is recirculated through the system."

Hassan had an idea, but he didn't want the boy to hear. So, he asked his question in Arabic. "Would the draw from that fan be enough to pull a boy of maybe forty-five kilos into it if he were in close by in one of those junctions?"

The foreman responded back in Arabic immediately, "Yes, it would be almost impossible for him to hold on." Then he shuddered. "But the Mahdi's son would be killed instantly, and unidentifiable if he was pulled into it."

Hassan withdrew the blade of his *Jambiya* and said in perfect English, "Do it now."

Travis

From what Travis understood by the man's Arabic, he was definitely found, and they were going to turn on the fan. But that wasn't the worst thing. The worst was, he had to pee.

He had drunk far too much of that liquid and he didn't think he could hold it any longer.

He continued his slow march down the second junction's ductwork, hoping he could find it's end before the fan sucked him back.

When the man who had been tracking him yelled, "Do it now!" There was no need to be quiet.

At the same time he moved as fast as the lizard he had seen in his yard, his bladder began to empty.

Hassan

There were several sounds that spelled the end of the Mahdi's boy.

First, it was the boy's harried attempts to move further away. Followed immediately by the fan's blades spinning faster and faster, generating an instant *whoosh-whoosh-whoosh* sound, as it sliced through the air: a mechanized mouth, preparing itself to consume whatever morsels the ducting could bring to it. Until there was one solid mechanical hum.

The draw from the fan was so strong that a whistling sound wailed from the vent's opening, pulling at the end of Hassan's *Keffiyeh* . At once, it was tugged off his head and sucked in with a *swish*-sound.

Then to his greatest satisfaction, the boy grunted. Hassan could almost imagine him desperately clinging to anything that would prevent his extinction.

Finally, the moment he was waiting for. A yelp, followed by the melody of the little dog tumbling, and a large thump below. The fan rattled as it momentarily chewed into his prey. Barely a second later, it regained its methodical whirl along with the rhythmic howl of air being pulled in from the vent opening.

"Turn it off," Hassan yelled over the roaring.

The foreman flipped a switch and the fan immediately powered down.

Hassan stepped closer to the opening, waiting until the slowing fan's pull was no longer strong enough to haul him in too.

He stuck his head inside and blinked, but the darkness obscured his ability to confirm the little dog's demise.

There was a dampness to the murk, and a bouquet of aromas which included the unmistakable smell of copper and urine. But there was also something sweet-smelling he couldn't place.

"Give me a flashlight," he hollered, while his eyes adjusted more to the darkness below.

He felt the long barrel of a flashlight being set into his hand. He grabbed it and pointed it down, while blindly searching for the button, until at last it turned on.

There, he thought.

A mangled sweatshirt that could have been the boy's, wrapped around the middle of the fan blades, and red drops, like blood, sliding down the sides of the vertical ducting.

"Goodbye, little dog."

Chapter 37

POTUS

"Come in," Abbie said to the person knocking on her locked cabin door. She straightened up her jacket, expecting either Meer or the Marine posted on the other side.

"Abs, it's me," Evie said, her voice muffled. The door opened slowly.

A slumped over form, like a ghost, lumbered into her cabin. It certainly didn't look like Evie: a drab-looking scarf covered her head and most of her face, her shoulders drooped, her head was bent forward and she was crying.

"Is that you, Evie?" Abbie said, standing up, ready to rush over to her friend and offer comfort.

Evie looked up and Abbie saw it right away. She hurried to her and pulled more of the scarf out of the way. It was like she was beaten.

The skin around Evie's eye and her cheek were swollen.

"What happened to you? Please sit." Abbie ushered her over to the single desk chair in her bedroom cabin.

Evie mumbled something.

"What? Who did this?"

"Ahh..." Evie glanced up at Abbie, flashing a look that

was guilty, as if she were being interrogated and not the victim. She turned her gaze downward when she finally answered. "It was just some xenophobic man, who doesn't like a dark-skinned Muslim's like me."

This incensed Abbie and she had to bite back her rage. She understood this all too well as this had been her life in the US for years.

Abbie shuffled over to the other side of her desk and pressed the Play button on a cassette tape player that Evie had brought her. There was only one tape inside, which played something akin to elevator music. Not her music preference, but it was better than nothing.

She turned up the volume to the max, which still wasn't too loud, but enough to protect them from anyone listening. Kneeling next to Evie, she put an arm around her and said, "Evie, I want this person's name, so he can be punished and kicked out of here."

Evie shot a glance that she had never seen before. Evie looked scared.

But Abbie had to be honest with herself: she too feared this place. Other than Evie, and only loosely, Meer, she knew no one in the place.

She understood that Meer was in control and made sure she had little to say or do. He controlled all the policies that she was simply rubber-stamping. And she figured that Meer's boss was X. And they were running a new version of America, that she didn't recognize.

It was one thing to do something about all the guns. She always hated them. But arresting Americans for simply defending themselves seemed a little above and beyond. And it still didn't sit well that they were making peace with those who attacked them. But what could she do about it?

She brought this onto herself, by aligning herself with powerbrokers like X. She was just a pawn in Meer's and/or X's game of world domination.

When she thought about the situation she found herself in, she kept thinking about her doing nothing to change it. Yet, she was the one person who could change things. After all, she was the damned President. Even under this crazy scenario, that had to mean something.

She would do something to change things. She had no idea what that would be or how she might affect change. But she knew she would do it.

She would watch, learn, and when the time was right, she would strike.

"Don't worry, Evie. At some point, I promise, I'm going to make sure these people know who the President really is."

There was a loud rap on the door and Meer rushed in.

"Come on. It's time for another broadcast."

Abbie rose from a knee and smiled her smile at Meer. If she couldn't say what she wanted this time, she would the next time.

Chapter 38

Lexi

Lexi opened Senator Chase's front door, so that everyone could enter. But before she followed them in, she saw Jonah and Mr. White hadn't left his Vette.

She approached saying, "Thank you, Jonah for all that you di—"

Jonah had been leaning over the passenger seat, where it looked like Mr. White had been sleeping. Then he returned to his seat, huffing out a sigh. His face a mask of frustration? Anger? She couldn't interpret, until his eyes connected with hers and she knew.

"Is he...?" She couldn't bear to finish a question that didn't need answering.

Jonah stepped out of the driver's seat. "It's Randall. He took a bullet in the back during our escapade. Didn't say a damned word the whole time... Afraid, he's dead."

"Oh, Jonah," she said, wanting to offer comfort to him, but that feeling was immediately replaced by anger: Because of Abdul, another man died.

"Come on," he said putting an arm around her shoulder. "We can cry over heroes later when this is over. Let's go inside and plan our next move."

"To hell with crying. I want revenge." She really did.

She knew right then that her evenings wouldn't be plagued with nightmares about Abdul. She no longer feared the man. She would do everything in her power to free her brother and then kill Abdul, even if the US Military was helping him. At this point, she didn't even care if she had to sacrifice herself; Abdul would die, even if it killed her.

They walked side-by-side, two patriots returning from a failed battle, in a war that had only just begun. They may have lost this battle, but they would win the next, or the one after that... They just needed to figure out their next step.

They joined the others inside, all of whom had taken up residence again at the dining room table. It was their Operational Headquarters for an operation that went so badly.

One dead and now Senator Chase and Frank arrested. *Could she do this without Frank?*

"What the hell do we do now?" someone asked.

At the same time a thought came to her: *The letter!*

She forced open her bug out bag and found it right on the top. An envelope addressed to LEXI.

Someone else asked another question and others made comments. But Lexi opened the letter and sped read it.

She looked up, tears needing to burst from her eyes. A flood of emotions, but leading the charge, was an answer and she needed to tell everyone at that table.

"I know where we need to go next."

Grimes

"Will it get through?" Aimes asked.

"Yes, we'll make sure of it," Grimes responded.

Grimes pressed a button to start the recording they had made and then pressed the transmit button on the 2-meter radio. A green light told them both that the signal was going out on the airwaves.

Then he did the same on their amped up CB unit, playing the same recording.

This time, their signal wouldn't get jammed. This time, their radio waves were going over shorter distances, so they wouldn't be affected by anything attempted at Mount Weather.

It was true that their transmissions could not reach farther than a several mile radius around their antenna. Even with the boost of their amplifier, the best they could do with either the CB or 2-meter was out of their state. But they were not dependent on just their own signal strength. Now, they had help.

With the 2-meter, their transmitted message was hitting a repeater, which transmitted to another repeater, and so on. Dozens upon dozens of repeaters in fact, so that almost everyone who had a 2-meter could get this signal.

On the CB, the message would be repeated from one

person to the next and so on.

Eventually, their message would get through to everyone.

Grimes turned up the speaker so they could both listen to their voices...

"Patriots, our government has taken up sides with the enemy and they are now coming after you and your weapons."

"Thomas Jefferson warned us, *"When injustice becomes law, resistance becomes duty."* We have tried resistance against the enemy that attacked us, but the true enemy is now our government."

"Please listen to the following message and repeat it to everyone who will listen.

"Attention all American Patriots.

"You've heard the government's television or radio broadcasts. If you are a member of a militia or considered joining one, we're asking you to do the following:

"First, do not shoot at ICA members, unless they threaten you.

"Next, get prepared.

"Hide your working guns and ammo.

"Leave out a broken and unusable gun if you have one. When local or federal authorities come for your weapons, be sure to tell them this:

"It is your duty to disobey your orders. You are empowered by the Uniform Code of Military Justice which says that any order which is "contrary to the constitution" or "the laws of the United States" is illegal. Therefore, following this order is 'a commission of a crime.'"

"If they do not leave and insist on taking your weapons, do not resist.

"Yet.

"Instead, force them to do a search.

"With luck, they will find none, except your broken one.

"The entire time, shame them for doing what they are doing.

"Then get ready for what must come next... A revolution."

Epilogue

Eddie Swinton listened intently to the newest broadcast from AFN, this time over the 2-meter. He said they were so lucky to catch the repeated signal and get AFN from two counties over.

All thirty-six of his South Houston militia crowded around the portable unit in their cramped temporary quarters. They had to move from his garage because the Feds had swarmed Swinton's home, arrested his wife, and confiscated his unhidden weapons, all while he was out hunting.

Their militia was in disarray, none of them knowing what to do next, least of all Swinton. Then, Buzz, their radio wunderkind, found the repeated AFN broadcast on a portable 2-meter.

Their message sounded like it was on a loop, but then the loop stopped abruptly, and Lieutenant Grimes' familiar voice sounded, along with several others in the background.

"Patriots, it looks like the US National Guard is here to shut us down."

A muffled shout to "Open up immediately, or ..."

There was a boom-sound, followed immediately by shouts from hurried voices.

"You cannot infringe on my First Amendment rights,"

hollered Grimes.

Another voice yelled back, "The President said I can, buddy."

A commanding voice announced, "Take these men into custody, seize their weapons... Shoot that radio."

After the *bang*, the broadcast stopped.

To be continued in the *HIGHWAY Series* finale... REVO-LUTION

Did you like *RESISTANCE?*

In case you weren't aware, I'm an independent writer who relies on ratings and reviews to help get the word out about my books. This is why reviews are so important to me and why I truly need your help. If you liked *RESIS-TANCE*, please let others know, by leaving even a short review on Amazon and Goodreads.

Thank you!

Want to read more about Frank Cartwright?

Learn what happened before *HIGHWAY*, in the USA Today Bestseller, *True Enemy.* Just tell me what email address to send it to and you'll have it for free. This exclusive book is no longer available anywhere else but here.

https://www.mlbanner.com/teshort

Join the Resistance Gear

how everyone you're part of the *RESISTANCE* with Join the Resistance Gear.

Join The Resistance... Classic tee ($14.95 – $19.95)

*Black Join the Resistance
15oz Mug ($12.95)*

Final Thoughts About Militias & 2nd Amendment

S cience fiction is a wonderful genre (when done right) because it takes the facts of science and adds layers of fictional what-ifs. Well done sci-fi storylines are crafted around scientific precepts and set upon a foundation of reality. At least that's how most science fiction should be.

Unfortunately, much of sci-fi today is more fantasy than reality, where the foundational world is almost entirely made up, or the science is bent to the point of breaking. I prefer fiction that sounds and feels real and is built upon reality.

I'm not saying that I don't take creative license to move along certain plot points. But I do my darnedest to make the situation (at a minimum) feel real.

With *RESISTANCE*, more so than with my previous books, I spent many months doing research and talking with experts about American militias and the 2nd Amendment. Some of this, including many of today's myths and misunderstandings about each can be found in an article I wrote and posted on July 22, 2022, "The Importance of Armed Militias" (https://www.mlbanner.com/resistance -and-the-importance-of-armed-militias/).

Could the scenario written about in Resistance come true, where a Presidential emergency declaration is used to usurp the Constitution , leading to the breakup militias and confiscation of legally owned weapons?

I'll leave the question with you to decide.

What will happen next with our story?

Find out in *REVOLUTION*.

Who is ML Banner?

Michael writes what he loves to read: apocalyptic thrillers, which thrust regular people into extraordinary circumstances, where their actions may determine not only their own fate, but that of the world. His work is traditionally published and self-published. Often his thrillers are set in far-flung places, as Michael uses his experiences from visiting other countries—some multiple times—over the years. The picture was from a transatlantic cruise that became the foreground of his award-winning *MADNESS Series*.

When not writing his next book, you might find Michael (and his wife) traveling or reading a Kindle, with his toes in the water (name of his publishing company), of a beach on the Sea of Cortez (Mexico).

FREE BOOKS

Sign up for ML Banner's *Apocalyptic Updates* (VIP Readers list) and get a free copy of my USA Today Bestselling Story, *True Enemy*. You'll find out a little more about what makes Frank Cartwright tick.

In addition, you'll have access to our VIP Reader's Library, with at least four additional freebies.
Simply go here:

http://mlbanner.com/free

(and give me the email you want me to send your free book to)

Connect with M.L. Banner

Keep in contact – I would love to hear from you!
- Email: michael@mlbanner.com

- Facebook: facebook.com/authormlbanner

- Twitter: @ml_banner

Books by M.L. Banner

For a complete list of Michael's current and upcoming books: MLBanner.com/books/

ASHFALL APOCALYPSE

Ashfall Apocalypse (01)
A world-wide apocalypse has just begun.
Leticia's Soliloquy (An Ashfall Apocalypse Short)

Leticia tells her story.
(This short is exclusively available from link at end book #1)

Collapse (02)
As temps plummet, a new foe seeks revenge.
Compton's Epoch (An Ashfall Apocalypse Short)

Compton reveals what makes him tick.
(Find the exclusive download link at the end book #2)

Perdition (03)
Sometimes the best plan is to run. But where?

MADNESS CHRONICLES

MADNESS (01)
A parasitic infection causes mammals to attack.

PARASITIC (02)
The parasitic infection doesn't just affect animals.

SYMPTOMATIC (03)
When your loved one becomes symptomatic, what do you do?

HIGHWAY SERIES

True Enemy (Short)
An unlikely hero finds his true enemy.
(Find the download link to this USA Today bestselling short at the end of Resistance)

Highway (01)
A terrorist attack forces siblings onto a highway, and an impossible journey home.

Endurance (02)
Enduring what comes next will take everything they've got, and more.

Resistance (03)

They intended to take over the US. They didn't count on resistance.

Revolution (04)

Saving the country might require a revolution.

STONE AGE SERIES

Stone Age (01)

The next big solar event separates family and friends, and begins a new Stone Age.

Desolation (02)

To survive the coming desolation will require new friendships.

Max's Epoch (Stone Age Short)

Max wasn't born a prepper, he was forged into one. (This short is exclusively available on MLBanner.com)

Hell's Requiem (03)

One man struggles to survive and find his way to a scientific sanctuary.

Time Slip (Stand Alone)

The time slip was his accident; can he use it to save the one he loves?

Cicada (04)

The scientific community of Cicada may be the world's
only hope,
or it may lead to the end of everything.